DEAL KILLER

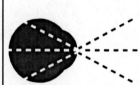 This Large Print Book carries the
Seal of Approval of N.A.V.H.

A DARBY FARR MYSTERY

DEAL KILLER

VICKI DOUDERA

WHEELER PUBLISHING
A part of Gale, Cengage Learning

GALE
CENGAGE Learning·

Farmington Hills, Mich • San Francisco • New York • Waterville, Maine
Meriden, Conn • Mason, Ohio • Chicago

GALE
CENGAGE Learning

LIBRARY OF CONGRESS CATALOGING-IN-PUBLICATION DATA

Doudera, Vicki, 1961–
    Deal killer : a Darby Farr mystery / by Vicki Doudera. — Large print edition.
        pages ; cm. — (Wheeler Publishing large print cozy mystery)
        ISBN 978-1-4104-7023-2 (softcover) — ISBN 1-4104-7023-7 (softcover)
        1. Women real estate agents—Fiction. 2. Serial murderer—Fiction. 3. Murder—Investigation—Fiction. 4. California—Fiction. 5. Large type books. I. Title.
PS3604.O895D423 2014b
813'.6—dc23   2014009119

Published in 2014 by arrangement with Midnight Ink, an imprint of Llewellyn Publication, Woodbury, MN 55125-2989

To Ed, who makes it all possible.

ACKNOWLEDGMENTS

I'm thankful for the assistance of many who helped with *Deal Killer.*

First, a big thank you to my faithful manuscript readers Lynda Chilton and Ed Doudera, whose comments and careful edits are so appreciated.

Much appreciation to my fellow real estate agents around the country and in Maine, above all, Scott Horty and the team at Camden Real Estate Company, including the trio always willing to lend a hand: Christopher Brown, Jeanne Fullilove, and Brenda Stearns.

Thanks to the real Debbi Hitchings for supporting Safe Passage and lending her name to Darby's legal counsel.

Thank you to my literary agent, Tris Coburn, and the folks at Midnight Ink, including editors Terri Bischoff and Connie Hill; publicist Beth Hanson; and book designers Donna Burch-Brown and Lisa

Novak. Thanks to illustrator Dominick Finelle for a Big Apple cover.

Finally, a huge thank you to Darby's fans everywhere. You make writing a real pleasure!

PROLOGUE

"What the devil . . . ?"

Miles Porter stood at the threshold of his office, a look of confusion contorting his face. Papers were strewn over his desk's thick surface, a desk chair was broken in two, and a drinking glass had spilled its contents and then been smashed. He ran a hand through a thick shock of hair and noticed the yanked-out drawers. *Someone's been in here,* he realized, his bewilderment turning to anger. *Some lunatic's destroyed the place.*

He nearly jumped when he spotted the shadowy figure.

"Who the hell are you? What are you doing here?"

The intruder lifted his hands palms up, a gesture meant either to placate or show he was unarmed. *Or both,* thought Miles.

"Waiting for you, obviously." His voice was deep, slightly accented. He showed no sign of rising from the leather armchair in the room's far corner.

Eastern European, guessed Miles, He glanced toward the stacks of papers strewn across his desk and knew the real reason his office was in shambles.

"Bloody hell! You've been rifling through my things!" Miles pocketed the keys to the door and grabbed his phone from a worn messenger bag. "I don't know why you're here, but I'm ringing the police."

"No need for that, Mr. Porter."

"Oh really?" He punched in 911.

With a swift gesture the man sprang from the chair and yanked the cell phone from Miles's grasp.

"Don't be an idiot." The clipped words rang out like gunfire in the still afternoon.

Miles spoke through clenched teeth. "What are you doing here?"

"I'm looking for something."

"And what would that be?"

"One of your students' assignments."

"What are you talking about? Which student?"

"Natalia Kazakova. She's written a paper that I must have." He waited a beat. "Immediately."

"This is absolutely ludicrous! You came here to steal someone's research? Who the

10

hell are you?"

"My name is Alec Rodin." He tossed the cell phone toward Miles who caught it with one hand. "It's important that I find what I need."

Miles noted the man's wiry build, his tailored suit, and expertly trimmed beard. He looked like a movie star, or a model, and had the confidence bred in someone with good looks.

Alec Rodin . . . Had Miles heard the name before?

"Do you even know Natalia?"

"Quite well."

"She's never mentioned you." Natalia was a serious student, bright and focused on her journalism studies.

"Really?" He lifted his eyes. "That's odd. We are engaged to be married."

Miles kept the surprise from registering on his face *This guy's a good fifteen years older than Natalia.* "You're her fiancé?"

"Indeed. I am here from Moscow on a short visit." He leaned back in the leather chair. "She should never have come to New York." He shook his head. "Her studies here seemed harmless. Creative writing — what could that hurt?" He said the word creative with such scorn that it sounded shameful. "Now I learn she is studying investigative

11

journalism."

"She's a talented writer."

He shrugged. "Perhaps. I found part of her paper this morning and was not struck by her talent, but by the danger she is in." He shot a cold stare in Miles Porter's direction, his good looks suddenly threatening. "My little Natalia is in peril. The topic she has chosen . . . it could get her killed."

Miles thought a moment. Natalia Kazakova had been in to see him that morning as well, clutching a steaming cup of coffee, her eyes bright as she described her subject: stolen royal real estate in modern-day Russia.

"How do the imperial castles of St. Petersburg explain your unwanted presence in my office, Rodin?"

The man gave a harsh chuckle. "I hardly expect you to understand the ramifications of Natalia's story, Mr. Porter. In fact, I doubt if you understand the situation at all. I don't have time to explain, and truthfully, it is better for you if you remain ignorant." He swung his eyes toward the door. "Now, I need any hard copies of Natalia's paper and the electronic file."

"Oh, please!" Miles shook his head. "This is turning into the plot of some melodramatic soap opera — something my granny would watch on the BBC! Even if I gave you that assignment, don't you think I'd keep a copy or two?" He made his voice hard. "Get out of my office right now, and I won't report you to the authorities."

"You're refusing to show me my future wife's work?"

"You can read Nat's story on Sunday. Page five of the *Times.*"

Alec Rodin's head jerked so quickly that Miles Porter nearly chuckled. "Surely her writing is not of that caliber . . ."

"No, not yet, but give her a few years. She wants to pursue a graduate degree, or hasn't she mentioned that yet?"

The Russian's face darkened. "Unfortunately that will not be possible. Natalia will be returning to Moscow as soon as the semester ends."

"What if that is not what she wants?"

Miles saw an imperceptible clenching of the seated man's jaw. "Mr. Porter, Natalia is an heiress to a large fortune. Her place is back in our country."

"I see. You're marrying Natalia for her money."

"The details of our arrangement are none of your business, but let me assure you, I have plenty of resources without the Kazakova billions." He rose to his feet and faced

13

Miles. "Trust me — this marriage is a very advantageous match for Natalia. Her doting father would have it no other way."

Miles, silent, detected a touch of contempt.

Rodin's face hardened. "I really don't have time for conversation, Mr. Porter. I need you to give me that paper."

"Pity, but it isn't here."

"What are you saying?"

"Natalia came by this morning and took it back."

"Why?"

"Because I'd read it and given my suggestions. Now she's making changes. It's what we journalists call editing."

Alec Rodin's lips curled at the sarcasm. "I see." He turned toward the door. "I hope you realize that you have put your little student in grave danger."

Miles had a sudden image of Natalia's eager face, bruised and bloodied. He had no doubt that the Russian businessman, despite the elegant suit and careful manners, was capable of extreme violence.

"Rodin? If you so much as harm a hair on Natalia . . ."

The man faced him and gave a rough laugh. "Yes?"

"I will kill you."

Again Alec Rodin laughed. "You will kill me?"

"Damn right."

"Ah, the British sense of humor. So refreshingly odd." Once more his look grew stony. "Goodbye, Mr. Porter. Let us hope for the best for poor Natalia."

Miles watched as Alec Rodin left the office. What the devil was the guy talking about? Was there really something newsworthy in the undergrad's paper? Had she uncovered some sort of scandal, perhaps? Miles took a steadying breath, relocked the door, and then pulled Natalia's essay from his messenger bag. He sank into the cracked leather armchair, and with total concentration began to read.

Peggy Babson paused outside the ladies' room, shaking drops of water from her hands. Once again, the paper towel dispenser was empty, and she was flinging her fingers like some dog after a swim. *You'd think that a hoity-toity school like Columbia could remember to refill things once in a while,* she thought, but no, half the time the dispensers were empty. She sighed. Thank goodness she carried her own supply of tissues in her handbag! You never knew from one day to the next if the custodians would remember to restock the bathrooms.

Her hands still damp, Peggy peeked over the railing, watching the ramrod straight back of the stranger head down to the first floor. Well, he had quite a nerve, getting Professor Porter all riled up like that! Peggy hadn't heard the whole conversation, but her intuition told her the unknown man was to blame. Miles Porter was a gentleman, and an English one at that, and he would never stoop to unbecoming behavior. *Although he had sounded pretty angry . . .*

She felt her plump cheeks pink up at the thought of Miles. What with his square jaw line and muscular build, he was handsome as all get out, what her Queens-born mother would have called "a real dish." And then there was that British accent, like that actor Hugh Grant, or the really hunky one . . . Colin Firth. She sighed. Hopefully he'd stay for more than just the semester. Miles Porter made her dreary days in the stuffy building more appealing, made it much easier to get up each day and come to work.

Peggy glanced at her watch. Only two, but she felt like leaving for the day. *It's the first nice day of spring,* she thought, *and I'm entitled to enjoy a little fresh air.* Pulitzer Hall was virtually empty, and she couldn't imagine any of the staff needing anything so desperately that they couldn't wait until tomorrow. Would anyone complain if she skipped out early? Not Miles Porter, that's for sure. She gave a guilty grin. Thank goodness Charlie Burrows was away on sabbatical! *Too bad he's coming back at all,* she thought. *Too bad Miles Porter can't stay here forever.*

With a soft sigh, Peggy Babson blew out the vanilla candle burning on her desk and locked the door of her tiny office. She tiptoed down the wooden stairs to the lobby, pulled open the door, and stepped out into the sunshine of the April afternoon.

Alec Rodin leaned against the brick building and lit a cigarette. He inhaled a few times and then pulled out the card he'd taken from the drawer of the cluttered oak desk.

Miles M. Porter, he read. *Investigative Journalist.* He fingered the high-quality paper stock, noted the phone number, and placed the card back in his breast pocket.

The man had been totally uncooperative, and yet Rodin had not felt the need for physical violence. *He has no idea of the stakes involved,* Rodin mused. *No clue as to what Natalia has stumbled upon.* He shook his head. The man called himself an investigative reporter, and yet he had not done his homework. He was ignorant, unaware of the price people were willing to pay for silence.

Rodin looked over his shoulder with a quick glance. Was it his imagination, or was someone following him? From experience, he knew that danger lurked where one least expected it. He inhaled from the cigarette and steadied his nerves. There was no need to feel jumpy.

He had sensed nothing strange in Moscow, before boarding the private jet for America. His business associates were typically brusque, but that was their way. Many of them were already multimillionaires, joining the burgeoning Russian upper class. It would have been unimaginable decades ago, this sea change in his country. Everyday life had been so bleak and hard that few dared to dream of a prosperous life.

And yet it had happened. The reforms ushering in capitalism and the accompanying corruption had given men like him the opportunity to gain wealth, one way or another, and now the country was fast becoming the home of more billionaires than anyone could have imagined.

The mid-afternoon sunshine was warm on his angular face, but Alec Rodin barely noticed. He took another drag on the cigarette and pondered his next move. Pressure on Natalia was going to be the only way to squash the whole thing. Fortunately, he knew her many weaknesses.

He tossed down the cigarette and ground it beneath his heel. There was no time to waste. He needed to find and destroy Natalia's paper, obliterate her research, and get her home, hopefully with her mind on something besides journalism. Rodin wasn't entirely sure what that something could be. Natalia had little interest in outdoor activities. She did not ride horses nor show expensive dogs. Her hobbies were few, her only interests intellectual. He frowned.

A pair of young women passed him by, chattering gaily. One of them wore a brightly patterned sarong-type carrier that held a red-cheeked baby wearing a pink jacket. Rodin glanced at the baby and she smiled, a thin line of drool hanging from the corner of her lips. Of course! The answer was literally staring him in the face. He pictured Natalia's womanly figure rounded with the flush of new life. She was not too young, and he was ready for a son, or a daughter if fate so decreed. Yes, motherhood was the answer to the whole situation. It would certainly keep Natalia busy and out of harm's way.

Anxious now to be back at his fiancé's penthouse, he glanced around for a cab. Getting a taxi on this corner was unlikely, given that a high percentage of the passersby were students, and most of them were on tight budgets. *Unlike Natalia,* he thought with a smirk. Thanks to her father's fortune, she was probably the richest woman enrolled at the university.

He rounded the corner of the building and headed toward Broadway. A shadow passed over the sun, and once more he had the unsettling feeling of being followed. Quickly he ducked into a dark passageway and surveyed the street.

The space between the buildings was narrow, too constricted to be called an alley. Peering out from the gloom, Alec scanned the sidewalks, seeing nothing to arouse his suspicions. Only throngs of animated students, wearing sweatshirts emblazoned with the university's logo, enjoying the warm breezes of spring.

He was about to step back onto the sidewalk when he heard a skittering sound. He tensed, his hand going instinctively to the inside pocket of his jacket. He was ready to confront whatever had made the noise when a lean rat scrabbled from the shadows, dodged Rodin's feet, and darted behind a nearby dumpster.

Rodin exhaled. Was this the way life would be now that he'd made his fateful decision? He scanned the street once more. Was the deal he'd made worth it?

He thought again of Natalia, this time with an urgency he'd never experienced. He'd make her understand why her research was so dangerous, and he'd do it with kindness. Instead of bullying, he'd try patient explanations.

He glanced back toward the dumpster. The rat peered out from under the metal, its head cocked and still. The rodent was listening intently, every muscle tensed and alert. *We are both listening,* realized Rodin. *But for what?*

And then he heard a sound he could never have imagined: the dull thud of steel encountering his own hard bone.

He felt an immediate and piercing pain and gasped with the force of it. The sensation was all consuming — he could only react to it — and yet a corner of his brain worked to pinpoint the source. *The center of my back,* he realized, *between my shoulder blades.* He tried to turn around and staggered.

It feels as if . . . He tried to identify the

intense throbbing. *It's as if something has gored me, something sharp and long, like the horn of a bull.* The pain intensified as he slowly turned.

A sword-wielding figure crouched in the shadows.

In the dim light Rodin could not determine details. Was it a man or a woman, someone he knew, or a stranger? An image from a book on Russian history filled his brain, a depiction of an ancient, saber-clutching soldier. He visualized the caption. *Ready for battle stands the Cossack.*

Rodin clutched the wall of the building for support. He tried to scream, but could not get air. He felt the terrible certainty of imminent death, and yet he could not believe what was happening. His mind refused to accept what he now saw — the long blade arcing through the air, the steel glinting, even in the darkness. He tried to lift his arms in defense. They seemed disconnected from his torso, useless appendages that could not follow his brain's commands. He watched helplessly as the metal plunged forward.

The dark attacker thrust the deadly weapon into Rodin's chest. Blood spurted in a pulsing fountain, the smell rich and metallic. Rodin sank to his knees, his chest a gaping crater filling rapidly with blood. Burbling sounds came from his lips as he felt the sword being pulled outward. A vision of the Baltic Sea, the feeling of the waves racing in and out, flitted into his mind. He had planned to take Natalia to the coast for their honeymoon.

Again Alec Rodin saw the flash of silver. Who was this fighter? How had he found Alec so quickly? The questions darted and then vanished, as light and inconsequential as clouds.

He took a shuddering breath, sensing it could be his last. He closed his eyes. Even before the swordsman made his final thrust, the one in which the saber would slice open his heart, the Russian surrendered. Not to the mysterious raider in the alley, but to his real enemy, the one who would take the killing blow.

Alec Rodin surrendered to death.

ONE

"Darby! You can't imagine how good it is to see you here in New York!" Miles Porter pushed aside the door to his office and wrapped the slim woman in a tight embrace.

"Tough day?" Her words were muffled in the soft fibers of his cashmere vest. She felt the warmth of his skin and inhaled the scent of him: bayberry, mingled with a hint of something studious, like stacks of hardcover books or the shelves of a quiet library. It had been two months since she'd last hugged the handsome Brit, and she'd missed him, but there was something about Miles that felt different. A tightness in his normally fluid movements, the way his square jaw was clenched — all telltale signs of stress.

"A tough week, now that you ask," he answered. He gave her a quick squeeze and then pulled away with an appraising grin. "Let us have a look at you, Darby Farr. Still five foot five or so, long dark hair, and slender build, I see — nothing's changed there."

"I feel like I'm a source in one of your investigative reports!" she said. "Want to know my weight, too? How about noting the new wrinkles around my almond-shaped eyes?"

"Where?" Miles pretended to scrutinize Darby's oval face. He laughed. "I'm sorry, love," he said, ruffling her glossy mane in a playful manner. "My head's been too wrapped up in my teaching. I just finished correcting a pile of essays, including some of the worst drivel you can imagine. Some of them made me laugh out loud. And these are college students!" He shook his head. "The way I should be greeting you is to tell you how lovely you are. And that's just what I'm going to do once we get out of here. Unless you're too tired from your flight?"

"No. I took a nap from Chicago to Kennedy and feel fine."

"Any problems getting here?"

"No — everything went smoothly. My flights were on time, and getting into Manhattan was a breeze. I grabbed the bus right outside of the airport and here I am."

"I wish you'd have let me pick you up."

"You know me, Miles. I like to do things

myself." She pulled her small suitcase into the tiny office, so crowded with stacks of books and papers that it felt barely bigger than a closet. Glancing past the tall professor, Darby saw his oak desk piled high with reports and magazines. It was pushed up against a burgundy-colored wall which held several framed diplomas. A scuffed swivel chair with a thin, tired-looking pillow on the worn seat stuck out from the desk, and a leather armchair, wedged between the desk and the wall, held Miles's tweed jacket.

"This has to be one of the tiniest offices I've ever seen." She glanced at the woodwork, which was richly stained and highly glossed, oddly formal for a room so small. The space had one high, grimy window, impossible to see out of, although it did let in light. Darby sensed more than saw the weak rays of an April afternoon sun struggling to penetrate the little room's gloom. *A jail cell,* she thought. *No wonder Miles is stressed out.* "How did the professor before you ever manage?"

"Charles? He has a large den at his apartment, as you'll see. My guess is he doesn't spend any appreciable time here. But I think it's important to hold office hours when the students can come in for a chat." He shrugged. "Although not many of them take advantage of it. Rather shoot off an email than make a personal visit, I suppose."

Darby's eyes swept the accumulated clutter like the real estate pro she was when back in Southern California. Her eyes were trained to pick out telling details, no matter how disarrayed the environment. "Someone did drop by recently."

"A most unpleasant bloke," Miles muttered.

"No, I'm thinking one of your female students?"

Miles furrowed his brow and then nodded. "Ah, yes, you're right. Natalia was here this morning. Natalia Kazakova. She's a senior at the college hoping to enter the School of Journalism. She stopped by for a little chin-wag about the program. Nice girl, Russian, and a fairly decent writer. Flair for the dramatic, though, and that can get one into a muddle."

"What do you mean?"

"She's working on a pretty hard-hitting article, and is finding it difficult to keep emotions out of the picture. That's one of the toughest things about becoming an investigative journalist — that, and developing a healthy sense of skepticism."

"I thought she was just an undergrad?"

"She is, but she got permission from the

Dean to take my course on Investigative Techniques." He frowned. "Oddly enough, Natalia's appointment was followed a few hours later by an unexpected visit from her fiancé."

"Is he a student as well?"

Miles shook his head. "No — a Russian businessman. I gather he's at least fifteen years older than Nat. Probably here to keep tabs on her, make sure she's not having too much American fun. I didn't much care for him, and our conversation got a trifle heated. But the whole thing's none of my business, now is it? I'm just here to teach my classes and then be on my merry way."

"You say that, but I know that's not the kind of person you are, Miles. If you didn't like this guy — whatever he's called —"

"Alec Rodin."

"Well, I'm sure there's a good reason. What about Natalia? Is she in love with him?"

"Who knows? I suppose he's a dashing sort of guy, but the only thing that I can see she's passionate about is a career in journalism. She's got a real talent for sniffing out stories. I think she's got a shot at the graduate program."

"How does her fiancé feel about her plans?"

"That was part of our argument. Alec intimated that he wasn't going to allow her to continue further studies. Said her place is home with him in Russia."

"That's an archaic attitude. What kind of a relationship do they have?"

"Apparently an extremely complicated one." Miles leaned over to kiss Darby's cheek. "Unlike ours, which has been smooth sailing from day one."

Darby tilted her head, knowing Miles's comment was tongue-in-cheek. She and the investigative reporter had been navigating the choppy waters of romance for nearly a year, and it wasn't always a straight course.

They'd met in Maine, on the island of Hurricane Harbor, where Darby had been summoned by her dying aunt Jane Farr to wrap up a seemingly simple real estate deal. Miles, a reporter for the *Financial Times* of London, was on the island to interview Jane about high-end waterfront property, and ended up interviewing Darby instead. That meeting had ignited something between them, a spark which smoldered slowly over the coming months as Miles traveled to Afghanistan for a posting with a combat unit there. Since his return, they had seen each other several times — in California and, most recently, on Hurricane Harbor —

but still had not determined what shape a future together might take, or if, indeed, there was to be one.

"Let's get out of here and talk about something more hopeful," he continued. "Solving the energy crisis, for instance."

"A topic on which I happen to have some excellent ideas," she said, flicking off the light while he scooped up his jacket. She waited until he had shrugged it on before leaning over to pick up a cardboard cup from the floor beside the chair.

"Aha," he said, pointing, "so that's how you surmised someone had been here! The old coffee cup clue." He grinned. "But how did you know my visitor was female?"

"Fibers from her miniskirt. They're barely visible to the naked eye, but if you look closely . . ."

"What! You can't be serious."

She laughed and rotated the cup to show the purple lipstick stain marking its rim. "An educated guess, my dear Watson."

Miles opened the door of the cramped office. "Remind me never to cheat on you, Darby Farr. You're much too clever for me."

"Exactly." She reached over and squeezed his arm, enjoying the feeling when he wrapped it around her and pulled her close. Her phone buzzed and she pulled it out of a pocket, took a glance, and shoved it back. "So where are we headed?"

"There's a great little bar around the corner. I thought we'd stop in there for a drink — unless you'd like to go directly to the apartment."

"A drink first sounds great."

Miles grabbed Darby's suitcase and they headed toward the stairs, their feet tapping on the worn wooden floors. Rounding the corner of the curving hallway, their progress was halted as two men stepped forward and blocked their path.

"Miles Porter?"

"Yes?"

"I'm Detective Benedetti and this is Detective Ryan. We need to ask you some questions."

Miles gave a quick glance at Darby as the speaker, a short, plump man in his late fifties, and his younger, thinner partner flashed New York City police badges.

"What is this about?"

"A Russian businessman named Alec Rodin." Detective Benedetti held the journalist's gaze. "Know the guy?"

Miles nodded. "Met him today. He came up here to my office — well, the office that I'm using for the academic year."

"What time?"

"After lunch — around two p.m., I suppose. He asked me questions about a student's class work, and then he left."

"That's it?"

"Yes."

"Did you give him your business card?"

"I don't think so." He noticed that the quiet cop — Ryan — was taking notes. "I didn't give him anything, but he had sorted through my things before I opened the door."

The two detectives exchanged quick looks.

"You mean he broke into your office, Mr. Porter?"

"Not exactly. I'd gone down for coffee and a sandwich and left the door unlocked, so he didn't have much of a challenge. Rodin was sitting in my armchair when I entered, and I could tell he'd been rifling through my papers."

"What was he looking for?"

"Said he needed one of my student's assignments." Miles cleared his throat. "Look, I don't understand why you need to know all this. What's Rodin done? Has he harmed Natalia?"

Again the men exchanged glances. "Natalia Kazakova?" asked Ryan, his pencil poised in midair.

"Yes. She's my student. He claims they're

33

engaged."

"Ms. Kazakova is unharmed."

Darby spoke quietly. "And Rodin?"

Detective Benedetti turned his milky eyes toward her before sliding them back to Miles.

"Rodin isn't doing so well. He's dead."

"Dead? That's not possible. I saw him only a short while ago —"

"Yes, so you said — 2 p.m." Ryan's voice was dry. "Where did you go after Rodin left your office?"

"Nowhere — I mean, I stayed here in the building." Miles nodded at Darby. "I was waiting for my friend's arrival."

"Your name?" Ryan's pencil hovered over his pad.

"I'm Darby Farr." She spelled her last name. "I'm visiting from Southern California."

Miles ran a hand through his hair. "I can't believe Rodin is dead. How? He was too fit for a heart attack, and you wouldn't be here unless it was suspicious . . ."

"That's correct, Mr. Porter." Benedetti shifted his weight and thrust his hands into a rumpled jacket. "Alec Rodin was fatally stabbed about a block from here."

"Christ." Miles shook his head.

"Were there any witnesses?" asked Darby.

"None so far." Benedetti frowned. "We found your business card in the deceased's pocket, Mr. Porter."

"He must have taken it from my desk."

"Evidently. Can anyone confirm that you've been here in the building since Rodin left?"

Miles shrugged. "I don't know. I haven't seen anyone else. There aren't too many people here late in the afternoon, especially when the weather is like this."

"I see." The detectives shared a glance. "Thank you, Mr. Porter. We'll be in touch if we have more questions." Detective Benedetti extended his hand and Miles shook it. "Goodbye, Miss Farr."

"Goodbye." The two men turned and headed down the stairs.

Miles put his hand to his head. "I can't believe it, Darby. That man — Alec Rodin — was here only a few hours ago, and now . . ."

"Did he say anything out of the ordinary, Miles?"

"What do you mean? I thought it was strange that he wanted Nat's paper."

"Did he seem afraid? As if he was in danger?"

Miles shook his head. "No. He intimated that Natalia could be in trouble if the subject of her paper were known. His exact words were 'she was in over her head.' Poor girl. What a shocker."

"Have you read her paper?"

"Yes. As soon as Alec left I read it. It's an interview with an unnamed source about the theft of Russian palaces in St. Petersburg."

"A historical piece?"

"No, modern day. Natalia's source claims that the current Russian government is illegally taking possession of Imperialist buildings — vacation homes, palaces, residences — and handing them over to powerful politicians."

"Interesting. But didn't this kind of thing happen years ago, right after the Revolution? Why is it newsworthy now?"

"I'm not sure. Natalia's source is an exiled royal, who claims to have all kinds of evidence against a Russian government agency." He searched her face. "Do you still want to head on over to the pub and talk? Or would you rather go straight to the apartment now?"

"No, the pub is fine. You can tell me all about this over a drink."

Miles held open the door. "Exactly. And you can tell me whether you think Nat's news story is what killed her fiancé."

■ ■ ■ ■

Three and a half miles south of Pulitzer Hall, Sergei Bokeria sat on a gray upholstered couch and observed the unfolding drama between his employer and his charge. The bodyguard's massive bulk dwarfed the sofa. It was as if he were sitting on a piece of furniture made for a child, the way his torso squeezed on to the cushions. To the casual observer, he appeared relaxed. The jowls of his face draped down from prominent cheekbones as if in repose, and his watchful eyes seemed nearly closed. But the restful image was deceiving. The big man had chosen his position only meters from the penthouse door deliberately, and he was not at ease. His hands, spread on the sofa's armrests, were tensed, and the large muscles of his powerful body were coiled and ready for action.

His gaze took in both the girl and the image of her father on the computer screen as they grappled with the news of death.

Mikhail Kazakova spoke first, his Russian resonant, deliberate.

"Natalia, I am deeply sorry. You know that Alec was like a son to me." The businessman's fleshy face was puckered, his brow a

37

series of furrows. He reached up with a manicured hand as if to comfort the young woman through the screen. As if she could feel the touch, she flinched.

"Papa." It was a quiet reproach, said as she turned away from him, closing eyes that were accented with full, dark brows. A hand went to her lips. From his perch on the couch, Sergei could see her fingers trembling.

"How did it happen?"

"He was surprised in an alley, and . . ." Mikhail sighed. "He was stabbed several times."

"My God." She looked back at her father through a long fringe of choppy bangs, streaked blonde like the rest of her hair. "Poor Alec. I can't imagine such a frightening death." Her voice trailed off.

"I am flying to New York as soon as possible. I will make all the arrangements."

"Thank you." She was quiet a moment. "Why did the police contact you and not me?"

"They couldn't reach you, I suppose. You can ask them that when they question you, which they inevitably will."

"But I had nothing to do with it," she protested.

"Of course not. But it is a murder investigation, and they will talk to everyone they can think of."

She nodded. "I guess you're right." She bit her bottom lip. "In a way this makes things easier."

Mikhail Kazakova pursed his lips. "Alec's death? What are you talking about?"

"It solves a problem."

"You're spouting nonsense. I should think you'd realize that the murder of your fiancé creates all sorts of problems, starting with cancelling the wedding."

"Please Papa, don't pretend you didn't know."

"Know what?"

"That I wasn't happy." She rose from the mahogany table where she was sitting and went to one of the large windows overlooking Manhattan. Raising her voice, she said clearly, "Alec's death means I'm released from my obligation."

"You say it so distastefully!"

"That's because I didn't want to marry Alec! I never wanted to be his wife. I don't want to go back to Russia. It was something you arranged."

"He would have been a good husband," he said woodenly.

"In what way? Because he was wealthy? I don't need his money, or anyone else's for that matter — you know that."

"He was a handsome, intelligent man, well-connected . . ."

"Yes, that's it, isn't it? You liked him for his connections and what they could bring you."

"I can't believe you are speaking to me like this."

"Why, because I'm telling the truth? The only reason you arranged my marriage to Alec Rodin was because of what the situation could do for you. You must have known that I didn't love him."

"You're too young to know what is good for you."

"But not too young to be married off to someone with ties to the FSB!"

"That's ludicrous!" On the computer screen, Mikhail's face was crimson.

"Is it?"

"Yes! Alec was a real estate developer, for God's sake, not some ex-KGB. Honestly, Natalia, your imagination is too vivid."

"That's not what Alec said."

"What do you mean?"

"I mean that he knew I was right! He didn't deny it. He was involved in the FSB, and for all we know, they're the ones who killed him."

"Natalia! I insist that you stop talking

like this. Those studies of yours are warping your mind. You have no idea what you are talking about."

The young woman spun around, practically hurling herself at the computer. "That's just the problem, Papa. I know exactly what I am talking about! At least Alec recognized that. I don't know the extent of it, but it's big. Theft of property, money laundering — our new secret service has their fingers in all the pies. People like you refuse to see it, because you don't want to know. You want your private jets, your dachas and designer suits —"

"And apartments in Manhattan?" His voice was dry. "You seem to forget who bought you your place, Natalia, all six thousand, three hundred and forty-five square feet of it."

"I haven't forgotten." She gestured toward the windows that revealed the jewel of Manhattan — Central Park — in all its sprawling beauty. "How can I? It's exquisite, Papa, and you know how much I love living here. But I don't need something so opulent or so large. I don't need ten bedrooms!"

"We have been over this before, Natalia. The penthouse is an investment. And having the extra room means I can visit you whenever I can leave Moscow."

Natalia nodded. "I suppose that since I'm going to stay here . . ."

"Stay in New York? Tell me you're not still thinking about this ridiculous degree?" On the computer screen, his face was pinched and red. "Your fiancé is not even buried and you are making your plans? Honestly, Natalia, your lack of emotion worries me. Your mother would be appalled."

She bit her lip but said nothing. On the screen her father shook a finger. "I'm leaving now to finalize arrangements for Alec's body. He will need to be flown back to Moscow for a funeral. You like to write stories? Start coming up with one that explains why you will not be there."

Mikhail Kazakova's image disappeared. A few moments passed before Natalia turned to the massive man seated on the couch.

"I did care for Alec," she said, after a few moments of silence. "You know that, Sergei, don't you? Whether he was FSB or not, I cared for him. But I didn't want to marry him." She wiped her eyes.

Sergei rose fluidly to his feet, more gracefully than one would expect for such a large man, and offered Natalia a tissue.

"Why is it my father can never see the truth?" She dabbed her tear-streaked face with the tissue.

Words were not needed, so Sergei said nothing. Instead he pictured Alec Rodin — dead, his body lying lifeless and cold in the morgue. Whether he'd been a part of the organization Natalia described or not didn't matter, nor did Mikhail's schemes or dreams.

Sergei wanted to feel relief that Natalia's doomed engagement was over, and yet he felt vague discomfort instead. He glanced at the penthouse door as a saying of his grandmother's came back to him in a rush: *Beda ne prikhodit odna.*

Trouble never comes alone.

Two

The tea kettle whistled and Peggy Babson poured herself a cup of steaming water. She added a tea bag from a little plaid box and stirred in a packet of artificial sweetener. From a cabinet she pulled a flowered porcelain plate and placed two gingersnaps upon it. Before closing the box, she took one more. When the cabinet doors were closed, she kicked off her pink leather ballet flats, moved two piles of newspapers, and settled down in the converted porch with a new fashion magazine to enjoy the last of the afternoon sun.

A knock on the door interrupted the quiet and startled her boxer, Pete. His yapping was insistent, high-pitched, and annoying — probably why he had been at the shelter in the first place. "Sshh!" Peggy admonished, shushing Pete's growling as she went to the entryway and peered out the peephole.

Two men stood on the stoop, looking slightly bored.

Cops, thought Peggy, her pulse beating a little faster. She watched quite a lot of crime shows, especially the ones featuring psychics, and knew what police detectives looked like. This section of the Rockaways wasn't the kind of neighborhood where she had to demand to see identification, but she opened the door just a crack all the same.

"Ms. Peggy Babson? I'm Detective Benedetti, and this is Detective Ryan. May we come in?"

She glanced at their badges, proud at having divined their professions correctly. *I really am quite gifted,* she thought.

"Of course." She led the two men — a short, stocky one and his taller, more youthful companion — through the living room, explaining away the piles as best she could. "I'm doing some organizing," she said, moving a stack of newspapers from the porch's worn couch. "What is all this about?"

"We'll get to that in a moment." The heavier one was clearly in charge. "We have a few questions to ask you, Ms. Babson. Will that be okay?"

"Sure. Ask away."

"Fine. Now, you work in the city, correct?"

"Yes. Columbia School of Journalism. My

45

office is in Pulitzer Hall."

"I see. Were you at work today?"

"Of course. In fact, I just got home."

The men glanced at each other.

"I did some shopping on the way," Peggy said quickly. "There's a small supermarket right by the train station. Buy one get one free on Thursdays, and it's not one of those giant ones where you spend all your time hunting for things."

"I see." Detective Benedetti nodded and looked at his watch. "Ms. Babson, what time did you leave work today?"

She gave a guilty glance downward. "I usually leave at four-thirty, but it was such a nice afternoon that I skipped out a little early."

"And what time was that?"

"Umm . . . close to three I think? But that isn't something I do very often . . ."

"We understand. Now, Ms. Babson, did you see or hear anything unusual while you were in your office or leaving the building?"

She shook her head. "It was very quiet. That's why I figured it was okay to go home."

"Did you see anyone coming into or leaving the building?"

"No."

"You didn't see anyone at all the whole

46

afternoon?"

"Well — yes, there was a man with a heavy accent. He was in talking to Professor Porter, and I saw him going down the stairs."

"What kind of an accent?"

"I'm no expert on languages or anything, but it sounded Eastern European."

"I see. So you saw him from your office?"

"No, I was coming out of the ladies' room and I heard his feet on the stairs. I looked over the railing and saw the back of his head as he left the building."

"What was he doing in Pulitzer Hall?"

"I don't know. Ask Professor Porter."

"Miles Porter?"

"That's right." She felt her cheeks flush just thinking of him. "It's warm in here! Let me open a window . . ."

Peggy Babson shoved aside a few cardboard boxes that were in front of the window, pushed up on the sash, and glanced toward the detectives. Was the younger guy smirking a little? She pretended not to notice. "Where were we?"

"You were telling us that you heard Miles Porter speaking with this man," prompted Detective Benedetti.

"Yes. It sounded as if they were arguing, although I'm not sure what it was about."

"Did you hear anything at all? It's very important."

She thought back. "I heard Professor Porter tell him to stay away from someone, and then I heard the man laugh."

"Anything else?"

She bit her lip. "Miles Porter said something else to the man and he laughed again. A minute or so later I came out of the restroom and saw him leaving."

Detective Benedetti tilted his head. "Would you say Miles Porter was threatening the man? What exactly did he say?"

Peggy Babson looked out the window. A fat robin was on a little patch of soggy grass, searching for a worm. Her parents, when they'd lived in this house, had kept birdfeeders full to the brim in the backyard, but Peggy didn't have time to keep all of them up. She swallowed and looked into the cloudy eyes of Detective Benedetti. "I don't know."

She saw them glance at each other as they rose from their chairs, heard them explain that the strange man she'd seen descending the stairs was now dead, stabbed in an alley off Broadway.

"Dead?" She shook her head, feeling her heart rate pick up a few beats. "Seems impossible."

"Call us if you think of anything else?" Benedetti said, handing her his card.

She promised she would.

But as Peggy Babson watched the detectives open the doors of a compact car and drive slowly down the street, she could scarcely concentrate on the words they'd uttered. She locked her front door with a distracted motion and smoothed the folds of her skirt. There was one image in her mind as she headed toward the kitchen where she'd pour herself a small Chardonnay and fix a plate of cheese and crackers.

Professor Miles Porter and his killer good looks.

The bar was called Pomegranate, and although it was rapidly filling up with the after-work crowd, Miles managed to find a quiet table where he and Darby could sit down and talk.

"We won't stay long, love," he said, ordering them each a drink. "We have dinner reservations at a little place that I think you'll love. Hope you're hungry."

Darby thought back to the last time she'd eaten. "I'm looking forward to dinner, put it that way. But I'm dying to hear about Natalia's story. It must have had something to do with Alec Rodin's death."

"He seemed genuinely concerned for her safety, I'll admit. Maybe I should have given him the bloody thing."

"Given the timing, it doesn't seem as if it would have helped."

Their drinks arrived and Miles paid the tab. "Cheers," he said, lifting his drink to Darby's.

She tasted the cocktail and shook her head appreciatively. "A perfect Manhattan — whiskey, sweet vermouth, and bitters."

"That's right." He sat back and watched, waiting for her to say more.

"What?"

"You know." Miles gave a teasing smile.

"Know what?"

"Come on, do your amazing thing and tell me what kind of whiskey is in the drink. Or the age of the vermouth."

Darby couldn't help but laugh. On several occasions when she and Miles had been together, she'd demonstrated her exceptional palate memory, a unique gift that enabled the young woman to identify many tastes and scents with uncanny accuracy.

"It's not a parlor trick, Miles." She took another sip of the cocktail.

"I know." He sounded contrite. "You can only recognize what you've actually tasted in the past, right? And I take it rye isn't one of them?"

Darby held back a grin. The disappointment in his voice made her think of a small child denied a favorite candy. She looked into his earnest face.

"True, I've never tasted rye whiskey. But this drink is made with Kentucky bourbon, and that I actually have sampled."

"Aha!" He gave a triumphant smile and then frowned. "But I thought a Manhattan was made with rye?"

"If I tell you the history of this cocktail, will you tell me about Natalia's paper?" Her brown eyes twinkled in the bar's low light.

He nodded. "It's a deal."

"Okay, then, here's the story. Originally, the Manhattan was made with American rye whiskey, that's true. During prohibition, it was difficult to get rye, but corn was cheap and abundant, so bourbon flowed freely. Hence the whiskey in a Manhattan began being replaced with bourbon."

"Wasn't it Winston Churchill's mother Jennie who first requested the drink?"

"That's the legend. Lady Randolph Churchill requested a drink made of whiskey, vermouth, and bitters in 1874 at the Manhattan Club, and this cocktail was born." She tilted her head, enjoying the way Miles hung on her every word. "Would you like to know what's in our drinks tonight?"

"Do tell," Miles said, reaching for her hand, "and then we'll get more serious, I promise."

"Okay." She took another small sip. "I believe the bourbon in this drink is Maker's Mark, which comes from a distillery in Loretto, Kentucky. I sampled some at the San Francisco World Spirits Competition last year, and I'm pretty sure this is it. There's one little difference from what I tasted, which makes me wonder if this could be a special variety called '46' which is aged a little differently."

"You got me. Chances are our waitress won't even know."

"The bartender will. I'm not up on my vermouths, nor do I know much about bitters, but I can tell you that what we're drinking is properly called a 'Sweet Manhattan'."

"What do you mean?"

"There's a tiny hint of cherry juice, and that wouldn't be in a straight Manhattan." She saw his face and quickly added, "I'm not complaining — in fact, I like it better this way."

He gave an appreciative whistle. "You're amazing, you know that?"

"Why, thank you, Mr. Porter." She

grinned. "Am I done performing now?"

"Yes. That means it's time for me to tell you about Natalia's research." He thought a moment. "Let me start at the beginning. The assignment was for my students to do a straight investigative story, using at least one source. I told the class that I would help flesh out their ideas if anyone needed a sounding board, but Natalia didn't seem to need assistance. I asked her at one point about her topic, and she said she'd met someone who had an amazing story."

"Obviously that person wasn't Alec Rodin," commented Darby. "Go on."

"Before this morning, I'd skimmed through her paper, but I hadn't really had a chance to read it. I knew she was writing about properties that were stolen from the Russian nobility at the time of the Revolution, and I questioned the relevance to today — much as you did yesterday." He paused and took a sip of his Manhattan. "However, what I discovered when I read it through is Natalia's claim that these properties are now being given to officials in the Russian government, all of whom are part of an elite organization called the FSB."

"I think I've heard of it, but I'm not sure."

"The FSB is the Federal Security Service — arguably the most powerful of the successors to the KGB. In the years since the fall of the Soviet Union, it has slowly taken on the responsibilities of a number of agencies, including, most recently, the Russian equivalent of the United States' National Security Agency." He paused. "The FSB is considered by many to be the foremost symbol of a resurgent and ever more powerful Russian central government."

"It's all sounding very Cold War-ish."

"I'm afraid that's true."

She shivered. "So the FSB is reallocating properties that were seized during the Russian Revolution. So far it doesn't seem as if Natalia's paper contains enough evidence to have aroused Alec Rodin's concern, never mind caused his death."

"I agree. It's a worthy story, but it isn't a smoking gun, so to speak."

"And this source . . . Natalia gave you no clues as to his or her identity?"

"No. It's tempting to think the person is here in New York. After all, Natalia told me that she'd 'met' her source. But in today's world, we can 'meet' people online easier than in person. Natalia's mysterious source could be anywhere."

"Good point, Miles." She took another sip of her Manhattan. It was nearly gone, as was Miles's, and she suspected he was ready for dinner, as was she.

He met her gaze. "Let me take care of this," he said, scooping up the receipt for the drinks.

Darby chuckled. Miles had already paid the tab and had no reason to go back to the bar, unless . . .

"You're right!" he exclaimed, trotting back to the table. "Maker's Mark 46."

"And the cherry juice?" She stood and shrugged on her jacket.

"Right again. The bartender apologized for making us Sweet Manhattans. He's absolutely gobsmacked."

"In other words . . ."

"Amazed. Next time we come in we get a drink on the house."

"Well, what do you know," said Darby, as Miles led her out of the bar. "Maybe it's a parlor trick after all."

Sergei watched the cook walk down the hallway from Natalia's room.

"She's on the telephone," the woman said, in Russian. "I told her that dinner was ready." Her lips pressed closely together so that myriad wrinkles formed around her mouth. "She sounds pretty happy for someone who just lost the man she was to marry."

The bodyguard frowned. He did not like

the cook and never had, although he did enjoy the hearty meals she prepared, especially her *pelmeni* — pastry dumplings filled with meatballs. "Isn't it time you went home?" he asked gruffly.

She sniffed and continued down the hall. A moment later he heard the main door slam.

He shuffled toward Natalia's room and paused outside, listening. Her voice was lilting, and although he could not hear distinct words, he knew she was speaking English. Suddenly she giggled and the sound was so unusual it made him start.

Slowly he turned and headed back down the hall. In the morning her father, Mikhail, would arrive, and he could deal with this impetuous daughter. Sergei's job was to protect her, not to babysit.

The big man reached the dining room where the long table was set for two. His stomach gnawed with hunger as he beheld the silver dishes, steaming with something fragrantly delicious. He eased himself into the chair made specifically for his girth and waited. Hopefully she would conclude her phone conversation quickly and come to dinner, but where Natalia was concerned, one never quite knew what would happen.

■ ■ ■ ■

"That was a fabulous dinner, Miles," murmured Darby holding his hand as they walked down Central Park West. Knowing her fondness for French cuisine, he'd taken her to a small but bustling bistro tucked a few blocks from Broadway. "Brings back such good memories of my mother's efforts to master every dish in Julia Child's cookbooks."

He chuckled. "I was hoping you'd like it, love. There are so many options for fabulous food in this city. I had a very difficult time deciding where we should go. Do you think Jada would have approved?"

"Yes, I believe she and my father would have enjoyed themselves there." Darby felt a quick stab of regret at having lost her parents at such an early age. They hadn't had many opportunities to visit restaurants other than the few on the small island of Hurricane Harbor, Maine, where Darby had grown up. Their death in a sailing accident when Darby was thirteen had seen to that.

The spring air had turned chilly and the trees lining the edge of the park shook in the wind. Darby thrust her hand — the one that wasn't holding on to Miles — deep into the pocket of her trench coat.

"Here we are, then." Miles stopped in front of an opulent limestone building which covered the whole block. Grinning, he nodded at the heavy front door. "Right this way to my Big Apple flat." He reached for the door and a uniformed doorman quickly appeared.

"Let me get that for you, Mr. Porter." The man ushered them in and grabbed Darby's small suitcase at the same time.

"Thank you, George." In a low voice he said to Darby, "I feel like a real New Yorker. I actually know both the night and day doormen."

Darby smiled appreciatively as she entered the lobby, her feet tapping on the polished marble floors. Crystal chandeliers spilled soft light onto an enormous flower arrangement of spring blooms. "It's lovely — a new building with old world charm."

"Custom English oak paneling," grinned Miles, gesturing toward the walls. "And a staff of forty. Makes me feel right at home."

"I'm sure." Darby elbowed the tall Brit good-naturedly. "You're from the landed gentry, I suppose?"

"You'll just have to take a trip with me at some point and find out."

"Oh, so that's how it works. You know everything about my upbringing, while yours remains shrouded in mystery."

"I've visited your island and found it perfectly charming. Now you need to fly across the pond and visit mine." He leaned over and kissed her lightly on the lips. "Shall we save the grand tour of this building for another time?"

"Yes. I'm ready to see Professor Burrows's pad, I think."

"Follow me." Miles steered Darby to a sleek elevator and pushed the button for the ninth floor. "Charlie's place is stunning, as you'll see, but the condominiums on the higher floors are supposedly magnificent. I'm told there are several full-floor pent-houses that exceed six thousand square feet."

"I'm impressed." Darby knew — as did anyone who sold real estate — that there were some of the most expensive and unique properties in Manhattan, covering everything from coveted pre-war mansions, to spacious lofts, to Donald Trump's fabulous towers. She also knew that this building, covering a full city block and across from the Park, was one of the more notable projects built in recent years, if not the star.

"How long ago was this built?"

"Five years, I think."

The elevator hummed to a halt and the doors opened with a quiet whoosh. "Here we are," Miles said. They stepped into a hushed hallway lined with sconces and framed artwork.

"I feel like I'm in a deluxe hotel, not an apartment building," murmured Darby.

Miles unlocked the door and flicked on the lights. *"Voilá, Mademoiselle."*

Darby was immediately drawn to the floor-to-ceiling panes of glass looking out on a darkened but still grand Central Park. "Wow, what a view," she breathed. "It's like the heart of the city is right there, waiting." She turned and took in the open living and dining space, noting the soaring ceilings and polished wood floors. "What's this, about twelve hundred square feet?" she asked Miles.

"A thousand, I think. It's one of the smaller units in the building, but Charlie was smart to buy it, don't you think?"

"Depends what he paid, Miles. If he got in on the ground floor, so to speak, chances are he is going to make a profit when he sells, providing the market keeps improving." She admired the sleek kitchen with its gleaming appliances, bearing the best names and brands. "Either Charlie had a decorator for this place, or his wife is pretty talented."

"Decorator. Mrs. Charles Burrows flew the coop just after they bought it. I gather our friend is a fabulous teacher but not quite the doting husband. He had an affair and she went back to wherever they were from."

Darby took in the comfortable furnishings, eyeing a particularly appealing leather couch. Suddenly she felt very tired, as if the flight from Southern California had finally taken its toll.

Miles made a sympathetic face. "Your busy day is catching up with you, love. Ready to turn in?"

She nodded, stifling a yawn. "As soon as I check in with ET. He's called a couple of times, so I'd better see what's up."

"A multimillion dollar deal, no doubt."

"That would be totally fine with me." Darby tossed her black hair and listened as her assistant Enrique Tomaso Gomez, or ET as she called him, answered the phone, his voice smooth and professional as always.

"New York calling San Diego," she joked, waiting for him to make a funny quip back.

He exhaled. "Thank goodness you've called. There's some trouble, I'm afraid."

"What's up?"

"Let me go into your office a moment."

She waited while ET, obviously wanting more privacy, changed phones. "It's the people who bought the property in Poway."

"The Davenports? Jill and . . ." she thought a moment. "Carl. That was back in December, I think. What's up?"

He sighed. "They called yesterday and then again today. They're very unhappy."

"Really? They were thrilled on the day the property changed hands."

"Yes, well, it seems that the addition on the back of the house has a moisture problem that the building inspector didn't see. According to them, it's fairly serious."

"Yikes. I can see why they are upset." She pictured the great room with its stone mantel and distressed pine floors.

"They asked for a mold expert and I gave them a few names. Hopefully, it's something that can be taken care of promptly."

"Was there any indication in the property disclosure information that moisture was, or had been, an issue?"

"No. I checked the disclosures and the inspector's report as well and there were no special notations regarding the addition." He paused. "I hope it will all blow over, but I wanted you to know."

"Thank you. You did the right thing in

contacting me. How is everything else going?"

"Fine. Claudia is listing a new executive ranch in Carlsbad, and I've booked you a few appointments for when you return. I'll send you all the information."

"Thank you, ET." Darby hung up her phone and turned to look out at the twinkling lights of Manhattan. It wasn't like ET to be so succinct. He hadn't even asked about her reunion with Miles, a subject of which he never seemed to tire. Was there more to the issue with the Davenports than her assistant was letting on?

She groaned and turned from the window. Images from her flight and reunion with Miles flitted through her tired brain, including the bulky figure of Detective Benedetti flashing his badge.

Was it her imagination, or did Miles seem to be uncharacteristically stressed? Usually the Brit was low-key and relaxed, but today Darby had detected an undercurrent of anxiety, even before they'd learned of the Russian's death. *Now I have my own issues to worry about,* she thought. *I can keep Miles company and get frantic over mold.* The idea did not cheer her.

Darby went to find Miles in the bedroom. He smiled warmly from the bed where he lay on his side, wearing only his boxers and reading a magazine. The muscles in his chest and arms were taut, well-defined, and as he flipped a page, Darby felt a surge of well-being edged with lust. Mentally she banished the strange encounters of the day, determined to put on something sexy as quickly as she could.

THREE

"Murder? No fricking way."

Sherry Cooper, dressed and perfectly made-up at only six-thirty in the morning, thrust her hands on her hips, stunned. A second later she reached for an enormous coffee mug and took a gulp. "The penthouse girl's boyfriend is the big guy, right?"

"No. That's her bodyguard." Gina Trovata shook her head as she licked strawberry jam from her finger. "The boyfriend's not here too often, but when he is, he goes down to the pool and swims laps." Gina herself was partial to the hot tub, so she saw who swam on a regular basis.

"I'll be damned. A Russian guy?"

"They're all Russian, sweetheart." Penn Cooper strode into the kitchen, his arms entangled in a vibrant silk tie which he knotted as he walked. "Alec Rodin is — or was — Natalia's fiancé. They found his body in an alley, apparently. He'd been, as they say back in Louisville, stuck like a pig."

"Holy sh— sugar." Sherry was making an earnest effort to curb her affinity for swearing, now that one of her sons had been heard trying out her colorful vocabulary. She narrowed her eyes and looked at her husband. "Maybe that means the penthouse will open up."

"I wouldn't count on it. Both father and daughter seem to love New York." Penn pointed at his tie and Sherry reached out to straighten it.

"Yes, but maybe they'll realize they don't need all that room." She glanced at her watch. "I'll text Rona in a little bit, see what she knows."

"Rona? I've told you, honey — Rona didn't make that sale."

"I know, Penn, but let's face it — the woman knows everything that goes on in this building. She's sold nearly every condo at least once."

"She didn't know squat when it came to that deal."

He's right, Gina thought, as she screwed the lid on the jam, licking her fingers again as she did so. She put it back in the refrigerator and pulled out a carton of eggs and some milk, listening for Sherry's response.

"It can't hurt to ask Rona. Then we

should talk to the Russians directly, too."

Penn frowned.

Gina reached for a bowl and a whisk. *Uh-oh,* she thought.. *Here it comes.*

"I don't see why we need that place, Sher. We're fine here." Above the colorful tie his square jaw was set, immovable, chiseled as if from granite.

"We've been through this a hundred times, Penn. This unit just isn't big enough."

"We've got four bedrooms! And some of them are big enough for a Little League team, never mind a couple of small kids."

"The boys need their own rooms. It's what every educator says, what all the self-esteem research bears out." Sherry was very big on self-esteem, mentioning it nearly every time she spoke about parenting. Now she waved a hand in Gina's direction. "Plus we need a room for the nannies." Gina arrived early each weekday to get the boys off to school and daycare, but there were two more care-givers who worked the afternoon and evening shifts, and sometimes stayed overnight.

"I agree that when one of our nannies spends the night she needs her own room, but I fail to see why it has to sit empty in the meantime. And I maintain that there is no reason why those boys can't share a few

67

rooms, for Chrissakes."

"I want that unit."

"I know you do, believe me, I know that." Penn shrugged on his suit jacket. "You've made that perfectly clear, Sherry. Never mind that Kazakova paid eighty million for it . . ."

"Eighty-three," Gina said, cracking an egg into a small ceramic bowl. The number was out of her mouth before she could bite it back.

"Eighty-three, then. How the hell are we going to come up with that?"

Sherry's smoky eyes smoldered. "Some of us don't have to 'come up with it,' Penn." Her voice dripped sarcasm. "Some of us already have it."

Gina knew from past arguments that although the Coopers were both hugely successful attorneys, Sherry made slightly more money than Penn, and had a generous source of inherited wealth to boot. Penn's response was predictable, and came as the milk splashed into the bowl and over the eggs.

"Do what you want," he muttered, moving fast toward the door. "I'm out of here." Gina saw him grab his briefcase.

The slam of the door reverberated for a few moments.

"Shit," said Sherry Cooper. "That didn't go well." She sighed and repeated the epithet, this time with more emphasis. "Shit."

"Mommy?" The eldest boy, Ryan, entered the room, sliding in his slippers on the wood floor as if he were skating, followed by a taffy-colored yellow Labrador retriever. The boy wore superhero pajamas and a worried expression on his seven-year-old face. "Nobody likes it when you use swear words."

Sherry reached out and gave the boy a quick hug. "I'm sorry, honey. You're absolutely right." She kissed his cheek. "Is Kyle awake?"

He shook his head. The younger boys, Kyle and Trevor, sometimes slept until seven thirty, with the baby, Sam, good for a half-hour after that.

As if contemplating the size of her brood, Sherry Cooper asked, "Gina, how many siblings do you have?"

It was a complicated question. But there was an easy answer, and that was most likely the one Sherry wanted.

"One sister," she said, picturing Paula, who had been born eleven months after Gina's adoption by an American couple.

"I'd like to have at least one more," Sherry

said absently, stroking Ryan's hair. She gave him a quick squeeze. "Mommy's got to get to work." Turning to Gina, she added absently, "Don't forget: no sugar on Kyle's oatmeal."

He was one of the largest men Darby Farr had ever seen.

At least seven feet tall, with a neck like a tree trunk and arms the size of standing rib roasts, he stood outside the door to Charles Burrows's apartment, a look of pure menace on his wide face.

"Mr. Porter?"

Darby's heart thumped as she checked the man's hands. No weapons, although his pure bulk was a threat in itself.

Miles's voice showed no hint of concern. "That's right. And you are?"

"Sergei Bokeria. I am here because of Natalia." He coughed, accentuating the gruffness of his voice. "May I come in?"

Although clearly not his first language, the man's English was very good, reflected Darby. It had none of the stiltedness normally present in foreign accents, and he seemed very comfortable speaking.

"Of course." Miles flashed a look at Darby as they turned back into the apartment. *Breakfast will have to wait,* it said. "Is Nat—

Natalia — okay?"

"Yes." The man looked around and Miles indicated one of the leather couches. He eased onto it with surprising grace. "She is naturally disturbed by the events of yesterday."

"The attack on her fiancé," offered Miles.

"Yes." He said it as if there were more to the answer.

"Are you a relative of Natalia's, Mr. Bokeria?"

He shook his head, a massive motion that made Darby think of a bull elephant. The antagonistic look on his face had not changed, and she was starting to think it was just his normal expression. "I am her bodyguard."

"I see." Miles's eyes met Darby's for a brief second. "Is Natalia in danger?"

The big man's jaw tightened. "Why else would one have a bodyguard?" He looked down at his fists, two knots of bone and flesh as large as footballs, and then back at the journalist. "She is the daughter of a wealthy man — an extremely wealthy man. That alone would make her a target. And . . ." He hesitated. "She is living in a dangerous city."

Darby wondered if New York were any more dangerous than Moscow, but said nothing.

"Is there something we can do to help Natalia?" asked Miles.

Sergei Bokeria nodded. "She would like to speak with you."

"Of course. Would she like to meet at my office?"

"She is too upset."

"We can schedule a visit," offered Miles. "Depending on where she is."

"There is no need. Natalia is upstairs."

"In this building?"

The bodyguard nodded. "She lives in one of the penthouses." He stood, and Darby felt as if he had blocked out the sun with his bulk. "I will go and get her."

As the door closed behind him, Darby turned to Miles. "I guess you haven't met your neighbors?"

"Apparently not! I suppose it makes sense that the Kazakova family lives here. This is one of the pre-eminent Manhattan addresses, and if her father is as wealthy as everyone keeps hinting . . ."

Darby grabbed her electronic notepad and did a quick search. She looked up and whistled. "I'd say so, Miles. Kazakova is one of the richest men in Russia. He's ranked in the world in fact."

"Bloody hell! He didn't make his money

as a reporter, I take it?"

"Ready for this? Fertilizer."

Miles's face wore an impish grin. "You mean to tell me his fortune is founded on —"

There was a knock at the door.

"Hold that thought," Darby said as Miles moved to answer it.

Sergei Bokeria stood at the door absolutely dwarfing a petite young woman with streaked brown hair.

"Professor Porter!" she exclaimed. "I did not know we were neighbors."

"Nor did I. Come in, Nat. This is my friend, Darby Farr."

"I'm sorry to hear of your fiancé's death," Darby said.

"Thank you." She sighed, and Darby could see the bags under her eyes and sallow circles marking the unlined face. "This morning it's really hitting me. Not just that he's gone, but that he was murdered. I mean, someone met him in that alley because they wanted him dead."

"Have the police established that?" Darby's voice was quiet, yet probing. "There are random acts of violence in every city."

"His wallet wasn't stolen, so it seems to have been planned out." Natalia looked down at her hands. "And there are other

73

things that are strange."

Miles flashed a look in Darby's direction. "Natalia, why don't you and Mr. Bokeria have a seat? Can I get you both a cup of coffee or tea?"

Natalia answered for both of them. "Thank you, but we are fine. Professor Porter, I know you have a class this morning, and I don't want to take too much of your time."

"It's early. Please, take a seat and go on."

She took a deep breath. "Thanks. I have an art history seminar at ten, but I need to talk to someone, and I don't know where else to go. When Sergei called Pulitzer Hall and found out that you were here in this building, I knew I needed to see you as quickly as possible."

They sat down and Natalia turned troubled eyes on Miles.

"The police detectives on the case called me this morning and told me about the murder weapon."

"Some sort of a sword . . . isn't that their best guess?" Miles and Darby had heard a report on an early news show.

"They don't need to guess — they located it late last night near the alley where Alec was killed. It's an antique saber, long and tapered — the kind you'd see in a museum

74

collection." She hesitated. "It's Russian."

"That could be a coincidence," said Darby. "After all, just about every type of artifact is for sale in New York."

"That's true," added Miles. "I've seen European and Asian sabers in a little antique shop a few blocks from here. Certainly the police will be looking into all that."

"Yes," Natalia said. She looked at her bodyguard, who gave an almost imperceptible nod. "But there is more."

She flicked her streaked bangs out of her eyes and continued.

"Alec is — he was — a highly successful businessman in Moscow. Most of his recent work was in real estate development, but he had many interests. I think the American expression is, 'a finger in lots of pies.' " she smiled.

"Darby is our resident American," said Miles. "She's from a little island in Maine. Well, has Nat used the idiom correctly?"

"Perfectly. Now, Natalia, tell us more about Alec's profession. Did he have rivals or enemies?"

"No doubt he made many enemies in the business world, but I'm not sure if one of them was responsible for his death." She gave Miles a searching glance. "Do you remember, Professor Porter, my references to an organization called the FSB in my research paper?"

"Yes, it's the Federal Security Service, a kind of offshoot from the old KGB. You said that some people within Russia called them the 'new nobility.' "

"Yes." She turned to Darby. "The FSB is the main security service in Russia, and they enjoy unprecedented freedom — even more than the old KGB. The FSB can operate abroad, collect information, and carry out special operations without any oversight and no parliamentary control. Their budget is not published, and there is no record of how many officers belong. But some people estimate 200,000 people work within its bounds." She paused. "Including our prime minister, who has been involved in the FSB for more than ten years."

"Incredible," murmured Darby. "Did you go into great detail about this in your paper?"

"I only scratched the surface," she said. "And then I found out something very disturbing."

"Concerning your fiancé?" Darby's voice was kind.

"Yes." The young woman's eyes clouded over. Beside her on the couch, the bulky figure of her bodyguard was very still.

"What happened?"

"Alec read my article and became very agitated. He said at first that it was ridiculous. As we argued, he admitted it was true and that many people could get hurt if my work was published."

"It sounds as if he was afraid of what the FSB might do."

"Perhaps." She licked her lips. "He knew what they were capable of." She took a deep breath. "Alec admitted to me that he was a member."

Miles cleared his throat. "That explains why he wanted your research destroyed."

She nodded. "The police asked me if I knew anyone who would want Alec dead, and I said no. What do I tell them, that Alec was a part of an organization more powerful and more frightening than the KGB?"

"Yes," Darby said. "You need to tell them, Natalia. Not only will this information help them to solve Alec's murder, but it could keep you safe as well."

"Darby's right," said Miles. He made his voice gentle. "There's something you should know, Natalia. Alec came to see me yesterday."

"After our appointment?"

"Just before he was killed, apparently." Miles's face was grim. "Nat, he was worried

77

that you could become a target."

Natalia glanced at Sergei Bokeria. The big man extracted a large envelope from inside his jacket and placed it on the coffee table. Natalia opened it, pulling out a piece of paper upon which crudely made words spelled out a message.

"Read it," she whispered, her pretty young face wan. "I think you'll agree the time for worrying has passed."

The poodle's ribbon was red today, tied in a jaunty little bow at the top of its angular head. The animal sported a collar encrusted with sparkly red rhinestones, and Miranda would not have been surprised to see red polish on its pointy little claws. She took the dog's leash from the maid, a skinny, pale thing who always looked petrified, and headed toward the elevator.

The Coopers' lab, Honey, was a gentle, mellow dog that seemed to enjoy the antics of the poodle. Today it was one of the nannies, Gina, who had handed Miranda the leash, while in the background a toddler shrieked.

Together the lab and the poodle, Mimi, were easy to manage, but throwing her third client into the mix made it a challenge. Korbut, who lived in the rarified air of the top floor penthouse, was a young wolfhound eager to play rough with Honey, and he seemed to think that Mimi would make the perfect toy.

Miranda headed back into the elevator, herding in the dogs before pushing the button. It was not an unpleasant job, and it did leave her free to use most of the day in other pursuits. And there were fringe benefits as well.

The elevator glided up to the top floor.

Miranda stepped out and approached the penthouse door. Beside her, the poodle let out a little bark of excitement and was quickly shushed. Miranda pushed the buzzer. Behind the door, the wolfhound was whining, anxious to join his canine companions in a walk.

Miranda couldn't help but smile as she watched Mimi dance on her little feet, cocking her head to the side and causing the ribbon to flip-flop. She knocked again, trying to ignore a rising feeling of irritation. What was it about rich people and their sense of time? No matter how clear you made it that you were on a schedule, that you actually *worked* for your living, they never seemed to get it. Whatever they were doing — even if it was a big fat nothing — was more important than somebody else trying to make a buck. She thought back to all of the excuses she'd heard over the years, including a few from Natalia Kazakova herself. Every lame thing from "I just ran to the Starbucks," to "I forgot what time it was." *Ugh!*

This was why she'd insisted on having keys for all of her clients.

"Guess I've got to root around in the backpack," she said to the two leashed dogs. Stuck in the penthouse, the wolfhound gave a muffled snort of frustration. "Hang on, Korbut — we're working on it."

Miranda took off her backpack and began searching through it when the elevator arrived and its doors slid open. A powerfully built man clutching a briefcase emerged. He wore a black vicuna coat, open over a polo shirt, and jeans. On his feet were tasseled leather loafers, no socks.

"Miranda," he said, striding toward her. She saw that his heavy-lidded eyes were bloodshot.

Miranda stepped back, keeping the dogs between them.

"Don't come near me."

"That's not the greeting I was hoping for." He reached out over Honey's broad back and tried to stroke Miranda's dark skin. She flinched.

"*Milaya,* I'm sorry."

"Don't be sweet-talking me. You blow me off without a word . . ." Her brown eyes flashed.

"It was urgent business, but still, I should have let you know."

"Damn right." Her tone softened. "You look like hell, Mikhail. Where have you been?"

"I only just arrived. Something happened yesterday . . ." He paused. "Natalia's fiancé was killed."

"Alec? How?"

"Murdered. Up by 114th Street."

"God . . . how terrible. I liked him, at least I thought I did. I know you didn't feel the same way."

"That's not true! I arranged the marriage, for Chrissakes!"

"You said your feelings had changed. Or don't you remember?"

"Of course I remember, Miranda. It's just that . . . Well, Natalia is very upset. If she knew about our conversation . . ."

As if on cue, the elevator doors opened and Natalia emerged, trailed by Sergei who wore his usual dark expression.

The girl's eyes locked on them. "Miranda?" Her gaze glided from the dog walker to Mikhail. "I didn't realize you

81

knew my father."

Miranda swooped toward the girl, wrapping her in a hug. "Honey, I have just heard about Alec. I am so, so sorry."

Natalia nodded numbly. "It's awful." She swayed a little on her feet as Miranda released her hold "Papa . . ."

Mikhail moved swiftly to his daughter's side. He pulled her tightly toward him and closed his eyes. She was crying, big, gulping sobs, while he stroked her streaked hair.

Miranda flicked the leashes and the dogs trotted obediently to the elevator. Korbut would have to miss his walk today. She pushed the button, got in, and descended without a word.

FOUR

"YOU ARE NEXT," mused Miles, remembering the words spelled out on the threatening letter to Natalia Kazakova. He pulled on a tweed jacket and pocketed the apartment's keys. "I can't say that I like the idea that Alec Rodin's killer is after Nat."

"Perhaps," said Darby. "I agree that whoever wrote the note knows about Alec's death, and the relationship between Alec and Natalia. Whether the author of that letter is the actual murderer — I'm not sure." She slung a small purse over her shoulder.

"I think she's in danger, but she didn't seem keen to follow our advice and go to the police, did she?"

"No, Miles, she didn't. Truthfully, I'll be surprised if she tells them."

"Sergei and Natalia's handling of that paper means they've destroyed any evidence — fingerprints, you name it."

"If there were any to begin with. According to what Natalia said, we could be dealing with a very sophisticated operation here."

"The FSB?"

"Exactly. Miles, I think we need more information on that organization."

"Agreed. I've got a colleague back in London who covers Moscow. I'll see what he knows about the FSB, without revealing anything to him about Nat or her article."

"Good idea." She cupped her chin in her hands, thinking. "So the murder victim worked for a top Russian agency shrouded in mystery, the sword that killed him was a Russian saber, and now Natalia, a lovely young Russian heiress and the deceased's fiancée, appears to be in grave danger."

"Appears? I'd say she's in it up to her Russian shoulder blades. I'm surprised you'd think otherwise."

"You know me, Miles. I tend to be on the skeptical side. I mean, what's the connection? Natalia doesn't seem to be a genuine threat to anyone."

He pushed the button for the elevator and waited for Darby to enter. "Nevertheless, she's got to contact Benedetti and Ryan and tell them about that threatening note. Maybe they can find the connection."

"Yes. In the meantime, it's lucky she has a

bodyguard."

"Indeed," Miles said drolly. "Our friend Sergei looks as if he could stop a speeding freight train."

"Do you think that her father has any idea of what's going on? She never once mentioned him."

Miles shrugged. "He's the fertilizer magnate, correct? Maybe she doesn't want to deal with his . . ."

"Sshh!" Darby giggled as the elevator stopped on the fifth floor. The doors opened and an elderly lady entered. She was wearing a smart navy suit of soft wool, and her gray hair was well-coiffed and tucked under a little cap. On her stocking-clad feet were what Miles and his countrymen called "sensible shoes."

Darby nodded in her direction, but in true New Yorker fashion, the woman stared straight ahead and kept silent. When the elevator reached the lobby, she marched off first, barely acknowledging the doorman when he called out a hello.

"Ramon," said Miles, pulling the doorman's attention away from the tight-lipped matron. "This is Darby, my friend who is visiting from California. Darby, meet Ramon."

"No kidding! You're this sorry guy's

girlfriend, huh?" His broad face broke into a grin. Inclining his head as if to whisper, he said, "I like to kid old Miles 'cause he's so prim and proper, being an Englishman and all that." He cocked his head, giving the young woman an appraising glance. "What about you? You're from Southern California, right?"

"Actually, I was born and raised in Maine."

"Really? You sure don't look like you're from Maine. Not exactly white bread, are you? I can say that because I'm a mutt myself — Cuban and Polish. What about you?"

"My mother was Japanese and my father was a New Englander."

He whistled. "Well, there you go. No wonder you're so pretty and exotic. I'm always saying that we're all Americans, when it comes right down to it. Good old melting pot." He jerked a thumb toward Miles. "Except for Mr. Bean over here."

"Mr. Bean!" Miles was incredulous. "Can't say I'm too keen on that comparison. I was thinking Daniel Craig, myself."

"Ha! In your dreams, Porter, in your dreams."

"Brilliant, Ramon, now that you've thoroughly insulted me in front of my girlfriend, tell me, who was that handsome older lady who walked out just before us?"

"The one who can't give anybody the time of day? That's Mrs. Graff. She lives on the fifth floor with her maid, although I guess today you'd call her a 'personal assistant' or something. Usually Yvette — that's the maid — is the one doing the errands, walking the dog — you know. They've got a cute little poodle named Mimi. You hardly ever see Mrs. Graff leave the building. She's one of those rich, eccentric types — likes to keep to herself."

Not an easy feat with Ramon around, thought Darby.

Miles clapped a hand on the doorman's shoulder. "Thank you, Ramon. It's nice to know who my neighbors are, even if I'm only here for a few more months."

"Anytime, Miles. I know everyone in the building by sight, and nearly everyone by name. After all, there're only two hundred residences." He pushed open the door for them. "Where you headed?"

"I'm off to take Darby for a fabulous brunch."

"Can't do better than The Camellia." He glanced at his watch. "Nine o'clock. Want me to call for reservations?"

"Already taken care of, my good fellow."

"Tootles, then." Ramon gave a little bow. "I'll be seeing you again, Darby."

"Definitely," she said, smiling, as they strolled onto the sidewalk. Nudging Miles with her elbow, she teased, "Girlfriend, huh?"

"Yes," he said, pulling her close and giving her a hug. "*Girlfriend.* You know, I happen to like the sound of it."

"I see," she said. To herself she thought: *Me too, Mr. Bean.*

As they finished up their brunch of salmon and lox, Miles asked Darby her plans for her visit in the city.

"Plans? I'm here to see you," she said, wiping a dab of cream cheese from her lips. The Camellia had been every bit as good as Ramon had promised, and Darby was stuffed.

"Now come on, love, I know you better than that. You're here to spend time with me but you've got more than that on your Darby agenda."

"I can't believe you're saying that," she protested, pretending to pout. "I've barely landed and you're questioning my reasons for being here. What kind of a host are you, anyway?"

"A realistic one. Fess up, Darby, you're

planning to acquire a boutique agency here — or land a new listing. Am I right?"

"Wrong. I'm here to relax and spend time with you — when you're not teaching or grilling me about my motives."

"That's all? No properties to preview for any clients? No hot buyers to meet for drinks?"

She paused. "Not really."

"Not really? Aha! So you do have a secret real estate plan."

She laughed. "Hardly. But now that you bring it up, I did have an email from Hideki Kobayashi a few weeks ago, asking me to check on possible locations for his company in New York. I suppose that counts, right?"

Miles's rugged face wore a triumphant look. "That's my girl, always ready to make the next deal. So your wealthy Japanese businessman wants a slice of the Big Apple, eh? How will you get up to snuff on what's available in the city?"

"I won't completely — not in a week, anyway, but I can sure give it a shot. Of course, there's the small matter of licensing, too. I've managed to make deals in Maine and Florida, but I'm not accredited here." She waited as the waitress set their check in the middle of the table and discreetly departed. "I have a few leads on Manhattan brokers, including a guy from Maine who's a partner in a new start-up. I'll do my own research on properties, and then make a few calls. If I like what one of them has to say, I'll invite that broker to work with Hideki and me."

"Isn't Kobayashi the one who bought the island estate down in Florida?"

Darby nodded. "Yes. He fell in love with a waterfront compound that had belonged to a pro golfer." She pictured the acres of manicured grounds, guest house, pool house, and killer views of the Gulf of Mexico, and smiled. It had been one of her biggest sales to date, and had launched her friendship with the high-powered pharmaceutical executive.

"Don't you run the risk of losing Hideki to this chap if you refer him?"

"Me, lose a client?" Darby laughed before the memory of the Davenports and their displeasure flitted into her mind. "I'll refer him for this transaction only. Besides, Hideki is a friend, and very loyal." She took a sip of freshly squeezed orange juice and savored the sharp, clean taste. Her stay in Florida a year earlier had spoiled her as far as citrus was concerned, but this juice was every bit as good as what she'd enjoyed off the tree while staying on Serenidad Key.

She glanced at her watch. "Hadn't you better get to your class, Professor Porter? Your students will be waiting anxiously."

"Suppose so. I wish I didn't have to leave you to your own devices. You sure you'll be okay?"

"I'll be fine."

"Right. I'll be busy until mid-afternoon or so. Where should we meet? At the flat, or somewhere more exotic?"

"Let's talk later on and see how your day has gone."

"Fair enough." Miles paid the bill and leaned toward her. "Goodbye, my little real estate detective," he said, planting a kiss on her cheek. "One night in the city and you have a murder to solve." He shook his head. "Wish I didn't have to run but I'll speak with you soon."

Darby watched as he walked past the tables and exited the restaurant, a tall, good-looking man who never failed to turn female heads. She thought of Natalia, wondering if she had a little crush on Miles. Then the image of the crudely constructed death threat popped into her head.

She shuddered. *How would I feel if I received a note like that? Most likely, terrified . . .*

Rodin's killer was out there, somewhere,

and so was the person who had written that note. As Darby picked up her purse and prepared to leave the restaurant, she wondered if Miles was right and they were one and the same.

From the wooden bench that creaked beneath his considerable weight, Sergei Bokeria watched the door to Schermerhorn Hall, waiting for Natalia Kazakova to emerge. The day was shaping up nicely, he thought, feeling the sun warm against his face. It reminded him of his boyhood in the Ural Mountains, playing outside in the first nice days of spring. There had been a small seasonal creek behind his house, brimming with muddy water once the winter snows melted, and the little boys of his village often congregated there. They'd gather stones and try to dam up the creek, and he remembered the feeling of the icy water as it splashed over his hands, the sound of innocent laughter, and the smell of the damp earth beneath his boots.

The bench sat in a compact little park with a constant parade of students and faculty streaming past. Bokeria watched the groups laughing and gesturing animatedly, wishing Natalia was among them. She was a bright, personable young woman, and yet had failed to make any American friends while in college. Sergei was not sure why, but he suspected Alec Rodin had had something to do with it.

He won't be a problem any longer, thought Sergei. Privately he'd spoken to Mikhail about the condition of Alec's body, told him how it was punctured in several places by the sword. He, Sergei, had been the one to identify Alec's lifeless corpse when it had proven too much for Natalia to even contemplate.

A shout brought the bodyguard up short. Instantly he was on his feet, his hand going toward the concealed weapon at his waist. But it was only a trio of college boys, shrieking when their Frisbee became entangled in the limbs of an old tree. He watched them leap upwards, trying to dislodge it, and then tossing their shoes toward the disc. When one of their sneakers became caught in the tree as well, there was even more shouting.

Sergei glanced back at the classical classroom building and then at his watch. A feeling of unease began in the pit of his stomach and rose slowly upward. Natalia should have been out of class by now. She was nearly ten minutes late.

A loud rumbling made him jump. An image of tanks, rolling by during a Victory Day parade from his boyhood, flooded his brain. His family had journeyed to Moscow to be bystanders at the event honoring World War II veterans of the Red Army. He recalled the awesome sight of the waves of tanks — more than one hundred — and the high-stepping soldiers, numbering close to eight thousand. Just when Sergei had thought the extravaganza could not get any more magnificent, his father pointed to the sky. Overhead scores of helicopters, transport jets, and bombers zoomed, seeming to buzz the buildings.

This rumbling did not come from a Soviet-era tank, but from a Harley-Davidson motorcycle, driven by a man who might be Sergei's age, his hair, where it peeked from the helmet, starting to gray.

He let out a snort of exasperation.

All this talk of the FSB . . . what if it was true? Someone had sent that threatening message. What if Natalia's classroom paper was truly dangerous, and ex-KGB officers had somehow infiltrated the classroom and kidnapped her? His heart began to hammer and his palms, normally dry, grew damp.

He rose fluidly from the bench and took a step forward.

Just then the door to the building opened. Sergei paused, waiting and watching, his breathing irregular, until at last Natalia emerged. She was smiling — not her usual dreamy, faraway smile, but a big grin that made her face glow. Beside her was a tall young man wearing a business suit. He was smiling as well, telling her something funny perhaps, and gesticulating with long, gangly arms.

Sergei's mouth twisted into his own version of a happy expression. So she had a friend after all, and he was a good-looking guy. Could he have been the one on the phone with her before dinner? Sergei took several steps backward, eased himself back onto the bench and continued to watch.

Darby made her way back to Central Park Place, determined to make some inquiries on Hideki Kobayashi's behalf before sightseeing. Once again the air was soft and warm, with only the gentlest of breezes. She glanced across the street to Central Park, noting the trees that were starting to bloom, and felt the green expanse luring her in. *I'll sit on a park bench and make my calls,* she thought. *On a day like today, it's better than being holed up in Charles Burrows's condo.*

Moments later she was responding to emails on her smartphone, including one from her Japanese client. *Telephone me when you can,* his message said, *so we may discuss my real estate needs.* Darby glanced at her watch. Nearly noon. The perfect time to reach Hideki before he headed out for his customary lunch of sushi and seaweed salad.

The high-powered executive answered his phone on the first ring.

"Darby! What a pleasure to hear from you. I trust that all is well?"

"Fine," she said, smiling at a group of pre-schoolers preparing to picnic on a patch of scruffy grass. "I'm in New York — sitting in Central Park, actually — and I saw your email message. I thought we might discuss what you're looking for in the city — that is, if now is a good time for you to talk." She brushed away a bee and watched it meander toward a clump of flowering azalea bushes.

"Yes, your timing is fine." He paused. "May I ask why you are visiting New York?"

"I'm here to visit Miles Porter." She felt a flush rising in her cheeks. "He's the journalist who was in Afghanistan when we were negotiating your purchase of Tag Gunnerson's property."

"I remember." What went unsaid were the events of the past February, when Darby had nearly perished at the hands of one of

Hideki Kobayashi's associates. *Fine with me if he doesn't bring it up,* Darby thought to herself. *I don't want to talk about it anyway.*

The Japanese man gave a little cough. "I contacted you about property because Genkei has interest in opening an office in New York. I'd be looking to purchase a building — new, if possible — in a desirable location."

"What kind of square feet are you thinking?" Darby was jotting down notes in a small notebook that rarely left her side.

"Oh, I don't know, but at least as much space as we have in Tokyo." He paused. "I do have a small window in my schedule before I head there on Monday. I could fly up tomorrow and see properties on Sunday if you'd like."

Yikes! Darby didn't need to think about it — when a client like Hideki Kobayashi said jump, Darby Farr laced up her shoes to take a leap.

"Terrific. I'll make some calls and line up showings for Sunday."

"Then it is settled. I will phone you tomorrow when I am in the city."

"Do you need me to make you a hotel reservation?"

"No, no, that won't be necessary." He gave a discreet little chuckle. "I thank you for

97

your kind offer, but I have a suite on standby at the Ritz."

Okay then. "Very good. I'll look forward to seeing you on Sunday and touching base tomorrow."

"And I as well."

Darby clicked off her phone and leaned back on the bench. She felt the familiar surge of adrenalin that came whenever she was about to assist a client in spending a large amount of money. Granted, Hideki Kobayashi was in the early stages of looking at New York property — heck, he hadn't even begun to look! — but Darby knew the man well enough to know that he did not waste time in idle contemplation or planning. If he wanted an office building in a prime Manhattan location, he would get one, and he wouldn't spin anyone's wheels in the process. All Darby needed to do was find some good prospects for Hideki to see.

Quickly she thought of Miles. What would his reaction be to her needing to show property on Sunday? It wasn't exactly the way they'd planned to spend his free weekend together. And yet Miles understood the nature of Darby's profession, the way she made it a priority to respond to her clients in a timely fashion. *Maybe he'll want to come along.* She pictured the tall Brit and the compact Asian executive and smiled. *It was very likely they'd enjoy each other's company,* she thought.

Darby searched her contacts for the name of the New York broker she'd met while last in Maine. Todd something . . . *Todd Stockton.* Raised in Minnesota, he'd dropped out of college in the '70s and hitchhiked east to Maine. Somehow he'd scraped together enough money to purchase an old Cape, which he'd restored and then sold for a profit. Before long, Stockton had his real estate license and had bought, fixed up, and then sold a number of coastal properties. By the mid-eighties, he'd started his own real estate firm, and within a decade, grown it to be one of Maine's most profitable brokerages.

But that hadn't satisfied Stockton. By now a very big fish in a small pond, the entrepreneur now turned his sights on New York. He'd launched a start-up brokerage just before Hurricane Sandy hit the east coast, and positioned the company to help rebuild in its wake. His uncanny ability to find talented professionals to join him was working, and the Stockton Group was already a major player in many of New York's most lucrative deals.

Darby called his number and heard a deep

voice answer.

"Stockton here."

She explained how they had met a few months earlier and Todd Stockton gave a chuckle.

"Of course I remember you, Ms. Farr. I don't think anyone who meets you would ever forget."

So he's a flatterer. Darby rolled her eyes. "I don't know about that, but I did want to speak to you about a real estate client and his needs."

She could feel Stockton's focus sharpen over the airwaves. "Go on, please."

She described what Hideki Kobayashi wanted, without mentioning his name, and waited to see what Stockton would say.

"I'm going to send you several options right now, Ms. Farr, any one of which we can see on Sunday." He asked a few more questions and Darby answered. "And our arrangement?"

"A fifty percent referral," she answered. It was more than the standard — she knew that — but what the heck.

"Fine. I'll send along an agreement as well. Shall we plan to meet at eleven o'clock on Sunday, or earlier?"

"That will be fine. Let me know where and my client and I will be there."

She looked around the park and smiled. *This was going to be fun.*

A dark-haired young woman with a stroller stopped at Darby's bench.

"Excuse me, but are you a friend of the man in nine-thirty?"

"Yes," said Darby, recognizing the number of Charles Burrows's apartment.

"I'm Gina Trovata," she said, kneeling to check on the two children in the stroller. Deciding that they were fine, at least for the moment, she continued. "I work in the building, so I'm in and out of there a lot. I take care of Sherry and Penn Cooper's kids." As if on cue, the littlest Cooper let out a long sound that might have been a sigh.

"You're their nanny?" Darby asked.

"Yes — weekday mornings, although today I'm working until five." She checked her watch. "Anyway, I wondered if you'd mention to your friend — the man —"

"His name is Miles. Miles Porter."

"Okay then, Miles. Please tell him I'm opening a vintage clothing store, sometime soon, and if he has any sweaters or jackets he'd like us to sell, I'd love to know." She rummaged in a pocket and handed Darby a business card.

Darby looked up at Gina and chuckled.

101

"You mean to tell me that Miles is a trendy dresser?" She thought back to his tweedy jacket and Irish knit sweater. "I guess I hadn't noticed."

"I don't know his whole wardrobe, but yes, he seems to like the classics." She bent down to pick up a toy that one of the boys had tossed from the stroller. "The natives are getting restless — I'd better keep walking."

Darby stood and introduced herself. "I'm here for a visit. It's nice to meet you, Gina, and good luck with your new shop."

"Thanks." She pushed the stroller and grinned. "I can't wait."

Darby looked at the card again. *High Voltage Vintage,* it said. No address, just Gina's name and her phone number. Darby smiled and put the card into the pocket of her jacket.

Peggy Babson watched the hallway outside her office at Pulitzer Hall. She was watching for Professor Porter, hoping she would have a chance to ask him about Thursday's strange events. The dark-haired guy and his violent death . . . She shuddered. Thoughts of the stabbing were never far from her mind, whether she was flipping through a magazine, watching reality television, or trying to fall asleep. She knew it was because she was more sensitive than other people, more attuned to the spirit world. Perhaps if she had more information, she could both block out the bloody images and help the police with their investigation.

She glanced at the watch encircling her freckled wrist. Professor Porter had been in a rush that morning, nearly late for his eleven o'clock seminar. Catching his eye had been impossible. Now it seemed he was keeping the students later than usual, and the waiting was tiresome.

Her stomach growled. Not wanting to miss the British journalist, she'd foregone her customary one hour-plus lunch at the pizza shop around the corner in favor of a tasteless granola bar at her desk. She yanked open a drawer to see if a stray Hershey Kiss was tucked behind the stapler. No luck. Maybe she'd find something sweet further back, behind the tape dispenser?

Footsteps on the wooden floors outside her door made her pull back a pudgy arm as if she'd seen a snake.

"Professor Porter?" She stumbled to her feet, nearly tipping a mug full of cold coffee onto her keypad. "May I have a word?"

Hustling to the hallway, she nearly collided with a young woman clutching a laptop and a dead potted plant. Enormous black boots — the kind construction workers wore — made her bare legs look like matchsticks.

"Is the registrar's office in this building?" she asked.

Peggy shook her head and directed the young woman to the correct office. She looked like a child, with her knobby knees and air of uncertainty. Peggy sniffed. *I may not have gone to Columbia, but I have responsibilities — a job, a dog, and my own house.* She plodded back to her desk and plumped the seat cushion on her office chair. The rumblings of hunger had turned to gnawing pains.

"Ms. Babson?"

She looked up. Miles Porter paused in the doorway, a shock of brown hair falling over his forehead.

"Hallo," he said, smiling.

Hallo. She loved that, the way he sounded like he'd stepped off the set of *Downton Abbey.*

"Professor Porter! I didn't hear you in the hall." No doubt the clomping of the girl's heavy boots had drowned out his footfall. "How was your seminar?"

"Oh, they're all very antsy — thinking about finals and such."

"Yes, of course." She felt her face flush. "What about the poor girl who lost her fiancé? Natalia? Did anyone mention that?"

"Not to me, but I'm sure her classmates are aware and properly sympathetic." Miles raised a hand and she realized he was preparing to leave.

"I hoped we could chat a bit about what happened yesterday." She sounded shriller than she wanted and looked down at her nails. The polish was due for a change and they needed a good filing. "That man who was stabbed."

"Ah, yes. Horrible thing." He glanced at his mobile. "I'm off to meet a friend, but I have a few minutes."

A few minutes. She felt irritation mixing with her mounting hunger. "Have you heard anything about who may have killed him?"

"No, nothing." He frowned. "Did you meet the fellow? Alec Rodin?"

"Yes, well, that is to say, not exactly. I heard you speaking in your office, and then I saw him going down the stairs." She bit her lip. "Your voices were quite loud."

Miles Porter nodded. "Indeed. I became pretty angry, I'm afraid."

"Yes. I heard you quite clearly." She sniffed and felt the British man's interest pique.

"I threatened him — you may have heard that, although I certainly didn't mean it."

"You sounded serious to me." She blinked her eyes a few times. "Of course, I didn't tell the police exactly what you said . . ."

"Why, Ms. Babson?"

"Because you said you'd kill him!"

"My dear woman, I took an instant dislike to Rodin, but I never would have murdered the man. Tell the police whatever you'd like."

She lifted her eyebrows. "I must get back to work, Professor Porter. Good afternoon." She turned toward her desk as his footsteps receded down the hall, unable to resist a tiny smile.

"You'll never believe what the secretary at Pulitzer Hall implied," fumed Miles as he closed the door to Charles Burrows's apartment.

"Whatever it was, I can tell it wasn't good." Darby reached up to give the lanky journalist a hug.

Miles hugged her back, tightly. "Just looking at you makes me feel better, you know that?"

"I'm glad. Now what did the old witch say?"

He gave a slow grin. "She isn't exactly an

old witch, although she acts like one, but she said she'd overheard my rather heated discussion with Alec Rodin, but that she hadn't told the police *everything.* Emphasis on the 'everything.' Darby, she hinted that she'd withheld information. This may sound silly, but I felt as if she'd like to blackmail me!"

"Because of your argument?"

"Exactly. I told her she could tell the police whatever she wanted, and that seemed to shut her down."

"Good for you. Extortion only works if the victim is afraid of exposure." Darby had dealt with a blackmailer's destruction in Maine several months earlier and the experience was fresh in her mind. "Speaking of threats, any word from Natalia?"

"No. Her father must be here now, and I trust she's told him about that note."

"Let's hope." Darby pictured the crude letter and its message and sighed. "What about her article, Miles? Will anything happen with the information she unearthed?"

"I don't know. That's up to Natalia to decide. I've asked her for a few revisions, and to flesh out a little of the details, but I would never publish anything without having permission." He reached out and squeezed Darby's shoulders. "Enough shop talk. What have you been up to, love?"

Darby told him about her conversation with Hideki Kobayashi. "I hope you won't mind if we look at a few properties with him on Sunday."

"Not at all. Perhaps he'd like to dine with us on Saturday night?"

"That's a nice idea, Miles. I'll be sure to ask him." She grinned. "Guess where he stays while in New York?"

"Let's see . . . the Ritz-Carlton?"

"Exactly! How did you know?"

"I guess I'm not the only one with super duper powers." He reached out and tried to rumple her hair, although it was so thick and silky it refused to muss. "Hideki obviously likes the finer things. After all, he has you for his broker, doesn't he?" Miles winked. "Not to mention that the Ritz is one of the city's best hotels."

"Deductive reasoning. Sometimes it can work like a charm." She frowned. "I wish we could use it to help Natalia. I'll admit that I'm worried about her."

"I love your concern. Let's call her and check in, shall we?"

Miles found his student's number and gave her a call. A few seconds later, he was leaving a message. When he'd finished, he groaned. "Now I'm worried, too. Perhaps I should send a text?"

"Why not? It can't hurt." Darby checked her own phone and made a face. "ET needs me to contact the office. Excuse me for just a minute, Miles." Darby rose and went into the bedroom. Her assistant answered immediately.

"What's up? I saw your message to give you a call."

ET cleared his throat. "Bad news, I'm afraid. The Davenports are taking legal action."

Darby thought back to her earlier conversation with ET regarding the couple. "They called a mold inspector, I take it?"

"I'm not sure, but they've decided to pursue the matter in the courts."

"What were the results of the mold test?"

"I don't know that they've had one yet."

"So they're going after the building inspector?"

"That's not all." He swallowed, obviously unwilling to continue. "They're blaming Pacific Coast Realty for the mold problem, saying the company should have known about it."

"And when they accuse the company, they actually mean me."

ET sighed. "Darby, I hate to say it, but you are getting sued."

FIVE

The wheels of the world's most expensive baby stroller were stuck. Gina Trovata bit back a swearword before remembering that the baby and his fourteen-month-old brother couldn't yet talk, so technically it was okay to curse in their presence. That was the operating theory of her employer, at least. Perfectly fine to throw out a four-letter word in front of the little boys, but clean it up when in the presence of the bigger ones. Gina pushed hard against the curb of the sidewalk and the wheels finally straightened. She sighed. The urge to let loose a string of expletives had passed, and lucky thing — a trio of nuns had stopped to gawk at her charges.

Gina nodded in agreement as the black-habited sisters oohed and ahhed, their heads bent toward the babies. This wasn't the first time total strangers had stopped to admire the brothers. It wasn't their adorable outfits or contented babbling, but their striking good looks that won them praise, and their older brothers were just as handsome.

Gina had to hand it to Sherry and Penn Cooper — they did produce gorgeous, well-mannered kids. All four boys were blonde and blue-eyed, with sunny smiles and winsome personalities that never seemed to flag. Given the Coopers' clean-cut and wholesome good looks, the family might have stepped right out of a Ralph Lauren catalogue.

The nuns straightened up and smiled. An old custom came to Gina, a gesture of respect she had learned at a very young age. She placed her hands together at the level of her heart and bowed her head. The nuns beamed back at her, bowed their heads, and started silently down the sidewalk.

Who taught me to do that? Gina wondered as she watched the stooped backs of the sisters. She pushed the stroller into the park. *My adoptive parents? The nuns at the orphanage?* There were so many secrets in her background. Unlike Penn and Sherry's kids, she had no clue as to who had brought her into the world.

She stopped the stroller in front of a vacant bench and sat down. Maneuvering it so that the boys could both see her, she gave

Trevor a biscuit to munch on while she fed Sam. She removed a bottle from the stroller, unclipped Sam's safety restraints, and pulled him toward her on the bench.

It had been a lucky thing, running into the woman who was a friend of Miles Porter's. What had she said her name was? Darcy? Gina couldn't remember. She'd been Asian, very pretty, with dainty features and long, glossy hair. Her clothes, Gina had noticed, had been nondescript. Almost blah.

The baby nestled into the curve of her body and began to drink from the bottle. She smiled down at him, and then at Trevor, who gave a quick grin and then pointed at a passing cyclist.

"Bicycle," said Gina. "Can you say that Trevvie? Bicycle."

He grinned and chortled before popping the end of the biscuit back into his mouth.

Gina took her phone and gave it a quick glance. Almost quitting time, she thought wryly. She scrolled to a text from her friend and business partner, asking when she would have time to scout a new location. She texted back that she would be free that afternoon.

Trevor squealed. Gina looked up and saw that he'd tossed his partially chewed cookie to the ground. She fumbled in the stroller for a bottle for him and leaned back on the bench.

The park was a fabulous place to people-watch, and occasionally Gina spotted someone she recognized. Sometimes they turned out to be someone she knew, but more often than not, they were celebrities whose everyday clothing made them difficult to identify.

Such was the case with an elderly woman who was walking slowly toward the stroller. Gina had seen the woman before — she knew that — and figured she was someone famous rather than an acquaintance. An aging movie star or model? She scrutinized the woman's handsome, patrician face before letting her gaze fall to what she most enjoyed ogling: clothes.

Gina couldn't remember when she'd first become enamored of textiles, and in particular, vintage garments. Like so many things from her past, she had only dim recollections. A calico-patterned apron with red rickrack. A poufy gabardine cocktail dress. A scrap of hand-tatted Italian lace . . .

She took in the woman's outfit and nearly gasped in surprise. Strolling by her was a two-piece suit in navy wool with a cropped bolero jacket, three-quarter length sleeves, and four big Lucite buttons. Gina knew immediately that the classic outfit dated from the 1950s, and had a crepe lining and back kick pleat. She nearly salivated with desire. The suit was beautiful, and she had to have it.

Quickly Gina settled Sam back into his part of the stroller and strapped him securely in. The woman had passed by the bench and was now exiting the park. After checking the bench to be sure she hadn't left anything, Gina pushed off after the woman.

Trevor raised his little eyebrows in surprise but continued to suck happily on his bottle. Walking fast, Gina closed the gap between her and the suit's owner. Gina noted that her hair was dove gray, and curled softly under a little cap. On her stocking-clad feet were flat brown shoes.

Gina frowned. *Frumpy and totally inappropriate for the scale of the suit,* she thought. She pictured pumps in an apple green, along with a structured handbag in the same shade. The woman crossed Central Park West with the stroller hot on her tail.

Gina was running through pocketbook options when the woman stopped abruptly in front of the Coopers' building. To Gina's amazement, she turned toward the front door, where the doorman greeted her with a warm smile.

Gina followed at a discreet distance. She watched as the woman headed to the elevator and disappeared behind the closed doors.

Unbelievable! Gina was about to interrogate the doorman when Sam started to fuss. *I'll quiz him when these two are quiet.* After all, where there was one vintage suit there were many — just the kind of inventory she and her partner needed.

Darby Farr had always prided herself on her impeccable record in real estate, not so much regarding deals negotiated and closed, but regarding satisfied customers. It wasn't easy keeping people happy, but she had worked hard to do just that, and more important, pay excruciating attention to each and every detail so that nothing escaped her eagle eye when it came to the nitty-gritty aspects of her profession. Now, in the quiet of Charles Burrows's bedroom, she thought back over the Davenports' purchase of the house in Poway, California, and asked herself what she'd overlooked. Had there been any indication at all of any problem with the integrity of the property's addition? Were there any signs of moisture? Any strange odors or red flags she'd ignored?

The answer was no. The mold issue — if indeed there was a mold issue — was a complete surprise, not only to the sellers of the home, but to the building inspector and to Darby herself. There had been no evidence, no damp smell, no signs of growth — nothing.

Although . . .

Someone had mentioned something about mildew. Darby thought back. *We had been looking at the addition at the back of the house. The door frame . . .*

It was me, she remembered. *I asked the inspector if there was mildew around the frame of the door.*

And he had answered no.

There's a first time for everything, she thought, realizing it was something her Aunt Jane Farr used to mutter when life took her by surprise. Darby supposed that even Jane had had her share of unpleasant surprises in real estate, but Darby, a professional for more than a decade, had so far kept her reputation squeaky clean. Other than a recent ticket for speeding, Darby was what many would term a model citizen and an exemplary real estate agent.

She sighed and looked up the number for a lawyer she knew from her Aikido classes in San Diego. When the attorney answered the phone, Darby explained the situation as best she could. Debra Hitchings's answer came quickly, in a no-nonsense, clipped voice.

"I'll take a look," she said. "Try not to worry."

After thanking her, Darby squared her shoulders and went to find Miles.

Rona Reichels, fifty-eight years old, scanned her credit card bill with increasing alarm. A three-hundred-dollar dinner charge in mid-March, and another one at the beginning of the month. Fees for concerts at two hundred bucks a pop. Purchases at a tony boutique on Fifth Avenue totaling nearly a thousand. She narrowed her eyes. Her own bills were bad enough, but these? She shook her expertly highlighted chestnut-colored hair and angrily picked up her phone.

Where are you? She texted.

With a friend, came the reply.

Rona gritted her teeth. That was the problem.

Come home now. Hopefully the curtness of the message sounded like an emergency.

Can't. See you in the morning maybe.

I SAID COME HOME, she typed, waiting. No response.

Rona's telephone hit the surface of the

desk with a clatter. *Damn that girl!* Devin didn't care what Rona said, and hadn't since she was a child of five. *She is the most selfish, stubborn creature to walk the earth.* She cared only for her own agenda, and that agenda involved spending large amounts of cash.

Her temples throbbing, Rona reached up and massaged her head, hoping to relieve some of the tension. *I've got to get some more deals going,* she thought, the pain now like a drumbeat against her skull. *I need to make more money.* She picked up her phone again and scanned her email accounts. One client had a question about a good dry-cleaner. That can wait. Another was hoping to score tickets to the Yankees . . . could she help? She swore under her breath.

The condo's opulent walls seemed too close for comfort. Her pulse began to race and the jungle drums in her head beat faster. She closed her eyes, opened them to find the walls even closer. *Not now,* she thought. *Not now . . .*

Rona struggled to regulate her breathing before a full-fledged panic attack began. She pictured a calm scene — Central Park at sunset — and inhaled deeply. She saw a few people strolling, a slight breeze rustling the leaves, watched the sun dipping down behind the trees . . .

You've always lived above your means, said her father, his voice still bitingly familiar even a decade after his death. *You think you're so high and mighty. Little Miss Rona who doesn't want to admit she's from the Bronx, and that she's never going to amount to much of anything . . .*

She gritted her teeth against the voice, against all of the criticism she could hear in her head or heap upon herself. She told herself she would not give in to despair. And then, out of the blue, her cell phone rang.

"Ramon, the old lady in the suit . . . which apartment does she live in?" Gina pointed at the figure stepping nimbly into the elevator.

The doorman gave a lopsided grin. "Whazzup with Mrs. Graff today? Everyone's asking about her." He shook his head. "She lives on the fifth floor. Five-fifteen. You don't see her much 'cause she's one of those what you might call reclusive types. Yvette is the one you'd recognize."

The little boys were both napping, and one let out a soft snore.

"The skinny woman with the poodle, right?"

"Exactly." Ramon grinned at the sleeping

119

children and leaned back on his heels. "Why's everyone so fascinated with five-fifteen today?"

"No particular reason," Gina said, steering the stroller past the doorman. "Just curious."

The elevator was empty and Gina pushed in the stroller and selected the fifth floor. She'd learned a long time ago to go with whatever urges she felt, and, except for a few instances (such as that rock drummer from upstate) her instincts had been right.

The doors opened and Gina wheeled the sleeping boys to the condo. She hesitated for a split second, and knocked.

"Yes?" A hesitant voice, slightly accented, on the other side of the door.

Gina explained that she worked in eighteen-twenty-two and wondered if she could speak to Mrs. Graff.

"Why?" A faint accent. *French,* Gina surmised.

"I . . ." Gina hadn't really thought of what she would say, and her mind raced to come up with something plausible. "I think she dropped something in the elevator."

"What is it?"

"A credit card."

The door opened a crack, the chain lock still firmly in place. "I will take it."

Gina bit the inside of her cheek. "Well, uh," she stammered, "I was hoping to give it to Mrs. Graff in *person.*"

"You can give it to me, Mademoiselle. I work for Mrs. Graff and I can assure you, I'm completely trustworthy."

"I'd rather not."

The woman's thin face grew wary. "Where is this credit card? Let me see it."

"You see, I need —" The door shut firmly.

Gina frowned. In the background she heard another muffled voice, and then the maid's response. *"Personne."* No one.

Gina turned the stroller as Sam stirred in his sleep. She thought of the maid's snotty attitude. *"Merde,"* she muttered.

There was no sense camping out in front of the door if the reclusive Mrs. Graff hardly ever ventured out. *I'm not quite desperate enough to pull a fire alarm,* she thought wryly. *There has to be another way.*

The elevator doors opened and a dainty poodle trotted out on a leash, followed by the tall figure of Miranda Styles.

"Hey, Gina," the dog walker called out. "Just put a very tired Honey upstairs. She's gonna sleep all afternoon after our walk."

"Don't count on it," Gina said. "That dog's always up for something." She eyed the poodle. "Cute little thing. Whose is it?"

"Five-fifteen. I take her every day, same as Honey."

Five-fifteen? Gina smiled. "What's its name?"

"Mimi. You've seen her before, I'm sure. They've had her forever."

"Huh." She nodded goodbye to Miranda and headed into the elevator, maneuvering the stroller into a corner. Humming a little tune, she pressed the button for her floor. Thanks to Mimi and Miranda, she'd find a way into the condo after all.

Miles found Darby pouring over pages regarding mold detection. She'd told him about the Davenports, and that she'd contacted her San Diego attorney. Miles lent a sympathetic ear, assuring her she wasn't at fault.

"Come on, love," he said gently. "Leave the mold for a bit. I've contacted Natalia for an update and she suggested we meet in the park. What do you say?"

"An excellent idea. I could read through this stuff all afternoon and I don't know that it would do me much good."

"Exactly. After all, say worse comes to worse, which isn't going to happen, but just say these disgruntled people do win some damages, your insurance will cover it, right?"

"I suppose, but that's not quite it." She looked up into his face. "It's my reputation. I've always been so careful to get everything right, you know?"

"I do. It's the same way in my profession." He gave her a gentle smile. "I understand how you feel, really I do, but let's put that sharp mind of yours to work on poor Natalia's problems, shall we?"

Darby grabbed a light jacket and tucked her cell phone into the pocket. "Did Natalia sound worried about that threatening letter?"

"No, I wouldn't say so. She sounds much better, actually. Perhaps the police have discovered something to do with Rodin's death."

"Where are we meeting her?"

"There's a gazebo by the Great Lawn. It'll give us a nice walk in the April sunshine."

Miles slipped an arm around Darby as they exited the elevator and gave Ramon a quick wave. He was speaking with a tall man and barely acknowledged them.

"Looks like Ramon's in a deep conversation," Darby commented.

"The man's a chameleon," said Miles. "I've seen him be serious, flirty, funny, earnest, righteous — you name it, and Ramon can mold his personality to fit whoever he's speaking with. A first-rate salesman, selling life the way it should be on Central Park West."

Darby smiled. "The Way Life Should Be" was a popular slogan for her home state of Maine. "I'll believe you when I hear Ramon using some of your British expressions, Miles. That will be the true test."

He chuckled. They crossed the wide avenue and entered the park, passing a man selling chestnuts in small paper bags. Miles halted and pulled out his wallet.

"Here's the ticket," he said, taking his change and the chestnuts. "Have you ever tried these, Darby?"

She nodded and took one. They peeled them in silence before popping the warm meats into their mouths.

"Delicious." She took in the yellow-green leaves of the trees, the swaying daffodils, and bright green grass. "Spring. Growing up I didn't see what the big deal was, but the older I get, the more I appreciate this season."

"Rebirth and renewal," Miles quipped. "The promise of life after winter's icy grip, right?"

"Yes." She took a deep breath, smelled a

hint of something blooming. "It's intoxicating."

They reached the gazebo and paused. "Nat's not here yet," said Miles. He plopped on a wooden bench and patted it. "Put that little posterior next to me, Miss Farr, and let's pretend we haven't a care in the world."

She sat down and regarded him. "We both know what I'm stressed about."

"Yes." He craned his neck, looking for Natalia.

"What about you?"

"Me? I'm my jolly old self, Darby. Granted, I don't like being badgered by that Benedetti chap and the other policeman, nor did I enjoy Ms. Babson's nasty hints that Rodin's untimely death had something to do with me, but other than that, I'm just ducky."

She touched his arm. "Natalia and her bodyguard are here." His eyes flitted to the approaching pair and then back to Darby. "I hope you'll remember, Miles — I'm in your court just the way you're in mine. If something is bothering you, I hope you'll trust me to help."

He gave a tight smile but said nothing.

The story in the *New York Times* gave no new details regarding Alec Rodin's death, thought Rona, nothing that Sherry Cooper hadn't shared when she'd called earlier. The Russian man had been murdered a stone's throw from some of Columbia University's most important buildings, stabbed with a sharp object.

"He bled to death," Sherry had said, adding, "Broad daylight, but it doesn't sound as if there were any witnesses."

"What a shame!" Rona exclaimed, although what she'd wanted to do was clap her hands with joy. "Poor little Nikita."

"Nikita?" Sherry Cooper sounded puzzled. "If you mean Natalia, I wouldn't waste your sympathy. That woman will be fine. She's a twenty-two-year-old heiress who no longer has to marry the man Daddy selected. How sad can she be?"

"I see what you mean."

"The important thing is to persuade them — especially Mikhail — to sell the penthouse." Sherry paused. "Of course, I can always approach him on my own —"

"No, that wouldn't be wise," Rona interjected. "I've gotten to know Mikhail very well. Let me have a talk with him."

Now Rona was searching in her phone for Kazakova's number, having murmured a few more things about the "tragedy" and promising Sherry she'd find out about the penthouse as soon as possible. "I'm on it," she assured her. "I'll be back in touch right away."

Rona scanned old emails with increasing anxiety. It was here somewhere, she knew it. Mikhail Kazakova's contact information — but where?

At last she located his number, and a new set of anxieties surfaced. What if he'd changed his number? What if he only answered numbers that he recognized?

Her fears evaporated when the call was answered instantly with a clipped "Yes."

"Mikhail, it's Rona Reichels, from the third floor. We met a few years ago, when you first came to the city?" She was determined to keep things positive.

He grunted. "Yes."

"I'm calling to say how sorry I am about Alec's death." Her voice was smooth. "I can't imagine how you and Natalia feel at this very difficult time. If there is anything I can do, as a neighbor or a friend, I hope . . ."

"Thanks." He cut her off, and was about to hang up. She scrambled for time.

"I've made a little something — a cake — and wanted to bring it over. It's — it's a tradition here when someone passes away. Neighbors like to bring by food. It shows that they care."

She waited a moment. She was laying it on a little thick, like the frosting on this cake she'd have to hustle out and buy. "Are you home?"

"No." A second or two passed. Finally, "You've made us a cake?"

"Yes — chocolate. I'm sure Natalia will enjoy it. Take her mind off this terrible tragedy . . ."

"Perhaps." He paused again. "I'll be at the condo in half an hour."

"I'll drop by then." Rona hung up and sprang to her feet. She yanked her jacket from a hanger, tied it around a waistline that was just starting its middle-aged spread. Pocketbook in hand, she gave herself an order: *Get to a damn bakery — pronto.*

Darby thought Sergei Bokeria's face wore a kinder expression than earlier, but it was hard to tell when the man's natural expression was a perpetual scowl. Natalia, however, looked noticeably different. Gone were the dark circles, and although she still seemed pale, her demeanor was much more relaxed than it had been in the morning.

"I took a nap after my class," she confessed, when Miles asked how she was feeling. "I barely slept last night so it was good to get some sleep."

"I'm sure." Miles's voice was kind. "With finals coming up, you're going to need lots of rest." He paused, and asked gently, "What about the investigation? Have you heard anything else?"

She shook her head. "No. If the police have new information, they aren't sharing it with me." Her face brightened. "The good news is that I believe the threatening note I received is a joke."

"A joke?" Darby's voice was sharp. "What makes you think so?"

"I have a friend who says there's a guy who reads the newspapers and sends out letters, just to see what happens. Other people have received them, too."

"That's terrible — not to mention, criminal," Darby said. "Scaring people like that."

"I know, but it seems it's more of a prank than a real threat."

Miles glanced at Bokeria's bulging biceps. "The fact that you have Sergei on your side gives me a fair amount of comfort," he said. "Still, I think you have to be on the lookout."

Natalia nodded. "I know."

"Did you show the note to Detective Benedetti?" asked Darby.

"No. I want to put it behind me, and move on to other things." She tossed her head and her fringe of choppy bangs bobbed with emphasis.

Darby and Miles shared a glance. Just what "other things" did the girl mean?

"Do you need an extension on your paper?" Miles asked. "I'm happy to grant you one, considering the circumstances."

"Maybe." She bit her lip, looked into the distance. "Truthfully, I'm not sure if my heart's still in it."

Darby shot a glance at Miles. *He'll be disappointed,* she thought.

"I understand, Nat," he said kindly. "You've been through bloody hell. Tell you what — we can talk about it when you're ready."

She gave a shy smile. "Thank you, Professor Porter. Thank you for understanding."

Darby met Sergei Bokeria's eyes, searching his fleshy face for any sign of emotion. If the bodyguard had an opinion, he betrayed nothing.

Miles inclined his head toward Darby's as they watched the petite woman and her bulky friend depart. "What was that all about?"

"I'm not exactly sure. Natalia wants to forget about the threatening letter and doesn't seem the least bit concerned for her safety. She's willing to put her investigative paper — and presumably a new career — on the back burner, too." Darby paused. "I don't know what's going on, Miles, but if I had to guess, I'd say Natalia's in love."

Miles grinned. "Ah! You think she's met a prince, and he's swept her right off her feet. In other words, a bloke kind of like me, is that it?"

Darby reached up and kissed him. "Let's hope Natalia's that lucky."

Six

Friday afternoons in New York were full of anticipation. The weekend, with all of its promise, lay before the hordes of business-suited office workers like a treasure chest of possibility. Stiletto-wearing women longed for the comfort of forty-eight hours in flat shoes, and nannies, such as Gina Trovata, looked forward to a weekend free of diapers, oatmeal, and fraternal fighting.

Small wonder she found herself astonished when she volunteered to take a Saturday morning shift.

"Just the little boys," Sherry pleaded. "The big guys have tee-ball tryouts, and Penn's got to work."

"I'll be here."

"Great. He's going to have to stop these crazy weekend hours if we're going to have any semblance of a family life, but you know Penn — his work is like a drug. And after all, it is tax season."

Gina nodded. There were times she suspected that Penn stayed away for more reasons than just work, but she kept those suspicions to herself. Instead she smiled fondly at Trevor, reached down to hug him. "We had a good time in the park today, didn't we Trevvie?" He gave a sloppy grin before scooting off to find his older brothers.

Sherry kept an eye on his progress. "Does he seem as if he's doing any better?"

Gina answered quickly. "Definitely." Trevor was taking his time in learning to walk, a development which greatly worried his Type A mother.

A sigh. "I hope so." She brightened. "I've ordered in Chinese. Want to stay for dinner?"

"No, thanks." Gina gathered up her vintage Dolce and Gabbana. If she hurried she would just make the crosstown bus. "See you at eight."

The lobby bustled with activity as Gina worked her way through the executives returning home from work. She gave Ramon a wave, and when he called out, "Have a good weekend," told him to do the same. Stopping to explain that she'd be back in the morning to put in more time might mean waiting twenty minutes for another bus.

A couple pushed by her, talking animatedly. The young woman looked familiar, and Gina took in her petite frame and two-tone hair while racking her brain for the name. Then it came to her: this was the Russian heiress with the murdered fiancée. *Natalia Kazakova.* The man with her was tall, sandy-haired, and good-looking in an angular sort of way. His gaze was directed toward Natalia, and yet Gina noticed that he seemed to be scoping out the lobby by looking over, rather than directly at, her. Gina smirked. He obviously didn't realize he was already with the richest person in the room.

Where's the bodyguard? Gina asked herself. *Not like he's usually hard to spot or anything.* A moment later she saw the big, bulky man enter the building, his demeanor alert, a discreet seven or eight steps between his client and himself.

The bodyguard gave Gina a nod of recognition as they passed. *He's good,* she thought. *After all, I only met Natalia the one time.*

She left the building, emerging into the late afternoon sunshine and throngs of purposefully striding people. The mood felt light, as it should on a Friday in spring, but

Gina was remembering a very different scene, months earlier, when she'd first met Natalia. It was back in the fall — October, she realized — just before Halloween. In fact, it was the holiday (if that's indeed what a day devoted to disguise and way too much sugar really was — a holiday) that had prompted their meeting.

Gina's business partner, Bethany, had suggested they check out a new bar on the Friday before Halloween. When Gina demurred, complaining that she didn't own a costume, Bethany merely laughed. "I'll bring something for you and meet you right after work," she said. Gina couldn't think of any more excuses, and so she'd said okay.

The weather had been very different on that Friday afternoon.

Gina recalled a cold rain that poured down from gray skies, the kind of day that made Manhattan look its worst. Nevertheless, Bethany'd bustled in, costumes in hand, bringing along an extra one, because that was the way she was. "In case we meet someone else," she'd said. The outfits were minimal but striking, befitting two women hoping to launch a vintage clothing store: three exquisite feather hats, two sets of silk gloves, a mink stole, and a beautifully beaded purse.

"You call this a Halloween costume?" scoffed Gina. "I'm not going out in this lame excuse for a —"

"Ta-da!" Bethany brought the *piece de resistance* from behind her back: three grinning Barbara Bush masks. "Well?"

"Now you're talking." That was the thing about Bethany: she was full of surprises.

Gina smiled at the memory, dodging the passersby and continuing her route toward the bus stop. Where exactly had she and Bethany met up with Natalia? The elevator? Gina thought back . . . no, it had been in the spa. They'd headed down to the spa and fitness floor to get dressed and have a quick hit off a joint Bethany had smuggled in her raincoat, and who had they nearly collided with in the women's dressing room but Natalia Kazakova.

She was sweaty, and wearing workout clothes. Her face seemed pale, and the skin around her eyes puffy, as if she'd been crying. The two business partners exchanged glances before Gina spoke.

"Hey, you live in the building, right?"

A hesitant nod. "Yes. I'm called Natalia."

"Gina, Gina Trovata. I work for a family on the eighteenth floor. This is my friend, Bethany."

Nods were exchanged, and Gina continued. "We're headed out to have a few drinks for Halloween, and we have an extra costume. Why don't you join us?"

Natalia looked from left to right and seemed to consider the request. "I don't know, I —"

"We've got a costume for you," Bethany said brightly. "It's nothing crazy or anything. We're only going a few blocks from here —"

"I thank you, but I cannot attend." The woman gave a sharp downward nod as if to emphasize her answer. "I cannot."

Again the partners traded glances. "Is everything okay?" Gina asked. "You seem upset."

"I am fine." The young woman nodded emphatically.

"You've been crying . . ." Bethany's observation was interrupted by a noise that sounded like a bark.

"Natalia!"

The girl started, and responded immediately. "That is my bodyguard. I must go. Again, I thank you for your kind invitation. I will not forget it."

Gina remembered that she'd slipped from the room, her dark hair bobbing as she fled.

And that had been her one and only encounter with the wealthy Natalia Kazakova, until today's chance meeting in the foyer. And the man with her? Was he an old friend? A Russian relative visiting New York? Or someone she'd met in one of her classes? She tried to place the young man's face.

Gina reached the bus stop. She paused to catch her breath and saw the bus lumbering down the road toward her.

Out of a voluminous leopard-spotted pocketbook, Peggy Babson pulled Detective Benedetti's business card. She checked to see that no one was outside her office door and dialed the number.

He answered on the first ring. "Benedetti here."

Breathlessly, she gave her name. "I may have more information on the killing of the Russian man," she said. "The one who was stabbed near Pulitzer Hall?"

"Yes?" His voice was focused and sharp. She felt her heart beat a little faster. "What kind of information?"

"I'm not sure if it's the kind of thing I should say over the phone . . ." she let her words trail off suggestively.

"I understand, but I'm afraid you need to tell me some details over the phone, Ms. Babson. I've got a lot on my plate today, so shoot."

She bristled. "If you don't have time to hear my information —"

"Listen, I've got time to hear it, I just don't have time to come down there right now. You can come into the station if you'd like."

The very thought made her shudder. This wasn't working out at all the way she'd imagined. On television, the psychic mediums were treated so well . . .

"I remember very distinctly something that Professor Porter said to Alec Rodin while they were arguing in his office," she said.

"Yes?"

"Professor Porter said, 'I will kill you.' "

She waited for Detective Benedetti's reaction, twirling the phone cord around her index finger as the moments ticked by.

"I see. Why didn't you tell us this yesterday?"

"I didn't remember it. I've been very upset about the murder. After all, it happened right here, so close to where we work! It could have been me, Detective Benedetti, it could have been me."

"What motive would Professor Porter have for killing that man?" Detective Benedetti asked, sounding a bit skeptical.

"I sure as heck don't know! That's *your*

job, Detective."

"I appreciate your reminding me of that, Ms. Babson. Thank you for your call and don't hesitate to contact me again if you remember anything else."

Click.

Peggy stared at the phone in disbelief. Sarcasm? Skepticism? These were not at all the reactions she'd expected from Detective Benedetti. He'd sounded almost as if he didn't believe her! Hadn't he cared about the information she'd taken the time to relay? Why, Miles Porter could be a murderer, and the lead detective on the case wasn't even willing to come to her office to follow up a lead.

She contemplated her options. She could complain to Detective Benedetti's supervisor, give him a piece of her mind. She could go down to the station and ream out the Detective in person. Or she could investigate on her own.

That was it! He needed a motive, she'd find him a motive. She'd use her keen intuition and developing psychic abilities, just like the professionals on television. She no longer liked the tall Brit anyway. He was too full of himself, cocky. The very qualities she'd expect in someone who stabbed a poor foreigner in broad daylight.

Peggy Babson decided to formulate a plan on her commute back to Queens. Her pulse beat a little faster. She checked her watch and wished it were already time to leave.

"So which do you prefer," asked Miles as he and Darby rounded the corner of the park, "walking here or in the wilds of Maine?"

"Hmmm . . . a hard choice."

"Really? I should have thought you'd have blurted out your home state instantly. Those beautiful craggy cliffs and tall pines . . ."

Darby laughed. "You're right; I love the wild, untamed nature of Maine. But there's something special about places like this that generations of humans have carefully manicured, too. And I love the idea that way back when, people realized how important green space is, and preserved so much of it, smack in the middle of the city."

Miles nodded thoughtfully. "I see what you mean." A roller blader with a pink Mohawk skated gracefully past them, licking an ice cream cone as he passed. "And who's to say you can't see wildlife in Manhattan?"

She chuckled. "So what's on our agenda for tonight?"

"I was hoping you'd ask. I thought we'd go out for drinks and a nibble or two, and then I thought I'd bring you to see a genuine New York show."

"Really!" Darby smiled. "That's exciting. What will we be seeing?"

"I'm keeping it a surprise, but I'm sure you'll like it." His face was boyish, the most relaxed Darby had seen him since her arrival.

"Can't wait." She reached for his hand and sighed. It felt wonderful to be with him. She could almost forget the Davenports and their lawsuit . . .

She pushed her anxiety aside. Miles was right; the situation would take its course and there was little she could do in the meantime. She thought about Natalia, about the unexpected turn of events her life had taken with the murder of Alec Rodin.

"Were you surprised to hear Natalia say she was giving her investigative piece a rest?" Darby asked.

"The theft of the Russian palaces? No, not really. It's a shame, because she seems to have a good source, but let's face it: poor Natalia has too much on her plate right now. I'm sure she's overwhelmed with details for Rodin's funeral back in Russia, and who knows what her role is in all of that. Her finals are undoubtedly consuming any available energy she has right now. And, if you're correct in thinking she has some sort of love interest, why, it's no wonder she's distracted."

"I wonder about her father. He must be here, helping her get through this. She's awfully young to be dealing with a murder investigation alone. Wouldn't you think so?"

"She's got Sergei, remember that," said Miles. "As for Mikhail Kazakova, I don't know whether he is in the states or not, but I know someone who will know for sure."

"Ramon?" guessed Darby.

"Yes. We're nearly back at the building. I'll ask him — even if I have to endure being called Mr. Bean again."

The cake smelled rich and chocolaty, and Rona, who had a definite weakness for sweets in general, was practically swooning by the time she returned to Central Park Place. Ramon rushed to open the door for her and she gave a curt nod of thanks.

"Where's the party?" he asked, eyeing the bakery box.

"It's a gift for a friend," she sniffed, not wanting to let the doorman know she had a store-bought cake.

"Lucky friend."

"I didn't know you liked cake, Ramon. I'll

be sure to think of you the next time I'm out."

He smiled, and Rona made a mental note to buy the doorman a cake. After all, it was good business practice to suck up to anyone and everyone who could be a source of leads.

She took the elevator to her floor and hurried to the apartment. Once inside, she removed the cake from the box and looked for a plate on which to put it. Gingerly, she lifted it and placed it on the plate, happy to see that it fit nearly perfectly.

She pulled a rubber spatula from a drawer. Such a shame to destroy the cake's beautifully swirled frosting, but there was no way in heck it looked homemade. Scrunching up her face with distaste, she used the flat part of the utensil to smooth out the lovely peaks, until the cake seemed like something she might herself have frosted.

"Done." She picked up the plate and moved toward the door, setting it on a small table while she undid the locks. A scraping noise on the other side made her pause. Someone was trying to get in.

She scooted into the closet, her heart pounding with fear. Of all the times to get robbed! Just as she was on her way up to Kazakova's penthouse.

The door opened and a fair, freckled young woman entered, holding a large shopping bag. "Rona?" she called, immediately moving toward the cake. Before Rona could protest, a slim finger was scooping frosting from the side.

"Devin!" Rona squealed. "Leave it! I'm bringing it up to the neighbors."

"You are bringing food to someone in the building?" Her daughter's face was incredulous. "I don't believe it."

"Well, believe it. They've had a tragedy, and I said I would make them a cake."

The girl erupted in laughter. "What? There is no way in hell you made that cake. No fricking way."

"Oh, please! I spent more buying it than I would if I made it myself. Surely that's what counts." Rona shooed Devin away from the cake and picked up the plate. "Why don't you come up with me? You might get a look at the penthouse."

"I've seen the penthouse, remember? Back when you thought you were going to be the one to sell it."

Rona stiffened.

"But I'll come along, if only to see your face when you tell them you made the cake." She saw her mother's narrowed eyes and laughed. "Don't worry — your secret is safe with me. If there's one thing I know how to do, it's keep secrets."

"What's that supposed to mean?" Rona thought about the bills charged up by her daughter. She'd leave it for another time — the two were having one of the more pleasant conversations they'd had in years.

"Oh, nothing," Devin said lightly. "Hey, I think I'm finally going to be able to pay off some of the money I owe you, not to mention my college loans." She pushed the elevator buttons and reached out toward the cake.

"No!" snapped Rona, her annoyance turning to pride. "I make a pretty good cake, don't I?"

"Yes, Mommy," Devin said, her eyes artificially wide. "Your cakes are the best."

The two laughed softly. "So what is it, a new job?" Rona tried not to sound eager.

"A great opportunity," Devin said, as the doors glided open.

"What kind of opportunity?"

They walked softly down the hall to the door of the penthouse.

"Tell you later," Devin whispered.

Rona knocked on the door. "Showtime."

It was opened almost instantly by the hulking man Rona knew to be Natalia's bodyguard. Explaining the reason for her visit, she said, "I spoke to Mikhail earlier, and he was looking forward to seeing me."

The large man shifted his massive weight from side to side. "He is not here," he said. "Did you have an —"

"Who is it, Sergei?" The petite young woman Rona recognized as Natalia pushed open the door. "Is that a chocolate cake?"

"It sure is." Rona pressed past the bodyguard, balancing the cake as she walked. "I've brought it up with our condolences — mine and my daughter's — on the death of your fiancé. Such a tragedy."

"Thank you." Natalia's voice was more subdued. "It's been horrible." She looked beneath her fringe of ragged bangs. "I'm Natalia. Natalia Kazakova."

"Rona Reichels, and this is my daughter, Devin." Nods were exchanged.

"This is very nice of you," Natalia said. "It looks delicious."

"What looks delicious?" A tall man with a narrow face came up behind Natalia. His eyes met Rona's briefly, before lingering on Devin.

"These ladies live in the building and they've brought over a cake." She gave a small smile. "So sweet, isn't it Jeremy?"

The man nodded. "Looks good, too," he commented, before withdrawing from the doorway.

"Well, yes, we hope you enjoy eating it as much as I loved making it." Rona thrust the cake toward Natalia. "Will you ask your father to call me?" She presented a business card. "It's very important. As soon as he can."

"I will." Natalia smiled again. "And I will return your plate, as well. Which residence are you?"

"I'm in three-twelve."

"Thank you."

As they walked back to the elevator, Devin snorted. "Poor little rich girl."

Rona nudged her daughter. "Did you know that guy? He gave you a funny look."

Devin was horrified. "Mother, you have to be joking." She said it as if it were two words: Joe King. "I wouldn't be caught dead with a loser like that. If he gave me any kind of a look, it's because I'm a voluptuous woman, not a little Russian Goth girl."

Rona smiled. *My beautiful, brash Devin.* Why did she worry about this daughter when it was obvious she could tear the world apart and not think twice?

The curtain came down and the house lights went on, while the enthusiastic audience clapped and clapped.

148

"Miles, what a terrific show. There truly is nothing like a Broadway production."

"You sound as if you're about to burst into the lyrics of 'I Love New York,'" he joked.

She laughed. "Yeah, I just might!" Punching his arm lightly, she said, "I'm happy, that's all. Happy to be with you and to be doing the normal kinds of things dating couples do."

"Rather than solving murders?"

"Exactly. What's next?"

Miles traced his hand lightly down Darby's neck to her collarbones, over her breasts to her thigh. "I know what I want."

Darby's eyebrows shot up and he grinned.

"I'll give you a hint — it's what every man wants." He grinned again. "A juicy steak."

"Miles Porter!" She pretended to be aghast.

"Followed by sex, of course. But first, the steak. Our pre-theatre nibbles were hours ago, and have left me absolutely famished. Come on, I've got just the place in mind."

He led her farther into the theatre district to an old-fashioned steakhouse bustling with diners. Dozens of black-and-white photographs of famous actors and musicians lined the walls, waiters with giant trays and crisp white shirts hustled back and forth, and the smell of sizzling red meat wafted from the kitchen like a siren song.

"Porter, table for two," said Miles. The maître d'hôtel nodded and beckoned them to follow.

"You made a reservation?" Darby whispered.

"One has to, in this town. I figured that if we didn't want to come, we could cancel and make some lucky couple's night."

"Good thinking."

Once the pair were seated and enjoying a rich bottle of Italian Barolo, Miles asked about their mutual friends on the island of Hurricane Harbor, Maine. "What do you hear from Tina and Donny? Are they enjoying married life?"

"Very much so. They took a three-week trip to the Mayan Riviera back in March. Had wonderful weather, and loved the Mexican people they encountered at their beach house. Donny fell in love with the local cuisine, and Tina tells me he now makes his own tortillas."

"No kidding! Life takes us to some interesting places, now doesn't it?" He changed tones. "How about the Chief's wife?"

Darby's eyes clouded. "It's still very hard for Bitsy. I think she's doing some nursing work on the island. But on a happier note, I did hear from Helen Near down in Florida.

She's planning to spend some time out west visiting our mutual client Tag Gunnerson."

"Only Helen could hold her own against a pro golfer. Now what about your other client — Mr. Kobayashi? Are we still planning to meet with him on Sunday?"

"Yes, meet with him, and then find him a building to buy." Darby took a sip of her wine. "We'll get to meet the wunderkind Todd Stockton, too."

Their dinners arrived — a rare T-bone with wild mushroom sauce for Miles, and a delicate Steak Dianne for Darby. "Smells heavenly," she commented. "It's times like these that I'm glad I'm not a vegetarian."

"Eat up," Miles said wickedly, waving his fork at the cuts of beef. "You're going to need your energy."

Darby rolled her eyes and took a bite.

SEVEN

Gina overslept on Saturday morning, meaning she had to run from the bus stop to the Coopers' building, catching her breath as she waved at the weekend doorman. He recognized her from the few times he'd substituted for Ramon and waved her in. Once in the elevator, she glanced at her cell phone. Five minutes before eight. *Good.*

Sherry pulled open the door with the big boys in tow. Kyle was adorable in his tiny Yankees hat, while Ryan wore a small baseball glove into which he continually smashed his fist.

"You guys look like professionals!" Gina said. "Did you take a photo for your Dad?"

"What do you think I am, bad mother of the year or something?" Sherry grinned. "I took some, but here." She thrust a camera into Gina's hands. "Take another one, just in case mine didn't come out well." Gina complied, and then pulled out her cell.

"I'll snap a couple on my phone and send them right off to Penn." The boys posed reluctantly, antsy to be on their way.

"Great." Sherry turned and waved to her youngest two sons. "Have a good time with Gina, Trevvie — you too, Sam! I'll see you soon."

When the door shut behind them, Gina gave a quick glance into the kitchen. "Not bad," she said to the little boys. "Your Mommy actually picked up today." Gina was always careful what she said at the Coopers' house, because she suspected they probably had a nanny cam hidden somewhere, recording everything that happened. Not that they didn't trust her — she knew they did. But they were almost obliged, socially, to have something like that, just the way they had to purchase a two-thousand dollar stroller, summer in the Hamptons, and get their boys into top-notch preschools. When you were a New Yorker of a certain standing, you didn't really have a choice.

She recalled one conversation she'd overheard between Sherry and another Manhattan mom. Sherry had told the woman that a family from Kyle's preschool was moving to Westport, Connecticut. "Westport?" the woman asked, raising her eyebrows as much as the Botox would allow. "What a strange choice. I suppose they couldn't afford Greenwich?"

Gina put a few animal crackers in a bowl and offered them to Trevor. "Just one, Trevvie," she said as he filled his fist. "Can you take just one?"

He looked confused, and then released the cookies, grabbing only one in a pudgy fist.

"That's right!" Gina beamed. "Good boy!"

He chortled and shoved the cookie in his mouth, while Sam sang a tuneless baby melody of his own creation. Gina picked up a copy of *Architectural Digest,* thinking about her plan to see Mrs. Vera Graff.

Very shortly, Miranda would come for Honey . . . She dropped the magazine. Where was the dog?

"Honey?" she called. The little boys looked startled.

Trevor took the gummy cookie from his mouth. "Bow, bow."

"That's right, sweetie. Where did Honey go?"

She stood and looked for the dog's leash. *Gone.* Miranda must have come early.

Gina picked up the baby and sniffed his diaper. Not bad. She pulled a jacket on Sam and slid him into the stroller. Next, she scooped up Trevor and sniffed his diaper. *Good to go.* "Come on, Trevvie — let's take a walk." she said, placing him in the stroller and strapping him in.

She grabbed her pocketbook and cell phone, locked the door, and headed down the elevator to Vera Graff's apartment on the fifth floor. With the stylish suit in mind, she prayed her idea would work.

She pushed the doorbell and waited. A moment later, the voice with the French accent asked who was there. "I just saw Miranda, your dog walker," she lied. "It's about Mimi."

"Mimi?" The door flew open and a thin woman with a pinched face stood before her. "*Mon Dieu,* what has happened?"

"I found this collar after Miranda walked by, and I thought that perhaps it belonged to your poodle." Gina held up a rhinestone-studded pink collar that she had purchased the day before on her way home.

The woman, whose name Gina assumed was Yvette, scrutinized the collar. "No, no, is not Mimi's." She prepared to close the door. "That will be all —"

"Who's there, Yvette?" The composed older woman Gina had seen in the park appeared around the corner. "Hello," she said smoothly.

155

"Mrs. Graff, hello, I'm Gina Trovata," she said, pushing the door open and moving past Yvette. "I work for the Coopers in Residence eighteen-twenty-two. I'm their nanny." Gina indicated the boys, both of whom were staring at the strange women.

"The lawyers, correct?"

"That's right."

"Nice to meet you. They look like darling children."

The maid indicated the hall. "Very well, Mademoiselle, you may leave now."

"That's alright, Yvette. Let Ms. Trovata and the boys stay a bit. It's so infrequent that we have any visitors."

The thin woman shot a nasty glance at Gina but said nothing.

"Perhaps you will get us some tea?" Mrs. Graff raised her eyebrows and Yvette, scowling, scooted away.

"Have a seat, dear," the old woman said kindly, "and then tell me the real reason you've come."

Gina turned to see her expression. It was firm, but curious. "Mimi's collar . . ."

"You know very well that didn't belong to our poodle. After all, collars don't just fall off dogs, do they? How would Mimi stay on her leash without it? No, that sparkly collar is a ruse to get you in here, and I'd like to know why. Are you casing the joint? If so, you'll see we have very little of real value. A few antiques, but that's about it."

"No," Gina said quickly. "I saw you walking in the park yesterday, and you were wearing one of the most gorgeous suits I have ever seen." She took a breath. "Navy blue, big Lucite buttons . . ."

Vera Graff looked puzzled. "My suit?"

"Kick pleat in the back . . ."

"Ah, my 'Hitchcock Ingénue' outfit," she said softly. "It is an exquisite garment. I bought it back in the 1950s, and I've always felt like Kim Novak wearing it." She gave a little smile. "I don't understand why you've taken the trouble to run the Yvette blockade for my suit."

Gina took a breath. "I'm about to open a vintage clothing store with my business partner, Bethany," Gina explained. Usually she described Bethany as her friend, but "business partner" sounded more official. Of course, you had to make sure and say "business" partner, or another meaning could be construed.

"Go on." Vera's steel blue eyes reminded Gina of the stained glass windows in St. Patrick's Cathedral. Brilliant and brittle.

"I'm looking for inventory for the store. Beautiful things, such as that suit. I suppose you don't really need the money, but . . ." she saw something flit across the older woman's face. "I mean, your clothes are probably priceless to you . . ."

"How much would I make?" Vera Graff's voice was abrupt.

"We're a consignment shop, so you'd make money whenever an outfit sold. We'll split it with you. If you have more pieces like what I've seen, I'd say you'd have quite a few sales."

Vera Graff's look was shrewd. "That suit, as well as my other garments, were very expensive items when I purchased them," she said. "What kind of money are we talking about?"

"For that suit I'd ask three hundred dollars," said Gina. "At least."

The old woman's eyes widened in surprise. "That much?"

"Your things are collector's pieces. They're like artwork for people who appreciate them."

"I understand." She glanced down and fingered the hem of her olive green skirt. It was wool, probably a Pendleton, and Gina nearly salivated.

Vera continued. "I never bought anything unless I could buy the best. My Hitchcock outfit, for instance, came from a little boutique on Madison Avenue. I can still remember the day I saw it displayed on a padded hanger. Unfortunately, the store is no longer there." A moment later she met Gina's eyes. "It sounds silly, but my clothes have seen me through some very difficult times. My husband's illness, his death . . ." Her gaze wandered around the room. "Happy times, too, I suppose. I remember wearing the navy suit to luncheon on the Upper East Side at the Carlyle." Her face grew wistful. "My clothes are like old friends."

"If it's too much to ask —"

"I hate to part with my things, but perhaps it's time." Vera Graff pressed her lips together. "I like the idea of young people giving them another chance to shine." She placed her hands on her lap and gave a little smile. "It's settled, then. Wheel that contraption this way and come and see my closet."

Miles looked up from his laptop as Darby came into the living room.

"Good morning, love," he said, patting a space next to him on the couch.

She yawned. "You're up early for a Saturday."

"Woke up around four a.m., and, despite your deliciously warm body next to me, I couldn't get back to sleep." He reached up and kissed her cheek. "I'm glad you had a bit of a lie-in. Ready for coffee? Got some brewing in the kitchen."

"Sure. I'll go get us both some." She peered at the computer screen. "What's up?"

"An interesting email from Natalia. Seems she's had second thoughts about her investigative report."

"In what way, Miles?"

"She wants to beef it up and try to get it published."

"Is that possible?"

"I shouldn't think she could do it on her own. But if she co-wrote it with an established reporter . . ." he paused. "She's invited me up to the penthouse to talk about it. Care to tag along?"

"No — you go on ahead." Darby said it emphatically, even though seeing the penthouse held definite appeal.

"I told her you'd be coming, and she sounded glad. Perhaps your real estate expertise could prove helpful — after all, her subject concerns stolen palaces and such."

Twist my arm, thought Darby. "I'd love to come. What time did you discuss?"

"Nine." He glanced back at the computer

160

and frowned. "I'm surprised Jagdish hasn't emailed me back yet."

"Who's Jagdish?"

"Sorry — he's my buddy in London who covers all things Russian. I wrote him hoping to get more information on the organization Natalia discusses in her paper — the FSB."

"Gotcha." She rose to her feet and stretched. "Coffee run. Can I get you a refill?"

"Please." He handed her a mug with a photo of the Empire State Building. "One cream . . ."

"And two sugars," she finished. "I remember."

He grinned as she padded into Charles Burrows's kitchen and poured the coffee. Domesticity was kind of fun, she thought. Relaxing, and comfortable. She opened the refrigerator and hunted for the cream.

A low whistle came from the living room. "Our friend Charles Burrows is extending his sabbatical," Miles said, raising his voice so that Darby could hear him in the kitchen. "He's wondering if I want to stay on for the fall semester."

Darby grasped the handles of the coffee cups. "That's a nice offer," she called. She walked into the room and placed the cups on a coffee table. "Are you interested?"

Miles pushed his laptop to the side of the couch and picked up his coffee. "I don't know. For the most part, I've enjoyed teaching, and the city is a fascinating place to be. Brings me back to my old college days when I was a student here."

"I nearly forgot that you are a graduate of prestigious Columbia," Darby teased. "Have you been haunting some of your old watering holes?"

He grinned. "Here and there." He took a sip of his coffee. "The thing is, I wouldn't want to be here for the summer, really. Too hot and sticky. I'd need to figure that out."

"We could spend a month together in Maine," Darby suggested. "I'm renting my house a bit, but we could stay for several weeks in July. Go sailing in the cove, eat lobster every night, pick blueberries on Juniper Ridge . . ."

"Sounds heavenly." His smile was brief. "Truthfully, I've been thinking that a trip to England might be in order."

"Has anything happened?" Darby realized as she said it that she knew very little about Miles's family.

"Such as . . . ?"

"I have no clue, and I'm embarrassed to say that I know next to nothing about your life back in England. Have I really been so self-centered that we've never spoken about your friends and family?"

He reached out and ruffled her hair. "Yes. You're a wicked, wicked girl who doesn't give a fig for anyone else." He saw her dismayed face and laughed. "I'm joshing, love! I'm afraid that you know precious little about my family because I've wanted it that way."

"Why? Are they so very strange?"

He laughed again. "Terribly so! Eccentric with a capital 'E.' " He rolled his eyes. "My mother is on her third or fourth husband, and supposedly has her eye on an African chieftain as husband-in-waiting. My father is an actor and a ladies' man, with the wonderful knack of spending large fortunes in the blink of an eye. And my grandmother . . . Well, let's leave her for another time, shall we?"

"They sound very colorful. What about brothers or sisters?"

"I have one — a younger sister named Scarlett. She's normal — so far, at least." He grinned. "I think you'd like her. She's very level-headed. Guess you'd have to be, to survive growing up in a family like ours." He picked up his coffee cup and seemed to study it. "Would you come along, if I

163

promised to keep you safe from the really batty ones?"

Darby smiled. "Sure. They don't scare me." She chopped the air with her hands. "I've got my Aikido training, remember?"

"Thank goodness for that — you may need it." Neither one of them spoke of the many times Darby's martial arts moves had saved her life.

"And I can be a pretty colorful character myself, you know." She stood and picked up her coffee cup. "I can impersonate the Queen, for instance."

"You can not!"

"Can so." Darby lifted her nose into the air. *We are not amused . . ."*

Miles guffawed. "That is the absolute worst impersonation I have ever seen!" He grinned. "Do it again."

She laughed. "I'm headed for the shower, Professor Porter. We've got a nine a.m. meeting coming up."

He nodded. "I remember." His gaze was wistful. "I love you."

"I love you, too." She smiled, wondering as she left the room why his glance seemed almost sad.

Rona Reichels tried the number again and heard the same stupid message. She tossed her phone onto the silk comforter, disgusted. *I've left two messages,* she fumed. *I already sound like an idiot . . .*

Unbidden, an image of the penthouse popped into her brain, and before she could will it away, the familiar churning in her stomach began. *If only I had made that sale!* Her pulse quickened. It had been her deal to make, hers alone, and that asshole . . .

It doesn't matter now, she told herself. *The money would be gone by now anyway.* And yet she could not let go of her anger, two years later, over the injustice of losing out. *That would have been my biggest commission to date,* she reminded herself, the bitter knowledge gnawing inside her like acid. *I would have beaten Kiki Lutz, been featured in all the real estate columns . . .*

She seethed with resentment and self-loathing. Not even the news of her swindler's death could cool the anger simmering below the surface. *That deal was mine, mine, MINE!*

Rona stood and took a deep breath. Opening the top drawer of her dresser, she took a pill from a prescription bottle and swallowed it dry. She wouldn't let the penthouse slip through her fingers this time. If Mikhail Kazakova was planning to sell it, he would list it with her. Or else he would end up like that rat Rodin.

She headed toward her closet, ready to arm herself for battle in something expensive.

"Darby, Professor Porter, come in." Natalia herself opened the door, a smudge of something brown above her lip.

"You'll never guess what we are doing," she said, pointing at Sergei, seated at a glass-topped table overlooking the fabulous view. "We are eating the best chocolate cake in the world. For breakfast!" She smiled. "Would you both like a slice?"

"Count me in," Miles said, eyeing the half-eaten cake. "Did you make it yourself?"

"No, one of the neighbors made it and brought it by. Isn't that kind?" Natalia picked up a messy knife and cut a thick wedge. She licked her finger and scooped the cake onto a plate.

"Very," said Miles. "Not the sort of thing you think of happening in the big city, is it?" He glanced at Darby. "Cake for you?"

"I'd love a bite or two of your piece," Darby said. She watched as Miles took the plate and a fork from Natalia. "Who's your thoughtful neighbor?"

"Her name is Rona Reichels. She's a real

estate agent, and I think she helped my father buy this place." Natalia pointed at the table. "Have a seat."

"Hallo, Sergei," said Miles, taking a bite of the cake. "Wow," he said, his words slightly muffled. "This is delicious. You weren't exaggerating."

Sergei wiped his mouth with a napkin, apparently finished with his piece. "Good morning." He picked up his plate. "Do you wish to be alone, Miss Natalia?"

"No, Sergei, stay. You know everything I'm going to say, anyway." She gave the bodyguard a fond glance. "There's not too much that happens with me that Sergei doesn't know about. He's like a big brother to me — a sounding board. A true friend."

Darby watched as a slow flush crept up Sergei's enormous neck. *He genuinely cares for Natalia. It's more than just a job to him.*

The big man grunted. "I will take our dishes," he said.

Darby looked at Miles's plate with surprise. He'd finished the cake, polished if off in mere minutes, leaving barely a crumb. She raised her eyebrows as if to inquire about the bite or two that she'd expected.

He mouthed something back that looked like "sorry" and handed his plate to Sergei.

Natalia took a breath. "I know that I said

I needed a break from my studies, but I can't stop thinking about my paper. I feel like I need to get this information out, that I owe it to my source to tell this story." She glanced at Miles. "Professor Porter — why are you smiling?"

He chuckled. "For a good reason, Natalia. I'm happy to see you've got the bug."

"I don't understand. What bug?"

"It's a way of saying that you've got what it takes to be an investigative journalist. That feeling that you simply must write a story — that you owe it to your sources and the public to let the story be told — I know exactly what you mean, Nat, and I'm thrilled to hear you voicing your passion. This profession is more of a calling than it is a job. It gets under your skin, so that you can't imagine doing anything else. Do you understand what I mean?"

"Yes." She was nodding her head. "I can see that it is a big responsibility, too."

Now it was Miles's turn to agree. "Yes — and sometimes the truth will weigh heavily on you. I suspect that you already sense that." He put his fingers together so that they made a tent, leaned in closer. "How can I help?"

She gave a brief smile. "You are very kind. I hesitate to ask you, because I know you are very busy, but . . ."

"Natalia, I wouldn't offer if I didn't mean it."

She gave a grateful smile. "If it isn't too much to ask, I would like you to work with me on this story, Professor, so that we may bring all of our resources to bear. The places where you indicated that my work needs more detail — I'm not sure where to turn."

Miles glanced at Darby who gave him a subtle nod of encouragement. He cleared his throat. "I'm trying to get in touch with a colleague from the *Financial Times* who may be able to shed some light on the FSB."

"Thank you," she said. "As for my source . . ."

"I believe I indicated that you need to dig a little deeper."

She nodded, biting her lip. "She is not as forthcoming as I would have hoped," she said. "Perhaps there is a way that I could make her feel more comfortable."

Miles's face was quizzical. "What do you mean?'

"She talks with me, but in a very guarded way. I must prepare the questions ahead of time, and she insists we stay on topic."

"She sounds as if she is afraid," commented Miles.

"Perhaps that is true," Natalia said. "But I

think if you were to meet her as well . . ."

A knock on the door stopped their conversation mid-sentence. Sergei materialized from the kitchen, looked through the security hole, and nodded to Natalia.

"You may open the door, Sergei."

He complied, and a stylish, solid woman with full red lips moved into the room. "Natalia, dear, I thought I'd stop by to see how you are doing." She ignored Miles and Darby, swept eyes heavy with mascara toward the kitchen. "I see you're enjoying my cake."

"Yes," said Natalia, rising to her feet. "It's delicious." She indicated Miles and Darby with a graceful wave of her hand. "This is Professor Miles Porter, who is staying in Professor Burrows's apartment."

The woman's eyes seemed to narrow just a fraction.

"And this is Darby Farr, a friend of Miles's, who is visiting from California." Natalia gave a quick smile. "This is Rona, baker of the extraordinary chocolate cake we just enjoyed."

The newcomer gave what looked like a grimace, although Darby figured it was supposed to be a smile. "Rona Reichels," she said. Turning back to Natalia, she cocked her head to the side.

"I've been trying to reach your father all morning. It's very important that we talk."

Natalia's brow furrowed. "He left early for the airport." She cast her eyes down. "He's been working to arrange the transport of my fiancé's body back to Moscow."

Rona barely batted an eyelash. "Really? I should think he would answer his calls regardless . . ." She seemed to realize how crass her comments sounded and put a well-manicured hand on the girl's arm. "I'm sorry, dear. It must be terrible for you."

Natalia nodded. "It's very difficult. Fortunately, I have friends." She gave a grateful glance at Miles and back at Rona. "And cake! You must tell me how you make it."

A shadow crossed Rona's face, or so it seemed to Darby. "It is an old family secret. I'm not sure I can part with the recipe." She moved toward the door, casting a quick look around the penthouse "The place looks lovely," she said, her voice quieter. "I like what you've done in this living room."

"Thank you," Natalia said. "The decorator was someone that Alec knew." Her voice trailed off and there was silence.

Rona broke the quiet by opening the door. "I'll see myself out."

EIGHT

Most Saturdays, Peggy Babson went shopping, usually to one of the big malls on the outskirts of the city. It was a way for her to escape the destruction that still littered the streets of her Rockaway neighborhood, the giant piles of wood, insulation, and twisted metal from dozens of wrecked houses and businesses, hurricane damage that seemed to Peggy as if it would never completely disappear. Sometimes she took her girlfriend Leslie along, or arranged to meet her for lunch, but today she had a very different kind of excursion in mind.

From her closet, she dug through the piles of clothes until she found a comfortable pair of stretchy pants and a sweatshirt. She searched until she found two matching sneakers, laced them up, and grabbed a light jacket. She then locked the house and made her way to the Long Island Railroad, to take the route she endured Monday through

Friday, into Manhattan and Pulitzer Hall.

Before boarding the train, she thrust some money into the hands of a shopkeeper for a candy bar, yanked off the wrapper, and took several satisfying bites.

She chose a seat in the back of the car and planned her strategy. First, locate a key for Charles Burrows's office. The custodian would have one, and it wouldn't be hard to get him to open the door. Once in, comb through Professor Porter's papers for evidence — clues as to why he had killed the Russian.

Peggy thought back to Detective Benedetti's words concerning motive. She wasn't exactly sure why Professor Porter stabbed the man, but she was more convinced than ever that he'd done it. Slowly, an idea was formulating in her mind: Perhaps Porter had killed due to jealousy over Natalia Kazakova's affections. She remembered the girl's early morning visit — her garish getup and purple lipstick — and shivered. What did a man like Professor Porter see in a silly student? Here she was, out of school, working . . . She shook her head.

And then, suddenly, she knew what attracted Miles Porter to the undergrad. Money! Of course! Professor Porter saw dollar signs, yes, a way to supplement his dismal teaching salary and improve his lackluster life. Natalia was an heiress — the newspapers had said that — and Professor Porter was most assuredly impoverished. Weren't all untenured professors? Why else would he wear a threadbare tweed jacket and moth-eaten scarf? Why would anyone choose such a nomadic lifestyle, filling in catch-as-catch-can for absent teachers?

Peggy rubbed her hands together. It was all making sense. As handsome as he was, Miles Porter was a murderer, his motive the most basic of all: greed. She pulled the candy bar out of her pocketbook and enjoyed the last two bites.

"So you say your source — this woman — seems to be rather guarded when you talk about her past." Miles stole a glance in the direction of the chocolate cake and Darby couldn't help but smile. *He's ready for lunch,* she thought.

"Yes. If it is okay with you, Professor Porter, I will ask her if you can accompany me to our next session. Perhaps you can put her more at ease."

"I don't know if that will be the case, but I'm happy to help, Natalia." He glanced at Darby, telegraphing a "let's go" type look. She gave a nearly imperceptible nod.

"Natalia, I think it's time for us to leave you now," Miles said. "The cake was delicious — thanks very much."

"You are welcome." She seemed downcast, until an idea brightened her features. "Would you like a quick tour of the penthouse? It's pretty impressive and far larger than I need, but Papa always insists it was a good investment."

"I'd love to see it," Darby said, rising to her feet. "Wouldn't you, Miles?"

"Sure." He stood and stretched. "I'm ready."

Natalia led the way down a hall, pointing out the various bedrooms, dens, and office spaces. "This suite is my father's," she said, indicating a masculine-looking bedroom with large oak furniture and an enormous master bathroom. "He has his own office for conducting business while in Manhattan, as well as an exercise room, bar, and small kitchen. I tease him that it is like a private house within the apartment!"

Miles raised his eyebrows. "It's amazing," he commented. "How often is your father here?'

"At least once a month, more if he can get away. He seems to adore Manhattan."

"And you? Do you enjoy Manhattan as well?" Darby's voice was kind.

Natalia grew thoughtful. "I've loved my studies, but up until now, I was not enamored with the city. Truthfully, I have been very lonely here." She brightened. "But that seems to be changing, so I imagine I may enjoy much more of what New York has to offer."

"What's changed?" prompted Miles.

"I have a new friend." She looked away, obviously embarrassed, but Miles didn't seem to notice.

"Your friend — is he or she a student as well?"

"He is in finance," she said, her cheeks pinking up. "And very good at it, too. We met at Columbia a few months ago. He's auditing an art class."

Darby glanced in Sergei's direction. Did the bodyguard approve of this new friend, she wondered?

"I know what you're probably thinking," Natalia said, as her flush grew even deeper. "Jeremy sought me out because of my money. That's what I thought at first, too. Truthfully, it's what crosses my mind every time someone is nice to me." She opened the door to yet another room in her father's suite and continued. "But the funny thing is that Jeremy didn't even know who I was when we met. He thought I was from

Finland." She giggled. "He's just a regular guy — a smart guy — and a good friend."

"That's brilliant, Nat," Miles said. "We're glad for you."

"Yes," Darby added, thinking of the friendships she'd made over the past few months, relationships that had sustained her during very difficult times. People such as Tina Ames and her husband Donny, Helen Near, and, of course, the stalwart ET. "It sounds like he came at just the right time."

Natalia nodded. "He's been sweet since Alec's death." She sighed. "I don't know what I would have done without him and Sergei."

Miles gave a cursory glance at Mikhail Kazakov'as giant walk-in closet. It was clear he could care less about the seventy-plus-inch flat screen television, teak bar, or floor-to-ceiling mirrored workout room.

"Has your father met Jeremy?"

"Not yet," she smiled, "but I know they will like each other."

Darby smiled as well, feeling a stab of pity for the girl. Would Mikhail Kazakova appreciate the idea that Natalia was spending time with a virtual stranger who was fast becoming more than just a friend? How did billionaire parents deal with their children's love lives? As she followed Miles back down the penthouse's long hallway, Darby had a thought. For all of her money, Natalia Kazakova was hopelessly naïve.

Gina Trovata wheeled the stroller through the park, humming a tune and feeling as if life was a huge Christmas present, ready to be unwrapped. She couldn't wait until Bethany heard about the wonderful items in Vera Graff's closet, vintage garments that would soon be on display in their store! She smiled at the memory of the clothes, each one more exquisite than the last: a cobalt blue sweater-dress from the '50s, the kind that turned the wearer into an instant sex kitten; a green, leaf-print chiffon party dress, with a full skirt and sweetheart neckline; a cherry-red wool coat from the '40s, trimmed in Persian Lamb. She smiled when she thought of Vera's confession regarding the coat. "That was my sister's," she'd explained. "She donated it to the Salvation Army, but I marched right in there after her and took it back. Imagine!"

Gina could imagine, and had barely resisted the impulse to slip her arms into the coat's sleeves and let it swing around her body. "What will you ask for it?" Vera had whispered. "Four hundred," said Gina. "No — five hundred." She'd grinned at the older woman. "And I'll bet you that someone will pay."

The two had laughed like schoolgirls, clapping their hands over each exquisite piece of clothing. And yet Gina had sensed the malevolent presence of Yvette, lurking outside the bedroom, hating Gina for having vaulted over Vera Graff's impenetrable walls. Why did the woman put up with such a negative employee? Why not fire her skinny French butt and find a more pleasant housekeeper?

Gina shrugged off all thoughts of Yvette and turned her attention to the boys. They had been good as gold in Vera's dressing room, enjoying the parade of beautifully colored fabrics almost as much as the women.

Now, on an impulse, Gina stopped the stroller at an ice cream vender, buying the boys orange popsicles, and herself a blue raspberry Italian ice. She grabbed extra napkins and headed for the nearest park bench.

The boys would create a grand old mess in their pricey buggy, but Gina knew she'd have ample time to scour it clean before Sherry and the older boys returned. She'd let Honey lick it first — run it through the prewash cycle — and then get out the chemicals. Surprisingly enough, between the dog's thorough licks and the stain repellent fabric, the stroller always managed to look as if it were brand new.

Gina lifted her face to the sun, enjoying the cold sweetness of the frozen treat. She knew that Italian ice had nothing to do with Italy, and yet she couldn't help but pick it when she had a choice. The words of her adopted mother, Pauline Higgins, came back to her. She remembered the halting story the kind-hearted woman had related when Gina had asked the most difficult question of her life: am I adopted?

At first, the woman she knew as her mother said no. "But I don't look like you, or Dad, or Paula," Gina had persisted as only ten-year-olds can do. "I have dark hair and none of you do. I get good tans and none of you can. I like spicy food, and none of you —"

"Okay," Pauline had said, giving a sad smile. "I see what you mean. I am going to tell you a secret, Gina, but before I do, I want you to promise me something that's very, very, important."

Gina remembered nodding emphatically, her heart racing, her emotions a jumble of anticipation and fear. "I promise."

"You must never forget how much Daddy

and I love you. Can you promise me that?"

And Pauline had proceeded to tell Gina a story, one not unlike the fairy tales she read to her and Paula at night, once they brushed their teeth and washed their faces, and lay waiting in their pajamas on Paula's canopy bed. It even started with "Once upon a time," and ended with "and they lived happily ever after." A story of a castle (only it was called an orphanage) and some kindly witches (although they were actually nuns) and a magical baby, who the nuns found singing (or maybe it was crying) on the steps of the orphanage. "This baby was so beautiful that the nice ladies took her inside, and gave her lots of love, until a Mom and Dad who had always wanted a magical baby girl came from America to bring her to New York."

Gina had seen through the fairy-tale lingo, but she appreciated her mother's imaginative telling and didn't comment. "Where was I born?" she asked. "Which state?"

"Italy," Pauline said. "It's not a state, but a country in Europe. Let me show you where it is on the globe."

A gust of wind ruffled a discarded newspaper left on the bench beside Gina, and she glanced at it, her mind still focused on the memory of Pauline showing her the dusty globe and Italy. An image caught her eye: Natalia Kazakova.

Gina skimmed the story, which focused on the details of Alec Rodin's death, noting that there was never any mention of Natalia's mother. Plenty of references to Mikhail and his vast fortune, but nothing about the woman who had brought Natalia into the world.

Perhaps she and the heiress had something in common.

With the last spoonful of blue raspberry Italian ice melting on her tongue, Gina peered into the stroller where the popsicle-eaters slurped away in contentment. Both of them had intense orange staining around their lips, orange dribbles inching down their chins, and orange blotches on their hands and shirts, but other than that, they looked perfectly clean. She dabbed what she could with a few napkins, removed their empty popsicle sticks before they gouged out an eyeball, and began wheeling them home. She forgot about Natalia Kazakova, thinking instead that life was good, good, good — as sweet as a popsicle on a sunny spring day.

Rona did not want to tell Sherry Cooper the truth, and so she did what she frequently did in these circumstances: she lied.

"Mikhail is thinking seriously about listing the penthouse," she said, leaving a message in a conspiratorial tone. "He can't commit to it right now, of course, what with the murder and all, but he's assured me that when he makes a decision, I'll be the first to know. Which means," she added pointedly, "that you will hear about it before anyone else."

She hung up her phone and let out a frustrated sigh. Why the hell wouldn't he call her back?

All sorts of scenarios ran through her mind. Mikhail was deliberately ignoring her calls. He'd already found someone who wanted the penthouse. He'd decided not to sell it in the first place . . .

She knew this was the most likely of the three. Sherry Cooper's suggestion that the penthouse was now a sad reminder of Natalia's thwarted engagement was wishful thinking. There was a good chance that selling wasn't even something that had crossed Mikhail's mind, not even when his future son-in-law was found gutted in an alley.

But what if they did decide to sell? Should she go back up to the penthouse, try to ingratiate herself with the sickly-looking Natalia? Flutter her eyelashes at the bodyguard? *There are only so many cakes I can "bake,"* she thought wryly. What then? There had to be something . . .

Meanwhile, perhaps there were other opportunities within the building. The old lady, the one with the poodle and French maid, surely she was on her way out of her condo and into a nursing home? She'd already been old a few years ago, when Devin had babysat the poodle while the maid had some sort of operation. Now she must be positively ancient.

And Charles Burrows . . . Rona wondered what it meant that he'd let the gangly professor and his Japanese girlfriend house-sit in the apartment. Was he ready to part with his slice of the New York pie?

Rona whipped out her smartphone and found her old client's number. Settling back on her down-filled settee, she crossed her fingers and hoped one of her many plans would work.

"We never asked Natalia whether there's been any progress on the investigation into Alec's death," mused Miles, as he and Darby strolled toward the imposing façade of the Museum of Modern Art.

"That's true. I think she would have said

184

something if there had been any news, don't you?"

"Perhaps. On the other hand, she seems pretty preoccupied with this new man in her life. What was he called? Jeremy? I don't know if I like the sound of that."

"Which — his name, or the fact that she met him?" Darby laughed. "I think it's great that she has something to take her mind off the murder, and encouraging that she wants to followup on the investigation."

"I suppose. I guess I'm just surprised that she meets this fellow just as her fiancé gets killed. Kind of coincidental, wouldn't you say?'

"I got the impression that she's known him all semester. If he's been auditing her art class, they've known each other for a few months. Maybe she didn't feel comfortable spending any time with him because of Alec. And now . . ."

"Yes, I get it," said Miles. "But what's a stockbroker doing taking an art class? I don't think it's all on the up-and-up."

Darby laughed. "Maybe he trades in fine art." She looked up. "Speaking of, I'm really looking forward to seeing this museum, Miles. Coming here has been a dream for a long, long time."

He bent his head and kissed her lightly on

the lips. "I'm glad, love. Let's see as much art as we can possibly stand, have dinner with your Mr. Kobayashi tonight, and, in between those two noble pursuits, make time in the middle for some snogging at the flat." He waggled his eyebrows and Darby raised her glance heavenward.

"I've created a monster," she said.

"Right you have," he whispered, pulling her in for another quick kiss and a low, guttural growl. "A monster of love."

"Oh boy," she said, as they headed up the stairs and into the museum.

Gina was waiting for Sherry to write out her paycheck when a call came in from Bethany. Gina apologized and started to silence her ringtone.

"Go ahead, take it," Sherry urged. "Fine with me."

Gina answered and let out a squeal. "Really? Where?" She listened a few more minutes, said she'd see Bethany soon, and hung up, her face in a wide grin.

"Well?" Sherry had a hand on her hip. She passed the check to Gina. "Is it about the store?"

"Yes!" Gina continued to beam. "Bethany thinks she has found the perfect storefront, in an up-and-coming part of Brooklyn called Bushwick. The rent is reasonable, the building's in decent shape, and we can get in there May first."

"That's fabulous." Sherry reached out and hugged Gina. "I know how hard you've been working toward this." Her face crumpled into a frown. "I only hope this doesn't mean you'll quit."

"No." Gina's tone was emphatic. "No way, Sherry. I need this job and I love your boys. I won't be able to fill in on weekends, like today, but I'll still be here for my morning shifts, no problem."

"Whew." Sherry smiled. "That's a relief. So tell me, when do you think you'll open?"

"Very beginning of June, maybe even the first," Gina said. "As long as we keep finding inventory . . ."

"I told you I'd pass the word at the firm, right?" She took out her smartphone and typed in a note. "First thing on Monday, I'll send out an email."

"Thanks." Gina debated whether it was appropriate to ask Sherry for a favor, and decided what the hell. "I've made a great connection with one of the women in the building — Mrs. Graff. She lives on the fifth floor and has lots of items to sell." She bit her lip. "Would it be possible for me to borrow your car one of these days to take her outfits home with me?"

"Has she got that much stuff? Sure, Gina. You can take it tomorrow if you'd like. For all I know, Penn will still be working, and I think the boys and I will just lay low."

"Great. I'll check with Mrs. Graff and let you know."

"No need. The keys are here — so just use it whenever." Now it was Gina's turn to hug Sherry. "It's nice to see someone so happy," Sherry said wistfully. "By the way, I may have some good news of my own. Don't say anything, but it looks like there's a chance we'll be getting the Kazakova's penthouse."

"No — really?"

Sherry ran a hand through her bobbed blonde hair. "I've got Rona Reichels working on it, and she thinks it's a possibility. If it's meant to be, it's meant to be, right?"

Gina nodded, knowing that there was no way Sherry Cooper was a "meant to be, meant to be," kind of person. She was the type who recited the phrase because it was trendy, not because she put any kind of stock in it. Sherry Cooper was more of a "If it's something I want, then it's something I'll get," kind of gal.

"Anyway, keep it under your hat for the time being." Sherry gave a little wave. "See you later, Gina — I'm off to check on the boys."

Gina stuffed her check in her jacket pocket and grabbed her backpack. As she left the Coopers' condo, she wondered if it made sense to call Vera when she could check with her in person in a matter of minutes? Now that she didn't have to resort to trickery to get by Yvette, she felt more confident about knocking on the door of Vera's unit. She pushed the button for her floor and waited.

So far, rooting through the antique desk in Charles Burrows's office — now used by Miles Porter — had yielded nothing interesting. Nail clippers, gum, a few dusty bags of tea — that was about it as far as personal items. She'd tried holding them in her hands to see if they generated any visions, but her psychic abilities weren't cooperating.

None of the drawers were locked, and there were few other pieces of furniture to consider. A faded leather armchair, a nondescript desk chair, a coat tree with a ratty plaid scarf hanging from one of the hooks — Peggy Babson rose from her haunches, grunting in dissatisfaction.

Her forehead was sticky with sweat. She

189

blew air up from her lower lip, trying to dislodge her bangs, and sighed.

On the crime shows the detectives were always talking about motive, means, and opportunity. She'd established Miles's motive: he was after the wealthy Kazakova girl, and needed her future husband out of the picture. Peggy wasn't exactly sure what "means" referred to. Ability?

There was no doubt Miles Porter was physically capable. He was very fit, probably a bigger man than the Russian, and he wasn't a stranger to violence. She'd read in the faculty directory that he'd been a reporter in Afghanistan, where he'd no doubt seen all kinds of brutality on a daily basis.

Opportunity was the easiest. After all, Miles Porter was the last person to see the murdered man alive. She pictured the chain of events as if they were on television: Miles, shouting at the Russian, threatening to kill him. Rodin, stalking down the steps of Pulitzer Hall, never knowing he was being followed. Miles, running ahead to a deserted alley and waiting for his quarry. (Obviously, he'd had some sort of knife or sword — the murder weapon — here in the office, and had brought it with him to the fateful rendezvous.) She saw Alec Rodin ducking into the alley, saw Miles Porter strike.

And then he'd ditched the sword some-where and come back to Pulitzer Hall.

Peggy swayed unsteadily on her feet. She lurched toward the scarf and stuffed it in her pocket. It all made sense.

NINE

Saturday night in the penthouse, and Sergei Bokeria was troubled.

Something Mikhail Kazakova had said to him the day before did not compute. He'd pulled the bodyguard aside, asking him to tell the pilot he would fly back to Russia the next morning. "Tell him I do not want a repeat of what happened Wednesday," he said. He laughed and put a hand to his mouth. "No vodka," he'd whispered.

And so Sergei had phoned the jet's pilot, repeating what he was told, and the pilot assured him it would never happen again. Sergei had then told Mikhail that the plane would be ready first thing Saturday morning, and sure enough, Mikhail had departed that morning.

And yet something was bothering Bokeria — something that did not make sense. He was pondering it when Natalia flounced into the room, followed by her new friend.

"Sergei, you know Jeremy, right?"

The big man nodded.

Jeremy stuck out a hand. "We've met, but not really officially. Jeremy Hale. I want to thank you for keeping Natalia safe. She thinks the world of you."

Sergei nodded again. He'd already checked out the sandy-haired young man, and other than the usual things one would think of with red-blooded males and females of that age, he was glad for Natalia to have company. He stood and went down the hall so that they could have some privacy, even though Natalia said Jeremy was only staying a few minutes.

He flicked on the television in his bedroom and watched a cooking show for a few minutes. The chef, a good-looking Italian girl, was making some sort of bean dish, but Sergei could not stop mulling over Mikhail's words. "I do not want a repeat of what happened . . ." Obviously the plane's bar needed restocking. There was nothing strange about that, other than it was unfortunate that the liquor most enjoyed by Mikhail was the one missing. Such was life.

He thought about Alec Rodin's murder on Thursday afternoon. His trip to the morgue with Natalia to view the body. Her conversation with her father on the computer, because he was not yet in town.

Sergei snapped off the television.

That was it. Mikhail had skyped with his daughter on Thursday because he could not be with her in person, or so he had said.

Sergei dialed the jet's number again and asked when the plane had last flown to New York. "Wednesday," answered the scheduling coordinator.

Frowning, Sergei Bokeria tried to reason it out. If Mikhail had landed in the city on Wednesday, where was he the afternoon Alec was killed? And why had he let his daughter believe he was still in Russia?

He crossed to his bed and stretched his massive bulk across it. Mikhail had lied about his whereabouts. Had he lied about anything else?

Darby slipped away from Miles Porter's embrace, ignoring his groans of protest. "I'm headed to the shower, sleepyhead," she called.

"What time do we meet Mr. Kobayashi?"

"You can call him Hideki, you know," laughed Darby. "We meet him at seven." She entered the bathroom and turned on the shower.

"Can't wait," muttered Miles.

"What was that?"

"Nothing, my love. I'm anxious to meet your pharmaceutical friend."

Darby came back into the room, wrapped in a towel. "We'll have a good time with him, I promise. Hideki's an interesting guy. He's also a very valued client, and I appreciate your willingness to pitch in and help me entertain him."

Miles sat up and reached toward her, grabbing the edge of the towel. "Care to show me some of that appreciation?" He tugged on the towel.

"Miles," she chuckled, tugging back.

"But I looked at all those paintings with you . . ."

"True."

Darby shrugged off the towel and slipped back into his arms.

Rona Reichels narrowed her eyes at the CNBC program. It featured Manhattan's hottest broker, Kiki Lutz, discussing a multiple offer on one of her listings. Three Chinese businessmen had bid on the place — three! — and she was negotiating the deal with one of them. "The top bidder has a son coming to school in New York," Kiki Lutz informed her viewers, "so he's purchasing the fifty million dollar apartment. A 'dorm in the sky' if you will."

Rona grabbed the remote and snapped off the television. Who was Kiki Lutz to talk about dorms in the sky, when Mikhail Kazakova had been the first foreigner to do such a thing? He'd started the trend, right here on Central Park West, and Rona had been the one to . . .

She closed her eyes. To what? To blow the deal? To get screwed out of her commission by fast-talking Alec Rodin?

It's been taken care of, she told herself. *He's dead.*

She remembered meeting Kiki Lutz at some benefit for the library. She was the type everyone tried to suck up to, not that it would do you any good in a negotiation. Did Kiki Lutz ever lose out on lucrative deals? She was one of the new breed of real estate professionals who slept with their damn smartphones (it was rumored Kiki had eight of them, and answered more than one hundred emails a day), who claimed that real estate was a passion and that they were always available — always! — in "real time." *Well, forgive me for ever wanting to take a crap without taking a call from China at the same time,* Rona fumed. *Pardon me for wanting to go to Boca for a month, for thinking I was someone who could actually take a real vacation.*

Before the advent of phones that could do everything but cook you dinner, real estate agents had enjoyed some down time. They'd used good old land lines, and fax machines. Before that, they'd mailed documents back and forth. They hadn't been tethered to devices that they had to compulsively check every two minutes.

Kiki Lutz had sold sixteen units in Rona's building, and would doubtless sell more. Someone Rona had met at the pool had said Kiki was trying to find a rental so that she could experience living in the building, something she tried to do all over the city.

Rona felt her heart start racing. *When did I go from rising star to sinking ship? Devin . . .* Devin and her pricey private high schools, followed by a narcissistic "gap" year, and then a stint at a private college upstate, and her spectacular expulsion due to drugs. Factor in the rehab center, the one that was supposed to leave Devin clean and sober, only it ended up leaving Rona broke and bitter. Okay, not quite broke. That had happened once Devin had been caught shoplifting, and, instead of letting her beautiful daughter go to prison, Rona had hired the best litigation attorney she knew.

And lost.

She got up from the couch and lurched

toward the kitchen. Her father was right, she was a nothing, trying to live in an über-wealthy world that was way beyond her means. New York was not a place where you could be middle class, and Rona was starting to realize that's what she was.

Saturday night. Surely it was time for a cocktail.

Darby climbed up the steps like a pro, a new pair of pantyhose clutched in her hand. She'd discovered a run in the pair she'd brought from California and headed out to buy a new pair, refusing Miles's very kind offer to get them for her. "There are too many choices involved when buying nylons," Darby assured him. "Sizes, colors, control top —"

"Stop right there," he laughed. "You'd better go. Shall I come with you?"

"Nope. You take your shower. I'll only be a few minutes."

Taking a few stairs seemed a harmless way to get a little exercise, but by the fifth floor, Darby realized she'd need another shower if she kept on climbing. She exited the stair-well and headed down the hallway to the elevator, only to see a familiar person entering one of the apartments.

Natalia Kazakova.

Once the door was closed, Darby tiptoed to the apartment door to see the number. *Five-fifteen.* She remembered the doorman, Ramon, explaining that the reclusive Vera Graff lived there. Was she Natalia's source for the theft of the Russian palaces?

Darby rode the elevator to Charles Burrows's apartment deep in thought. Back inside, she heard the water running for Miles's shower, as well as his deep baritone singing a song by the Beatles, "Norwegian Wood." *He's not half bad,* Darby thought.

She turned on her tablet and did a search for Vera Graff. On the list of New York City property holders, she found Vera's maiden name: Ikanov. Quickly she typed it in as a search.

Nothing. Darby sat back, discouraged. *You can't expect everything to be easy,* she thought, vowing to look again with Miles's help. She was about to turn off her laptop when she decided to open her email.

Along with the usual requests for property information, updates from clients, and notifications of new listings, Attorney Debbi Hitchings had sent Darby a terse note.

The Davenports are indeed filing suit for damages on the mold issue. Looks flimsy to me. I don't see that they have much to go on, but will be in touch on Monday.

Darby groaned. "Much to go on" wasn't as comforting as "nothing to go on." She typed her thanks to Debbi and shut off the machine.

Back in the room, Miles had stopped singing and was already dressed. He noticed that Darby was still in her jeans and raised his eyebrows. "Six-thirty, love. We should head out the door in a minute or two."

"Afraid I got a little distracted." She explained seeing Natalia on the fifth floor, going into Vera Graff's apartment.

"Fascinating. So our reclusive Mrs. Graff is the source for Nat's story."

"So it appears. I searched for Vera's maiden name and looked to see if there is any news about her having been of Russian nobility. I didn't find anything, so we'll need to keep digging."

"Hmm . . . I suppose we should be searching under Graff, too? Perhaps it was her husband's family who was of royal Russian stock."

"Excellent point, Miles." She pulled on the pantyhose and reached for her dress. "If it is Vera, I suppose I can understand her extreme need for privacy. It must have been dangerous for her family back in the day."

"If everything Natalia's said about the FSB is true, it could still be dangerous for

Vera, especially if she starts making waves about stolen real estate."

"If Alec Rodin were a member of the FSB, it would make sense that he wouldn't want his fiancée digging up a whole lot of dirt on this whole thing, right? But why would someone kill him over it?"

"Maybe someone killed him wanting to protect Natalia."

"Her father? Sergei?" Darby turned her back to Miles so that he could zip her up. "Let me run a brush through this hair and I'm ready," she announced.

He watched her walk into the bathroom. "We'll take all this up another time," he said. "And I'll try Jagdish again. This whole thing is right up his alley. Meanwhile — you look lovely, messy hair or not."

"Why, thank you, Professor Porter," she said, coming back into the room. "Let's go meet the perfectly punctual Hideki Kobayashi, shall we?"

How did a person not get covered in blood when they stabbed someone? This was the question Peggy Babson was trying to answer as she traveled back to her home in the Rockaways. Obviously Miles had been wearing gloves — that was why there were no fingerprints on the murder weapon. He must have had some sort of lab coat as well, because wouldn't the splatter from a stab wound have been significant? She thought back through the vast array of crime scene reconstructions she'd seen on the cable networks and shook her head. If he had been wearing something, where would he have put it?

There was a dumpster in that alley, Peggy remembered, but surely the police would have checked it. She thought about the route back to Pulitzer Hall, wishing she had walked it following her search of Miles's office. It was odd the police hadn't found anything yet — or if they had, they weren't making it public.

The train pulled into the station and Peggy climbed down the steps and onto the platform. She walked around to the front, past boarded-up stores and mounds of rubble. This was one of the days she feared nothing would ever return to normal, that the "superstorm" that had destroyed her town had triumphed.

She said hello to the butcher on the corner whose meats her mother had purchased for years. He'd tried opening up after the disaster, only to find that his heart just wasn't in it anymore. In that way, he was like a lot of people living in these working class towns by the sea — downtrodden and discouraged. Last week, he'd announced his shop would close. *Another casualty of Hurricane Sandy,* Peggy thought, watching him head back into the building.

She passed his piles of trash, bundled neatly into black plastic garbage bags. Tossed on the top, obviously as an afterthought, was the butcher's soiled white apron.

Peggy paused. This was the kind of thing she was expecting the detectives to find in Manhattan. A bloodied apron, or scrubs, or lab coat — something Miles had slipped over his clothes before he killed Alec Rodin. She stood rooted to the sidewalk, contemplating the stained apron. Slowly she edged closer.

No one was watching and no one was nearby, but touching the cloth would mean transferring her fingerprints. *It doesn't matter,* she told herself. *It's not like this is the real apron Miles Porter wore.*

But what if it was? Or what if it could be? In the absence of anything else, wouldn't the police rather have *something* with which to incriminate Miles? *Besides, I can always decide to throw it away myself,* she thought. *Just because I take it now doesn't mean I'm going to use it.*

Peggy looked right and left, but she and the garbage bags were quite alone. Upon closer inspection she saw that there was an empty, discarded one on the muddy ground by the building. She scooted over to pick it up. Using it like a glove, she picked up the apron and managed to slide it inside without touching it. Quick glimpses to her right and left revealed that still no one was near.

Bag in hand, Peggy started back down the street, imagining the look on smug Detective Ryan's face when he found this latest evidence.

Darby enjoyed watching the chemistry develop and deepen between Hideki Kobayashi and Miles Porter. Here were two intelligent, international men, both believers in the power of hard work and careful preparation; both determined to succeed with their values and integrity intact. Hideki was older and more conservative than Miles, and yet they shared enough traits that this difference in style didn't seem to matter. "We've got one very important commonality," Miles would tell Darby later. "We both have an enormous sweet spot for you."

She smiled as the men chuckled at something. The evening was winding down, and

Hideki insisted on paying the bill for the dinner, saying it was not often that he enjoyed such stimulating company.

"I hope that we are successful in finding my building tomorrow," he said, his eyes twinkling. "And now, I am afraid I must return to the hotel for my beauty sleep."

They bid him goodnight and waved as he climbed into a cab. "Fancy a walk back home?" Miles asked.

"Definitely. I've been somewhat of a couch potato since I've been here."

"You've done a fair amount of walking, but none of those power runs, right?"

"Exactly. Maybe if I get myself up nice and early tomorrow, I can trot around Central Park for a while."

"You do that," Miles grinned. "I'll be home waiting for you, making coffee and toast."

She laughed. Just then, they heard a familiar voice saying their names.

"Darby? Miles?"

It was Natalia, her face wearing a radiant smile, arm-in-arm with a sandy-haired young man. "This is my friend, Jeremy Hale."

They shook hands and chatted briefly about the pleasant spring evening. "We just had a great dinner — Ethiopian food,"

Natalia gushed. "We sat on the floor. It was so unique! Tomorrow we're going to the opera." If it was possible, she smiled even more at her companion.

"The Met?" Miles asked.

Jeremy nodded. "We're seeing *Rigoletto*. Supposed to be fantastic."

"Jeremy's firm has season tickets," interjected Natalia. "Isn't that great?"

Darby marveled that a girl whose family could buy their own theatre was so taken with her boyfriend's good fortune. "Wonderful. I hope you have a terrific time."

"We will." Jeremy smiled down at Natalia. "Hey," he said, looking up, struck with a sudden thought. "Do you want to join us for a nightcap?"

Darby and Miles exchanged a quick glance. "Thanks for the invitation," said Miles, "but we've got an early day tomorrow. Best be heading home."

As they left the couple, Miles elbowed Darby. "I would say Natalia isn't spending too much time grieving over Alec Rodin."

"No. I can't say I fault her for wanting to have some fun. She's only — what — twenty-two or so? — and her engagement to Alec was obviously something Mikhail arranged."

"I agree. Jeremy seems like a nice chap.

Wonder which firm he works for?"

"Between the Financial District and Midtown, there certainly are enough of them in Manhattan."

"Quite. Seems like every other person in this city is in finance." He frowned. "Why do you think Mikhail was so keen for Nat to marry Alec? Connections? Security?"

"I don't know. I wonder if our friend Sergei has an opinion." As Darby said the words, she already knew Miles's next question.

"I wonder where the devil Sergei is? I didn't see him protecting Natalia, did you?"

Darby shook her head. "Do you suppose he gets a night off now and then?"

"He's not a very good bodyguard if he's not on the job, is he?"

"True." She stopped and faced Miles. "Speaking of being on the job, it really bothers me that a man was killed barely a block from your office and there are no leads in the case."

"Or none that we know of. Darby, this is New York City. I hate to say it, but there is an awful lot of crime that happens in a city of eight million people."

"I know it's not little Hurricane Harbor, Miles, but after all, this murder involves one of the city's wealthiest residents! Wouldn't you think there would be some pressure on the authorities to make some headway? Alec was killed on Thursday. Two days later, there seems to be no progress."

"And the first forty-eight hours are the most critical."

"Exactly."

"It's beginning to seem as if neither of the Kazakovas is concerned about the crime, isn't it?"

"Natalia isn't shedding any tears, that's for sure." She cocked her head to the side, thinking. "Did Rodin have any family, and, if so, are they demanding answers?"

"Let's hope they've been notified," Miles said grimly. He took Darby's arm and resumed walking. "We could contact the detectives and ask for an update. Whether they'll give us any information or not, who knows."

"I'd like to do that, Miles. I can't stand this feeling of being powerless." She sighed. "I supposed it has to do with this mold issue, too. I'm stuck waiting for the shoe to drop on that one, as well."

"These are the times that try men's souls," Miles said. "Women's, too." He pulled her closer as they continued down the avenue and toward the park.

■ ■ ■ ■

In Rona's dream, Devin was a little girl of six years old or so, and she was wearing roller skates. They were in a small park — Rona couldn't quite tell where — and had just finished an enormous soft pretzel. It was a sunny day, and Rona felt light and happy to be trotting alongside her pony-tailed daughter. The metal of the skates made a clacking sound when Devin hit them together, and Rona could see from her little freckled face that she was working hard to keep her balance. Suddenly they were at the crest of a big hill, then up and over it, and Devin started picking up speed. Rona tried to run faster, but her legs wouldn't move. They were heavy things, rooted to the ground, as if she were stuck in a pile of hardened cement. All she could do was stand frozen, immobile, while her daughter careened down the hill.

She woke, took a moment to get her bearings. *Only a dream,* she told herself, feeling her racing heart slow a little. *Thank God.* The park . . . it did not exist, not with a huge hill like that. And Devin had never really liked roller skating.

Rona rolled over and looked at her watch.

Two-thirty in the morning. The point of the dream — if indeed there was a point, and Rona wasn't sure she believed in dream analysis — was that Devin was headed toward something and Rona felt powerless. *I couldn't help her in the dream, and I can't help her in real life.*

She rose, pulled on a silk robe, and headed to the kitchen. She took an individual portion of coffee and put it in her brewer. The familiar routine was soothing to her jangled nerves, and she took a deep breath while she waited.

You help her plenty! The voice sticking up for her was strident. All those bills you've paid, all her fancy trips to take ropes courses and gain self-esteem, all her clothes . . . *You have no reason to feel guilty.*

She pulled open the refrigerator and took out her fat-free half-and-half. Devin was on her own path now, nineteen years old and figuring things out for herself. *I never could tell that girl anything, anyway,* she thought. The only thing they communicated about was how much money Devin needed. Hopefully those days were over and Devin really had found a good job . . .

Rona took the mug of coffee and splashed in some half-and-half. She returned the cream to the refrigerator and entered the

210

living room. Outside, the sky was dark, the beams of the passing cars streaking through the night in an unending light parade. *Can I afford to keep living here?* She took a sip of the coffee. *Can I afford to leave, to lose the only contacts I've amassed?*

She hunted for her cell phone, texted a message to Devin: *You were in my dream. Roller skating.*

She waited. Devin was probably asleep in her apartment. The phone buzzed.

I hate roller skating. What are you doing up?

Couldn't sleep. What about you?

Coming home from a club with a friend. XOXO

Be safe, Rona texted.

Always, was the reply.

Rona smiled and sipped her coffee. The girl was her change-of-life surprise, a living, breathing, reminder of a brief love affair and even briefer marriage long gone, a stubborn, selfish child who had caused her mother an inordinate amount of anguish, and yet . . .

And yet I love her, Rona thought. *I do.*

TEN

Gina maneuvered the Volvo station wagon down Central Park West through light Sunday morning traffic, pulling into the motor court reserved for residents of the building. "Mrs. Vera Graff," she said, telling the uniformed man why she was entitled to park the borrowed New Jersey car in such a privileged spot.

He gave a brief nod. "Very good."

Once parked, Gina scooted into the building, taking the elevator to the fifth floor. Bethany had wanted to accompany her, but her shift at the restaurant came first. "I shouldn't take your parents' car," Gina had protested. "You ought to be the one driving it."

"Why is that? You're a much better driver than me. My parents don't care — they love you — and besides, I can't get out of work."

"The Coopers said I can borrow their car . . ."

"Yeah, but that's back in the city. This is easier. *Go ahead.*"

Reluctantly Gina had pocketed the keys, found the car, and negotiated the trip into Manhattan. Driving was nervewracking in the city — it always was — but at least Sundays were somewhat saner than the rest of the week.

Yvette answered the door with her customary glower, but to Gina's relief, said nothing. She stepped to the side, allowing Gina to enter, and moved soundlessly away.

Gina watched her sloping shoulders sneak off and shuddered. Yvette gave her the creeps, pure and simple. She reminded her of some aging movie star from the forties harboring a grudge against the whole world —

"Good morning, Gina," said Vera, breaking her reverie. "You were deep in thought."

Gina flushed. "I was just thinking —"

"You were thinking about Yvette, weren't you?" Vera gave a soft laugh at Gina's startled look. "It's alright, she can't hear us. She's gone into her bedroom, her little fortress of solitude."

"I'm sorry, Mrs. Graff, I didn't mean anything unkind . . ."

Vera bit her lip. "I know Yvette's behavior is very strange, but if she's cold and unfriendly, I'm afraid she has her reasons. That woman has had a very hard life, a struggle that left her wounded at a very young age. I'm not excusing her rudeness, but I am trying to explain it."

"Where did you and Yvette meet?"

"In Paris, just before the second war. My husband was a diplomat and we lived in several European cities. Paris was the last. Yvette worked for us and we became friends."

"Was she — was she as skittish as she is now?"

Vera nodded. "Worse, if you can believe it! She darted in and out of our apartment as if she were a terrified mouse. One day I found her sobbing on the stairs, and she told me some of her story." Vera sighed. "Her family history is traumatic, put it that way. She asked me not to repeat what I'd heard, not even to my husband, and I've kept that promise. But I, in turn, made her pledge to accompany us wherever we were posted, even back to the United States. She became our live-in housekeeper."

"That was very kind of you, Mrs. Graff."

"Oh, please — call me Vera." Her blue eyes were softer today, reminding Gina of the Hudson River rather than glass. "I don't know if it was kind or not. One does these things for certain reasons, and sometimes it appears to others to be something other than what it really was." She laughed. "Goodness, I'm sounding very philosophical in my old age. Suffice to say that Yvette, for all her crustiness, has proved to be a loyal friend, keeping a lonely woman company for many years now." She smiled. "And she's a decent housekeeper as well."

Gina shoved the car keys into her pocket. "I feel as if she doesn't trust me."

"Yvette? Of course not! She doesn't trust anyone!" Vera laughed, and then took a deep breath. "She suffers from extreme paranoia, along with some other psychological traumas. Right now, she insists that things are disappearing from the apartment."

"What kinds of things?"

"Parts of collections that we have here and there. A figurine of a horse — a glass paperweight. A rusty sword and its sheath . . ."

"A sword?" Gina's voice was quick.

"Yes. She's correct in noting that it's missing. I don't know if it was anything valuable, but it was quite old."

"Mrs. Graff — Vera — when did that sword disappear?"

"Oh, months ago." She thought back. "Let's see — I first noticed it missing in

February." She saw Gina's look of alarm. "What is it?"

"Maybe nothing," Gina said, giving a calming smile. Why mention that the Russian girl's boyfriend was killed with some sort of sword? After all, he'd been murdered blocks and blocks away, and antique swords were a dime a dozen in the city's flea markets and pawn shops. "Sorry — I'm being dramatic." She put a hand on Vera's arm. "Be sure to tell Yvette why some of your clothes are gone," she said. "I don't want her thinking I'm a thief."

"Indeed." Vera motioned for her to follow and they walked toward Vera's room. With blue eyes twinkling, she put up a hand and whispered, "We still have a few of those swords lying around. The last thing you need is Yvette chasing you around with one."

Darby and Miles were on their way out for a quick breakfast when they nearly ran into Detectives Benedetti and Ryan in the lobby.

"Good morning," Miles said, nodding at the two men. "Any new developments on the murder of Alec Rodin?"

"Nothing we can share, Professor Porter," Detective Benedetti said, shifting his bulky weight from one foot to another.

"Not with you, anyway." Detective Ryan's sarcasm was thick.

Detective Benedetti gave him a look. "We're here on other business, I'm afraid."

"Nothing's happened to Natalia . . . ?"

"Gee, Mr. Porter, we'd tell you about anything important, wouldn't we, Detective Benedetti?"

The older detective frowned. "Come on, Ryan."

Darby pulled Miles toward her and let the detectives pass by. "We can see you're busy."

When they were out of earshot, Miles snorted, "Right. Is it my imagination, or do those two men think they are God's gift to the world of law enforcement?"

They walked quickly out of the building and down the street. He pointed at a little diner wedged between several high-rises. "Mind the homeless guy on the corner. I always give him a little something, but he can be kind of aggressive."

They crossed the street, coming close to a figure crouched against the side of the building. He wore an oversized black coat and a neon pink knitted hat.

"I wonder who the detectives were going to talk to." Darby fished in her pocketbook and put a few dollars in the old man's coffee can.

"Who knows. There are more than two hundred units in that building, Darby." Miles stuck money in the can as well. "There you go, my friend." He opened the door of the diner, and the smell of toasted bread, grilled pancakes, and coffee wafted out, mingling with the man's muffled grunt of thanks.

The fat blue jay jabbed its beak at the smaller bird until it took wing, fleeing the solitary feeder that still dotted Peggy Babson's backyard. She watched dispassionately, not really noticing the chickadees darting back in for a quick bite, now that the blue jay had flown to the tall pine tree. She was thinking about the soiled butcher apron safe in its plastic bag in a corner of the den, now jammed nearly full with old toys, clothes, discarded magazines, and knickknacks and called the collecting room. Peggy wondered where the apron should go, and how long it would take Detectives Benedetti and Ryan to find it.

There was the dumpster near where Alec Rodin's body had been found, but that had been searched initially and would probably not be the best choice. There were places inside Pulitzer Hall — Miles Porter's office, the restrooms — and garbage bins outside the building, but of course those were emptied quite regularly.

No, it had to be somewhere the police had not searched initially and yet somewhere plausible.

Peggy knew, from watching her crime shows, that it was important to think like a murderer in order to work on the details of a case. She pictured herself as Miles Porter, hurrying down the steps of Pulitzer Hall, taking a short cut so that he could beat Alec Rodin to the narrow alley, waiting for him — and then striking. Miles would have grabbed the apron before leaving his office, of course. He would have tossed it on in a hurry in that dark alley. And then, when the deed was done, he would have wanted to get rid of it as soon as possible. But where?

The dumpster was the logical spot if Miles had wanted to toss it away right then and there. If he had held on to it, he might have continued down Broadway, and found a spot farther away. There had to be any number of places, and Peggy would find them before work on Monday. Once the apron was in place, she would monitor the situation, notifying the police herself (secretly, of course) if they did not find it.

She smiled and got up to make herself a second cup of tea. Dirty dishes had collected on the counter, but Peggy just pushed them aside. The tea box had a plaid design on the cover, and looking at it reminded Peggy of the wool scarf she'd found in Professor Porter's office. She froze, about to put the tea bag in her cup. What if the scarf was found with the apron? Miles, in his haste, yanked off both the bloody apron and the scarf . . .

A slow nod as she moved a stack of pots and put the kettle on to boil. *Yes, that would be the perfect touch.*

The slight man radiated energy, thought Darby Farr, reaching to shake Todd Stockton's hand. He had dark hair, graying at the temples, bushy eyebrows, and a firm grip. His attire was casual, yet professional — completely appropriate for a Sunday morning in the city.

"Great to meet you, Darby," he said. "I kept thinking we'd run into each other in Maine, and now here we are."

"This is Hideki Kobayashi," Darby said, introducing the quiet man beside her. "And this is Miles Porter, a friend and professor at Columbia."

"Miles is an investigative journalist, Mr. Stockton," noted Hideki. "I have brought him along to find anything unusual with the properties you show us."

Todd Stockton looked confused, but just for an instant, until Darby and Miles chuckled and he joined in.

"I'm hoping we don't uncover any deep, dark, secrets today, Mr. Kobayashi," Stockton said. "Darby has selected some great properties for you to see, and my goal is to help you purchase one at the best price. You'll find I'm very aboveboard."

Hideki bowed slightly, but when he looked at Darby he had a slight twinkle in his eye. *He likes being a bit of a tease,* she realized.

"I thought we'd start here," Todd said, indicating the high-rise behind him, "since it is one of my listings." He paused. "First, a little explanation. Manhattan is divided into three primary commercial real estate markets: Midtown, Midtown South, and Downtown. Within these markets are sub-markets with specific geographic boundaries. For instance, here in Midtown you'll find Bryant Park, Columbus Circle, the Garment District, Grand Central, Penn Station, the Plaza District, and Times Square. Midtown South has Chelsea, the Flatiron District and Silicon Alley, Gramercy Park, Greenwich Village, Hudson, Madison and Union Squares, and SoHo. Downtown is the Financial District — along with the

World Financial Center and the World Trade Center. Darby has given me her input, but naturally, one of your first decisions will be determining which submarkets you like.

"Let's head inside so you can take a look at what kinds of space you might need. I'm imagining you'll be one of the anchor tenants — meaning you'll be the largest company in the building. A consumer goods manufacturer was in this space, but has since relocated to New Jersey. I think you'll find the building would be a good fit for Genkei Pharmaceuticals."

Darby and Miles followed the broker and Hideki into the gleaming lobby and up several flights to see the several floors of available space. Darby listened to Todd Stockton's information about the building — the square footage, leasing particulars, and the like — but her thoughts kept roaming to Natalia, her research, and the death of Alec Rodin. Were the two things related? Was Rodin killed for what his fiancée had uncovered?

The next building, shown by New York's star broker Kiki Lutz, seemed more to Hideki's liking. "You can't beat the Flatiron District," she said, peering at him intently though large oval glasses. "Grand old buildings with a real mixed-use character, several lovely parks, good restaurants and shopping — I know your company would enjoy doing business in this part of the city."

She proceeded to show Hideki the features of the five available floors. Again, Darby found it hard to be as engaged as she would normally be. This time, her mind was on the Davenports and their mold issue.

Did the fact that Darby hadn't heard from her attorney mean that the suit had somehow gone away? *Magical thinking,* she told herself. *You haven't heard anything because it's the weekend.*

Miles came up beside her and put a hand on the small of her back. "You're far away, love," he whispered.

"Is it obvious?"

"Only to me."

She gave him a grateful smile, determined to be more engaged in the business at hand.

"Where're you off to, all dressed to the nines?" Miranda Styles grasped Korbut's proffered leash, her eyebrows raised with the question. Natalia Kazakova stood before her wearing a new outfit from the chic boutique the *Times* was calling "the hottest place to shop in town," and looking fantastic.

"The opera." Natalia said it almost bashfully, and Miranda did well to keep from smiling.

"Gorgeous — you and your clothes. You going with your new friend?"

"Jeremy."

"What about Tiny? He tagging along?"

Natalia rolled her eyes. "Of course. What can I do? I love Sergei, but . . ."

"Guess you can pretend you're a big celebrity requiring protection from the paparazzi, right?"

"That game gets old." Natalia glanced back into the apartment. She dropped her voice. "You're friends with my father, Miranda. Could you say something to him? I'm twenty-two years old, and I can't exactly have a normal life with Sergei trotting behind me all the time." She sighed.

"You know as well as I do that your father doesn't care what anyone else says regarding your safety. He wants you protected, and there's no way he'll give in on that, especially after Alec's death."

"Alec's death had nothing to do with me," she said darkly.

"What do you mean? Your father seemed to think so."

She shook her head. "Trust me. Alec was involved with shady things in Russia, things

224

that had nothing to do with me."

"I see. What kinds of things?"

"Government work." She shifted her weight from one foot to another. "My dad's paranoid, thinking someone's going to kidnap me. No one even knows who I am in New York! Besides, it's not like I'm the only wealthy college kid here. Look at all the Chinese kids. You don't see bodyguards with them, and they're worth more money than me."

"For some reason he feels you're in danger."

"Not me."

"You may think you're safe, but if you're father thinks otherwise —"

"I don't think it's me he's protecting."

"Then who?" It was Miranda's turn to sound exasperated. Beside her, Korbut whined softly. She glanced at her watch. "I'd better go. Listen, though — take my advice. Have a talk with your father. Tell him how you feel. Who knows? He might surprise you."

Natalia shrugged as if talking seemed a pointless exercise when it came to Mikhail Kazakova. She reached out and rubbed Korbut's ears. "Surprise me? We can't be talking about the same man."

"All I'm saying is don't assume the worst."

Miranda gave the dog's leash a tug. "Let's go, Korbut." She walked with the dog toward the elevator, calling over her shoulder, "Have a good time at the opera."

"Thanks," came the listless reply.

ELEVEN

The outfits, still on their hangers, were wrapped in protective plastic coverings and ready to be transported to Bethany's parents' car.

"Are you sure you don't need a hand?" Vera surveyed the clothes with a quizzical glance.

"That's okay. I can make a bunch of trips," Gina said. She picked up one bunch of hangers and contemplated another.

"I don't mind . . ."

Gina smiled. "You know, a little help would be great." She handed her pile to Vera. "Is that too much for you?"

"No, no, it's fine."

Gina picked up another bunch and the two started toward her apartment door.

"It may do me good to get some fresh air," the woman said. She waved an impatient hand in the maid's direction. "I'm fine, Yvette. Stop scowling at us." The maid sniffed and retreated to another room. "Honestly! Her attitude can be such a challenge."

"Why do you put up with it?" Gina asked, shutting the apartment door behind them. A hand flew to her mouth. "I'm sorry, I shouldn't have said that . . ."

"No, no." Vera rolled her eyes. "Believe me, I've asked myself the same thing." The elevator doors opened and they entered. "The short answer is that Yvette is my friend. The long answer . . ." She looked up, her blue eyes brilliant. "The long answer is more complicated. Another time, perhaps."

Gina was silent. The elevator doors opened and she led Vera slowly to the motor court, where the car was waiting. They spread the garments carefully on the seats and closed the doors.

"It feels like springtime," Vera said, her voice sounding light and carefree.

"We've had a beautiful stretch of weather, starting with that day I saw you in the park wearing your Hitchcock Ingénue outfit."

"That was the last time I ventured out. Before that, I don't think I had left the apartment for months."

"Really? Why? I'd go crazy if I didn't get outside every day."

"Maybe that's been my problem." She gave a wry look. "It may sound strange, Gina, but it's very easy to fall into bad habits . . . destructive habits. Things that can destroy your soul."

"I suppose. What about on a practical level? If you don't go out, who gets your eggs, milk, bread? Yvette?"

"Mostly we have them delivered."

Gina pointed at a delicate dogwood tree just beginning to bloom. "You can't deliver beauty like that."

The older woman smiled. "You are wise beyond your years, Gina, and your name suits you well." Seeing the young woman's quizzical look, she continued, "Your family name, Trovata. I believe it means 'found' in Italian."

"I think the nuns who scooped me up from the orphanage steps decided it was fitting," Gina said.

"Interesting. Well, I don't believe in coincidences," Vera said. "You were given that name for a reason. I can't help but marvel at the way you've helped me to find myself again, after all these years."

Gina opened the motor court's door back into the building. She smiled at Vera, waiting as the woman climbed a step. Vera swayed slightly, as if she was considering her next move, and then, while Gina watched, horrified, crumpled like a blossom in a harsh spring rain.

Sergei contorted his big body until he fit into the back of the cab and pulled the door shut. He directed the driver to follow the taxi directly in front of them, the one in which Natalia sat with her date.

Sergei looked out the window and fingered the ticket inside the pocket of his sport jacket. He loved opera, although *Rigoletto* wasn't one of his favorites, and he was looking forward to hearing at least some of the production. The issue was not his attention span. Ever since adolescence and his meteoric growth spurt, Sergei had found it difficult to stay seated in an average chair for very long. He was just too damn big.

He remembered his first opera, a production of *La Boheme* in Paris. Mikhail had brought Natalia there for her thirteenth birthday and insisted Sergei attend as well. He'd sat a few rows behind them, expecting to be bored to tears, and instead had found himself transfixed.

The costumes, the set design, the opulent surroundings, and best of all — the music, filling a void in his soul he had not even known he'd possessed.

Only severe cramps in his legs had forced Sergei out of his seat. Retreating to the back of the building, he'd stood by the fire exit until the final curtain dropped, as mesmerized as anyone in the place.

When the show was over, Mikhail had asked him for his opinion and Sergei had shrugged. "Something to pass the time."

His employer had narrowed his eyes and then laughed. "I do not believe you, Sergei! I see from your face your true feelings. The opera — it has climbed into your soul. Now it will be forever a part of you."

From that moment on, tickets to shows had appeared in Sergei's hands more often than he had dreamed possible. Nearly a decade since seeing his first production, the humble bodyguard was a knowledgeable aficionado.

He thought again of Mikhail's recent dishonesty and his face clouded. The man had not been in Russia when Alec Rodin was killed. He had been in New York. But where? And why?

The taxi pulled to a stop in front of the Metropolitan Opera Company. Sergei paid for the ride and lumbered out, keeping his eyes on the couple emerging from the other cab. Natalia's face was happy, and she was listening to something the young man,

Jeremy, was saying. Sergei noticed that she did not once glance about for his whereabouts.

He grunted with satisfaction. This was the way it should be. He had not liked Rodin, had not trusted the man, and was not in the least bit sorry he was dead. Natalia was right: the murder had removed her from an awkward situation.

Mikhail's manner at the time of Rodin's murder had been subdued. He'd seemed sorry that the man was dead, that the marriage was off, but now Sergei questioned it all. What if Mikhail had also been relieved? What if he, too, had seen the benefits of the young Russian's untimely demise?

Sergei stood in line a good dozen people behind Natalia and her date, not even trying to hear the young couple's conversation. Let them enjoy themselves. Let Natalia have fun . . .

He pulled his ticket from his pocket. Were these the same sentiments Mikhail Kazakova had felt once Alec was dead? Or — and this was the line of thinking Sergei forced himself to consider — had Mikhail envisioned Natalia's life without Alec before the fatal sword thrusts? Had he been the one to make the murder a reality?

Sergei accepted his program from a matronly usher and entered the hushed hall. He would think no more about it until the last note of *Rigoletto* had died away. For now, he would enjoy one of life's most sublime pleasures: the opera.

"She has a bad heart," hissed Yvette, wringing her hands as Gina and the motor court's manager helped a woozy Vera back into the apartment and onto a stiff-backed baroque loveseat. "She should not be working like a common laborer!"

"I didn't know." Gina's voice was morose. The manager gave a sympathetic nod and edged toward the exit. "She didn't tell me."

"She didn't tell me!" Yvette mocked, and there was real malice in her voice. "Why won't you just leave *Madame et moi* alone?"

The manager asked quietly if there was anything else, and hearing no response, retreated hastily into the hall.

Vera groaned. In a raspy voice she whispered something in French.

The maid glowered at Gina. "She says I must keep quiet, but I'm telling you this: if you ever —"

A knock on the door saved Gina from what she imagined was further scolding. Yvette sprang to her feet and pulled open the door. Rapid-fire, high-pitched yapping filled the room.

"Mimi!" Yvette bent to scoop up the poodle, murmuring endearments as the creature squirmed.

"Everything okay here?" Miranda Style's face in the doorway was quizzical. "I saw the motor court guy leaving . . ."

Yvette reached to close the door but Gina quickly stood.

"Miranda!" she called to the dog walker. "It's Gina, from the Coopers' unit. I was with Mrs. Graff and she passed out."

Creases appeared in Miranda's caramel-colored forehead. She pushed by Yvette and crossed the carpet to kneel by the couch. "How are you feeling now, Vera?"

"Dizzy."

Miranda reached for Vera's wrist, her jacket rising up as she did so. Gina saw a glimpse of her belt, and something else.

A holster, holding a small gun.

"How is her pulse?"

"Weak," answered Miranda.

"Of course it is," Vera protested. "I'm an eighty-five-year-old woman, not some Olympian."

"I think we should call an ambulance," Miranda said, standing. "They can rule out anything serious."

"No." Vera struggled to sit up. "I've had

these spells before, and going to the hospital doesn't help. They do all kinds of tests, and in the end the only thing that's happened is that I've been exposed to all manner of germs." Her voice grew stronger. "I'd like a glass of water."

Yvette scurried from the room, presumably to fetch it, and Vera's eyes met Gina's. "Listen, those clothes . . . if anything happens to me, take the rest of them to your store. My jewelry, too. Understand?"

"Yes, but you're going to be fine." Gina's eyes flitted to Miranda's. "She's going to be fine."

Miranda lifted her well-shaped eyebrows. "I think she should go to the hospital."

Vera waved a hand dismissively in Miranda's direction, the effort seeming to tire her. "Whatever money I make from sales is yours," she continued. "Deal?"

"Deal, but please let's not talk about this now." Gina put a hand on the woman's shoulder. "I could drive you to the emergency room. Skip the ambulance?"

"Non." Yvette hurried to her mistress's side and gave her a small tumbler of water. "Madame does not like hospitals," she spat.

"Yes, but . . ."

"Listen," Vera interrupted. Her voice faltered. "I've been making my own decisions my whole life, and I'm not stopping now, just when it starts to get interesting." She reached a wobbly hand dominated by a large diamond ring toward the glass, but Yvette ignored the gesture and lifted it to her lips.

"Merci." She took several sips, swallowing slowly, and then nodded at Yvette to remove the glass. "I'm having a series of little strokes. Hopefully one kills me, because I don't want to be stuck in a wheelchair or hobbling around with one of those walkers. But I'm not going to the hospital while I have any say in the matter." She leaned back against the couch and closed her eyes. "And now I think I shall rest."

Gina and Miranda exchanged glances.

"You heard Madame," hissed Yvette. "She wants to rest. *Allez!*"

Gina clenched her fists, wanting very much to use them against the malevolent maid. Instead, she followed Miranda.

"Take care, Vera," called the dog walker. "Let me know if you need more help with Mimi."

"Goodbye, Vera," Gina said, hating how final it sounded. She narrowed her eyes, prepared to meet Yvette's scowl, but the maid did not look up.

Snatches of a French folksong, hummed

very softly, met Gina's ears as she closed the apartment door.

Hideki Kobayashi shook Todd Stockton's hand and thanked him for his time. "I will speak with Darby," he said, "and ask her to communicate with you."

"Of course." Stockton's eyes met Darby's before flitting back to the older man's. "It was a pleasure to meet you."

Darby watched the slight figure of Todd Stockton navigate down the crowded street. He appeared to be a straight shooter, and yet there was something — she couldn't quite pinpoint what — that he kept under wraps. *Give it a rest,* she chided herself. *Not everyone's got some deep, dark secret.*

She glanced at Miles, engaged in small talk with the Japanese businessman. Nothing clandestine behind the Brit's sunny smile. He chuckled at something Hideki said and then turned Darby's way, catching her mid-stare. She felt her face flush.

"Gentlemen, let's go talk some business," she called out, hoping her cheeks weren't bright pink. "I saw a little coffee shop around the corner."

"I may need a little snack as well," Hideki said, his dark eyes twinkling. "Whenever I'm about to spend money I become famished."

"Then I'm sure we can find you something delicious to eat." Darby grinned at her client, aware of Miles's hand on the small of her back, inching down to tap her lightly on the butt.

"Hey!" she whispered. "Don't take my mind off my work, Professor Porter."

"Point taken. I'm going to head back to the apartment and let you and Hideki talk privately. Do you fancy a quiet night in tonight? I'd like to cook for you."

"That sounds terrific." Darby reached up and gave him a kiss.

"Hideki?" Miles raised his voice. "I'm heading out to let you and your star real estate agent talk dollars and cents. It was wonderful to meet you."

Hideki Kobayashi gave a slight bow. "And you as well, Miles. I'm sure we'll see each other again."

With a quick wave, Miles was headed down the street, already difficult to pick out in the sea of Sunday strollers. Hideki paused, put a hand on Darby's wrist.

"I hope I did not frighten your good friend away," he murmured.

"Miles?" she laughed. "He doesn't scare that easily, believe me." She steered her client toward the coffee shop she'd noticed earlier. "Here we are. I think if we grab a table in the back, we'll be able to talk."

The lunch crush was over and the restaurant, a modest place harking back to the 1930s, had several vacant tables. The air was redolent with the scent of grilled beef, pickles, and hot oil. Pennants from New York sports teams hung on the walls, along with framed black-and-white photographs of baseball players. A large glass case at the entrance held shelves of pies, many mounded high with cream. A waitress nodded when Darby pointed at a banquette in the back corner, and soon she and Hideki were seated and ordering a late lunch.

The businessman was quick to get right to business.

"I want the Flatiron District building," he said simply, spreading his hands in a gesture that was oddly elegant. "I think it is a most desirable location, and I like the mix of uses one finds there — residential and business. I believe that means it will be a good investment down the line."

The Flatiron property was the one represented by Kiki Lutz, who, with her trademark red-rimmed glasses and celebrity looks, had built her own empire as the star of a luxury real estate reality television show.

"I agree," Darby said, taking a sip of her water. "That was my favorite property as well. The space was in excellent condition, and leases for the other tenants seemed fair. Is this something you want to do now, or would you like to wait and see what else comes on the market? It's only April, and the next month or so may bring more options."

He leaned back in his chair. "More options, yes, but I may also lose this one."

The waitress arrived with Hideki's grilled cheese and bacon sandwich, and Darby's chicken salad platter. "Will that be all?"

"For now," Hideki said, sprinkling salt on a mound of French fries that spilled over onto a dill pickle. He took a bite of a fry and made a satisfied sound.

"I want to buy that building, Darby." He chewed happily. "Make it happen."

She picked up her fork and scooped some lettuce. "You got it," she said.

TWELVE

You know things are desperate when you start calling old lovers, Rona Reichels thought, fingering the small address book. She was in her bedroom, seated on the Egyptian cotton comforter that had cost a small fortune, even on sale. Idly she opened the small book to the letter "F."

Max. There was his number, written in faded blue ink, and as she read it to herself she realized she'd never quite forgotten it. Max Finnegan, the dashing actor she'd married on a whim more than two decades ago. She pictured his little garret in Greenwich Village, the tiny café where they'd shared bottle after bottle of cheap wine. It had been a glorious three months. She picked up her phone from the nightstand. *Can I really do this? Can I really call him out of the blue, and . . .*

And what? Rona wasn't sure. Ask him for money? Tell him about a daughter he never knew existed? It would all depend on how their conversation went, how convincingly she could still play the coquette. She wasn't interested in how the rest of his life was going — whether he was married, had children, and the like — all that seemed superfluous. *All I need is for him to still want me.*

She pressed the numbers on her phone and waited. A recorded, robot-sounding voice invited her to leave a message, and she did so, hoping the desperation she felt wasn't obvious.

Going back into the city now was tempting. Peggy Babson had to watch two back-to-back episodes of CSI to keep herself from marching down to the train station and riding into Manhattan. *If you want the plaid scarf, you need to wait until tomorrow,* she told herself. Getting into Miles's office on a Sunday had the potential to arouse suspicion, and that was the last thing she needed. *Patience,* she told herself. *Patience.*

She wondered how she should alert the police to the presence of the bloody apron and scarf. Anonymous phone call? Email? Emails were too easy to trace, unless she sent it from a public place like the library, but even then, you probably needed your card or something stupid like that. A good, old-fashioned phone call from a public phone (if she could find one) was probably the best way.

She still had not decided where to leave the items, but she figured she would know the right spot when she saw it. She had not ruled out a trash can within the building itself, especially since the upkeep of Pulitzer Hall was notoriously spotty.

Picturing the look on Detectives Benedetti's and Ryan's faces was worth all the trouble. The moment they realized that Miles Porter could, in fact, be guilty would be her vindication. It would be proof of her astute listening powers as well as keen intuition.

Peggy rose from her recliner and hustled into the kitchen. Rubbing her hands together, she reached for the ginger snaps and put the tea kettle on to boil. She pulled a plate from the cupboard and positioned three cookies on it. And then, because she was in the mood to celebrate, she added two more.

Darby decided to call Todd Stockton from the café, rather than waiting until she reached Miles's apartment. She gave the broker Hideki's terms for buying the Flatiron property, and asked that he forward the offer to her so that she could send it along to Hideki.

"Of course," Stockton said. "I'll get it done in the next ten minutes." He paused. "Did you tell me you're staying in Central Park Place?"

"Yes."

"What a fabulous building. I've brokered a few sales there and am hoping to get another listing soon. No doubt you've met the bulldog broker who thinks she owns the place?"

"I don't think so."

"You'd remember, believe me. Rona Reichels. One of those very territorial agents who can make any transaction miserable."

Darby remembered the cake-making visitor to Natalia's apartment and chuckled.

"I may have met Rona after all," she said. "But she didn't seem that bad to me."

"Try doing a deal with her and you'll see. The story is that she got cheated out of an enormous commission in that building, and she's still bitter over it."

"Interesting. What sale?"

"The premier penthouse."

Darby's interest piqued. "You're kidding. The one Mikhail Kazakova owns?"

"If he's the Russian billionaire, yeah."

"What happened with the commission?"

"I think the sale was arranged privately. Something like that." He paused. "Let me get that offer written up for you right now. Call or text if you have any questions."

Darby put down her phone and thought about Todd Stockton's comments. Was Rona still smarting, four years after a botched deal? Was her grudge strong enough that it had driven her to murder?

The call from Max Finnegan came in while she was dialing Charles Burrows's cell phone. Quickly Rona answered the incoming call, her heart beating a little faster at the prospect of speaking with her old lover. She gave a seductive hello and held her breath.

A woman's voice asked a simple question.

"How did you get this number?"

Rona explained that she was an old friend of Max's, and that she was hoping to speak to him as soon as possible. There was a long pause.

"I don't know how to tell you this," the woman said, "but Max is dead."

Rona felt the pit of her stomach sag.

"No," she managed.

The woman continued. "I'm sorry to say it so bluntly, but I don't know of any other way. Max died years ago. I'm his niece, and

I moved in to take care of him when things got really bad. I stayed on in his apartment."

"I see."

"I don't remember him mentioning you at all," she continued, her voice matter-of-fact. "If he had, I would have gotten in touch."

"Of course." Rona licked her lips, suddenly bone dry. "How did he die?"

Max's niece was silent for a few moments. "He had AIDS," she said. "He lived with it for a few years, but it got him in the end."

Rona fought the urge to run to the bathroom and vomit. Instead she turned off her phone, closed her eyes, and began to laugh.

It explained a lot. Why Max had been uncomfortable being in public with her. Why he took furtive phone calls for meetings. Why their relationship had never progressed beyond a few nights of drunken sex.

She didn't feel any emotion over his death, only amazement that she had never questioned his sexuality. When her laughter had finally subsided, she found a red pen and drew a line through his name in the old address book.

Once again Rona picked up her phone.

A masculine voice answered on the second ring, and this time she knew it was the right one. "Charlie, I've missed you," she purred.

"Tell me all about where you are, and when you'll be coming back to see me in New York."

"Why Rona," chuckled Charles Burrows. "I thought you'd never call."

Darby entered the apartment and inhaled the aromatic scent of rosemary and sage. "I'm home," she called out. She closed the door behind her and crossed to the little galley kitchen. "It smells heavenly!"

"Pork scaloppini," Miles said, wiping his hands on a dishtowel and then tossing it onto a counter. "To celebrate a deal, I hope . . . ?"

"We won't know for a bit, but I'm keeping my fingers crossed," Darby said. She pointed at a steamer full of vegetables. "Artichokes?"

"Yes, I'm trying a new Roman-style recipe. Glass of wine?"

Darby took one, smiling at the sight of Miles bustling about Charles Burrows's kitchen. "You look very at home here," she commented. "Have you thought any more about teaching another semester?"

"Funny you should say that. Five minutes ago, Charles Burrows called. He says someone's interested in buying the apartment, and he wanted to know my plans."

"Huh." Darby dipped a spoon in the scallopini sauce and took a taste. She gave Miles the thumbs-up sign and sighed. "Delicious."

"Thank you, my dear. We'll be ready in about fifteen minutes."

Darby leaned against the counter and took a sip of her wine. "So what did you tell Charles?"

"I said that if he was serious about staying abroad, I'd check with Columbia about teaching in the fall. I think I'd enjoy teaching one more semester, and it's a good opportunity. That way I can spend some time in England this summer." He looked into her eyes. "Hopefully with you."

Darby gave a very small shrug. "It's certainly tempting. I've never been to England."

"What better way to travel than with me as your guide?" He put his hands on her shoulders, and drew her close. "I want you to meet my family, crazy as they are. I want you to see where I'm from."

Darby took a breath. The image of the little house on the cove — the place where she'd been raised — flashed in her mind.

"So is he listing the apartment?"

"Who, Charles? Apparently not quite yet. I don't believe he thinks this so-called buyer is on the up-and-up, and he's not in any rush. He says that if Columbia wants to keep me on for the fall semester, he'd be happy to continue renting to me."

"That's good news."

"Yes. It will make things a lot easier if I can just stay put."

From the corner of the living room, a cell phone rang.

"That's yours, isn't it love?"

"Yes, excuse me." Darby hurried to the phone and checked the number. *Todd Stockton.*

"Bad news," he said, his voice clipped. "Kiki Lutz has another offer, and she says its better. Does your client want to step it up a few notches?"

"How much?"

"A mil and a half."

"That's a nice chunk of change. Can we trust her?" Darby meant that she questioned whether there really was another offer on the table, or if perhaps Kiki was merely trolling for more money.

"I wouldn't." He exhaled. "We can ask to see it in writing, if you want. You know how it is — it all comes down to how badly Hideki wants the building."

"I'll call him right now." Darby pushed her friend's cell phone number and heard the elegant gentleman answer. Quickly she explained the situation.

"Do it," Hideki said at once. "You know me, Darby — when I make up my mind, I don't want to move backward. Spend what it takes to get that building, and then let's get going on making it ready for my company."

Darby called Todd Stockton and conveyed the conversation. "I was thinking about playing hardball with Ms. Lutz, but my client really wants this building, and even with the higher price tag, I don't think he's overpaying."

"Agreed."

"So go for it then."

"Fine. Let me call her and get this wrapped up with a bow."

Darby hung up, drumming her fingers. Real estate agents had a duty to be honest, but that did not mean that all of them were. When it came right down to it, you had to take a lot of what you heard on good faith.

She reached for her wine and took a sip. It was a rich, red Barolo, chosen to complement the pork, and one of Miles's favorite wines.

Her phone vibrated and she picked it up. *Todd Stockton.*

"Done," he announced. "You can let

Hideki know he's in primary position."

"Great. I'll call him right now. Thanks, Todd."

"Thank you," he said. "Nice doing business with a fellow Mainer. Oh — I've got the scoop on what happened in your building."

Darby's interest sharpened. "When the Kazakovas purchased the penthouse?"

"Exactly. I figured if anyone would know, it would be Kiki Lutz, right?" He chuckled. "So, it was the boyfriend, the one they found stabbed in the alley. Rodin, I think was his name. Apparently he wormed his way into the deal and convinced Kazakova not to use a broker."

"Rona must have been livid. Obviously she didn't have an agreement in place with Mikhail Kazakova."

"Guess not." He paused. "We've all had crap like that happen to us, right? The people who ask you to find them a rental while they house hunt, and then after you arrange it all and show them endless properties, they make a deal with the owner and cut you right out."

"It's frustrating, for sure." Darby thought about the Davenports and the possible lawsuit hanging over her head. People thought selling real estate was easy, but the job was not for the faint of heart.

"I wouldn't put it past Rona to have knocked the guy off, even all these years later," Stockton continued. "According to Kiki, she's one vengeful bitch." He chuckled. "And Kiki Lutz would know."

Whack! The cast iron skillet came down on the block of ice, skittering it onto the floor.

Rona swore and let the pan clatter onto the counter. Nothing was going her way — nothing. Max was dead, Charles content to keep his apartment, and Mikhail nowhere to be found. Now she couldn't even get a piece of ice for her drink.

A key in the lock of her door made her stiffen. "Hello?" she called. "Who is it?"

No answer. She reached for the skillet and edged toward the door. "Hello?"

"It's me, Rona." Devin's voice called through the door. She pushed it open and regarded her mother with the skillet. "Jesus. What's gotten into you? I heard a loud noise . . ."

Rona lowered the pan and gave a dramatic sigh. "Trying to get some damn ice."

"What's wrong with your icemaker?"

"Jammed. Again." She regarded her daughter. "What are you doing here?"

"That's some kind of welcome, especially

when I'm going to give you this . . ." she jiggled a paper cup and the rattle of small ice cubes was music to her mother's ears.

"Excellent." Rona grabbed the cup and rinsed diet soda off the ice. She scooped the small cubes into her drink and took a large gulp. "Finally. Can I fix you one?"

"What've you got?"

"Scotch."

Devin wrinkled her nose. "No." Her eyes roamed around the kitchen. She wandered into the living room and plopped onto the couch.

"What's up?" she asked, picking up a magazine. "Any plans for your Sunday night?"

Rona followed her daughter into the living room and sat down on a leopard-patterned chair. "Dinner, but we had to cancel."

Devin's delicate eyebrows shot up. "I see." She tossed the magazine back to the table. "Too bad."

"What are you doing?"

"I've got a date."

"New boyfriend?"

She rolled her eyes. "Not exactly. A business associate." She reached into a pocketbook that was slung across her chest. "This is for you. Some of what I owe you." She

253

handed an envelope to Rona and leaned back.

Rona peered inside. A thin stack of one hundred dollar bills.

"How much?"

"Two thousand. It's a start."

"Yes, a good start." She narrowed her eyes. "What about your loans? Are you paying them?"

"They're being taken care of." She checked a cell phone that Rona hadn't realized she was carrying. "I've gotta go."

Devin stood. She was wearing makeup and a low-cut blouse that revealed her generous cleavage. "Bye."

"Thanks for coming over," Rona said. "And thanks for this." She held up the envelope.

"You're welcome." Devin gave a shy smile. "Bet you never thought you'd see any of what I owe you, huh?"

"I'll admit I'm surprised." Rona smiled. "Pleasantly surprised."

"Okay, bye." To her surprise, Devin leaned over and kissed her mother on the cheek.

She barely had time to say goodbye to Devin before she'd opened the apartment door and vanished.

"So, is Hideki happy?" Miles spooned some

sauce over the servings of scallopini and placed a plate before Darby. He'd set the table overlooking the park with two placemats and lit a wide sequined candle, and the effect was very romantic.

"Yes. He's all excited about opening a new division of Genkei Pharmaceuticals here in the city. I'll have to make sure he waits until he owns the building, before he starts tearing things down, but other than that, it's all good."

"Congratulations." Miles lifted his wine glass and they touched rims. "He's lucky to have such a wonderful broker."

"Remind me of how wonderful I am when I'm in the middle of a mold lawsuit, okay?" Darby grimaced. "Anyway, I'm not thinking about that tonight. I'm not thinking about anything except how happy I am to be here with you and this wonderful meal."

"Tuck in, then. See how it tastes." Miles watched as she cut a small piece of pork, dipped it in the sauce, and savored the bite.

"Delicious. The sauce is light, but flavorful, and the meat is cooked to perfection. You have many wonderful talents, Miles Porter."

"Mmmm." He leaned over and they kissed lightly on the lips. "Mind you, I can't cook a thing without having someone special to prepare things for, so there you have it."

"A symbiotic relationship."

"Exactly."

"Speaking of relationships, Todd Stockton told me an interesting story. Apparently Rona Reichels — the one we met up in Natalia's penthouse with the cake — was Mikhail's real estate agent."

"Lucky girl."

"Apparently not. She never got a commission when he bought in the building."

Miles whistled. "Which would have been what, close to a million dollars?"

"The property sold for $83 million. Figuring four percent for the commission, and then splitting it up — a million is probably about right. Enough to make anyone pretty darn angry."

"How did it happen?"

"According to Stockton, someone convinced Mikhail that he didn't need to use Rona." She waited until the Brit raised his eyebrows. "Alec Rodin."

"Mikhail's future son-in law."

"That's right. Remember, Alec was a developer in Russia. That's how he and Mikhail first met."

"Do you think Rona has held a grudge all these years?"

"I don't know."

"Would you?"

Darby leaned back and thought a moment. "I'd like to say no, that I'm above all that, but the truth is, Miles, that's a lot of money. If I felt like I worked for it, that I deserved it, yes, I'd have a hard time letting that anger go."

"Could that anger have pushed Rona to kill Rodin? Even after four years?"

"Perhaps if she has other stresses in her life, yes."

"Such as . . . ?"

"Some kind of health issue, money problems . . ."

"Yes." He put down his fork and knife. "Something that could have tipped her over the edge." He made a face. "Isn't it strange that we've heard nothing new about Rodin's murder? It's almost as if no one cares. Natalia has moved on, who knows where her father is, and there aren't any grieving relatives demanding answers. I feel like his death is a lost cause."

"I agree. I don't mean to judge, Miles, but I am surprised that Natalia appears to have forgotten all about her fiancé. There's something strange about her behavior."

"Could it be cultural?"

"I wonder. Her marriage to Rodin was arranged years ago, right? Maybe she didn't have very deep feelings for him in the first place. Maybe she loved him early on but then grew out of it."

"Maybe I'll discover more if she and I start working on this story."

"Any news on that?"

"No. I've left the ball in her court, so to speak."

"I see." Darby finished her meal and took a sip of her wine. "I'm stuffed."

"Don't say that — I'm taking you out for authentic Italian gelato for dessert."

Her dark eyes twinkled. "In that case, I have a little room left."

THIRTEEN

"Fancy a Monday morning walk in the park before I head off to class? Work off last night's gelato, perhaps?"

"Definitely." Darby accepted the steaming mug of coffee from Miles and peered out the window. "Looks like another nice day."

"Warm, too. I guess the weather turns nasty tomorrow, with rain showers, but it should clear up for your flight back to California on Thursday."

"Ugh. I don't want to think about going back to work."

"Really? That doesn't sound like you, love."

She sighed. "I know."

"Maybe you're growing tired of the whole West Coast thing?"

"I don't know. I love working with ET, but other than that, I feel like my ties are more on the East Coast now. There's Tina, and Helen, and Hideki, and . . ."

He looked at her expectantly. "And me?"

She wrapped him in a hug. "And you. Miles, I think it's getting harder and harder to leave you."

"Really?"

"Yes, it's . . . it's painful."

He kissed her deeply and mussed her glossy hair. "That's a good thing, love. One of these days you'll realize you don't want to leave me. Then you'll know how I feel every time you say goodbye."

Detectives Benedetti and Ryan were standing in the lobby as Darby and Miles exited the elevator.

"Gentlemen," Miles said. "We're certainly seeing a lot of you lately."

"I wish we could say we were here on a pleasant errand," Benedetti commented.

Darby and Miles exchanged glances. "Can you tell us?" Darby asked.

"Not really." He glanced around the lobby. "Next of kin notification."

"Dear God. Nothing to do with Natalia Kazakova, I hope?"

"No, Mr. Porter." Ryan squinted at the lanky journalist. "You're awfully concerned for Ms. Kazakova's safety. Why is that?"

"She's my student — that's why." Miles's voice was a trifle indignant. "She's been through a lot, and I only hoped . . ."

"Thank you for setting our minds at ease, detectives." Darby cocked her head toward the door. "We need to go, Miles."

He gave her a questioning look as she tugged on his arm. "Let's go."

"Why is it I feel I'm a piece of Turkish Delight, being stretched this way and that?"

"I could see they weren't going to tell us anything, so I figured we should get on our way," Darby explained. "Clearly, they have unpleasant work to do."

"Another tragedy involving someone in the building," said Miles. "I can't help but wonder who's about to get devastating news."

An attractive woman passed them with three dogs on leashes. One, a lanky wolfhound, dove toward Miles's sneakers.

"Hey!" he jerked away his foot.

"No, Korbut!" yelled the woman, yanking the dog's leash. She rolled her eyes. "I'm so sorry. He's got a thing for running shoes. Don't ask me why."

Miles chuckled. "As long as he hasn't a 'thing' for ankles, I guess."

"Is that Natalia Kazakova's dog?" Darby asked.

"Why do you ask?" The woman's eyes narrowed.

"We were in her apartment, and I recognize him."

"I'm sorry to sound so suspicious. Yes, this is Natalia's dog." She reached out a hand. "I'm Miranda Styles. I live in the building, too."

Darby and Miles introduced themselves.

"So you're in Charlie Burrows's apartment?"

"Yes." Miles eyed Korbut, who was now sniffing a trash receptacle. The other dogs, a fussy-looking poodle and an aging lab, waited patiently. "You know Charles?"

"I served a term on the residence owners' board," she explained. "Fortunately or unfortunately, you get to meet most of the residents." She reached over to scratch the lab's ears. "When is he coming back to New York?"

"His plans are a trifle up in the air, I'm afraid," said Miles.

"I see." Miranda Styles struggled to keep Korbut from once more investigating Miles's shoes. "We'd better head off. Nice to meet you."

"Interesting career choice, that," Miles commented. "Do you think it's the only thing Ms. Styles does?"

"From what I hear, dog walking can be pretty lucrative." Darby watched the brisk pace at which Miranda trotted the dogs along.

"Speaking of lucrative, what's next for your Mr. Kobayashi?"

"We're checking into a few things with the building, and then he'll buy it," Darby explained. "Genkei Pharmaceuticals will join the ranks of New York City's many corporations."

"Why did Hideki want to be here?"

"Oh, same as anyone, I think. It's the hub of the universe, right?" Darby smiled. "He's also an incredibly shrewd businessman. Manhattan is an investment. Barring some kind of disaster . . ."

"Another Superstorm Sandy? Or terrorist attack?"

Darby nodded. "Exactly."

"The thing is, no one can live their life in fear of things like that, can they?"

Darby stopped and scrutinized Miles's countenance. She thought back to that summer day, long ago, when she'd said goodbye to her parents, never knowing that their afternoon sail would lead to their deaths.

Have I been living in fear, she wondered? She thought of the anxiety she carried around regarding her unhappy clients, the Davenports, and their allegations of mold. She thought about her reluctance to make long-term plans — with Miles, with Maine . . . *With life,* she thought.

Her parents had not lived that way. They'd met on a chance encounter in Boston, fallen in love, married, and moved to Maine, with little thought of what an interracial relationship on a remote island might entail. They'd had a child, raised her on that island, confident that she'd find her way in the world, having known their love . . .

"What is it, love?" Miles's voice held concern. He reached out and rubbed Darby's cheek with the back of his hand, a tender gesture that caused her eyes to well with tears.

She let herself be enveloped in a hug. Later, she'd tell him that yes, she wanted to visit England, but for now she allowed him to comfort her in the midst of Central Park.

The basement of the Pulitzer building was a dusty, dark place, even at ten o'clock in the morning, but Peggy had thought ahead and brought a small flashlight. She'd already entered Miles Porter's office and removed the moth-eaten scarf, and it was safely inside the plastic bag along with the butcher apron. She shone the flashlight down the stairs, saw the giant hulk of the boiler, as well as the massive hot water tank. She frowned. It was pretty clear no one came down here. Important evidence would be a long time in coming to light if it were placed in the basement.

Reluctantly she climbed back up the stairs. This whole thing was becoming annoying and she felt an anxious itchiness that she associated with her penchant for collecting.

And then she saw it. A huge potted plant — a tree, really — in the corner of the entryway. The perfect place to put something if you were in a hurry to dispose of it . . .

Quickly she lifted the plastic bag over the plant's soil and released its contents. Bunched together on the dirt, the apron and scarf looked natural, as if they'd been tossed there. She stepped back. Yes, it was perfect.

Peggy stuffed the empty plastic bag in the pocket of her spring jacket. She found the custodian replacing paper towels in the downstairs bathrooms and reminded him to water the ficus tree outside her office. "You're probably watering them all today, right? Even the ones in the lobby?"

He nodded. "Just one of my many duties, Peggy."

She ignored the sarcasm and gave a heavy sigh. "I keep thinking the cops will make some headway on that murder."

"Now, what murder would that be? They're a dime a dozen in this city."

"The one that happened a block away, of course. The Russian fellow. I know the police are looking for evidence."

He slammed shut the dispenser. "Yeah, well, I'll be sure to keep my eyes peeled."

Later, when she saw the detectives enter the building, Peggy Babson could not resist a small triumphant smile.

There was a throbbing in her head, a dull, persistent ache that the migraine medicine couldn't touch, and Rona Reichels suspected, even as she gulped down a drink, that nothing would relieve her of the pain. If she could only sleep, she could forget about the pain, forget, too, about the death of her daughter, Devin.

How had the police detectives put it?

An accidental overdose.

A neighbor had thought it odd that the blaring music of Devin's alarm had not ceased after an hour, and had called the building superintendent. He'd knocked repeatedly and then finally entered her apartment, finding her sprawled across her queen-sized bed.

In her system was a toxic cocktail of

Valium, Oxycontin, and alcohol. "We see this happen more than we'd like," said the portly detective. "Unintentional overdosing on prescription meds. Sometimes the victim takes a sedative, gets confused or drowsy, and forgets they've already taken a dose, and then takes more. Or they take another drug. Unfortunately, when you add sleeping pills to the mix there's little difference between the amount that helps you nod off and the amount that can kill."

Rona hadn't known Devin took sleeping pills, but she wasn't surprised. She herself suffered from insomnia and took a sedative nearly nightly. As for the pain pills, Rona remembered a tennis injury — a torn rotator, or something like that? — for which Devin was treated last spring. Had that doctor been the one to prescribe Oxycontin?

"Was she alone?" Rona barely recognized her voice, which seemed to come from somewhere far away, as she questioned the detectives.

"We saw no evidence anyone was with her."

Rona had nodded. Devin, her lone wolf. She closed the door behind the men and collapsed on the couch, getting up only when she remembered the insurance policy tucked inside her dresser drawer.

■ ■ ■ ■

Eleven a.m. Gina dialed the number for Vera's apartment, praying that by some miracle Yvette would be out and she would not have to speak with her. Her prayers were answered when the clipped voice of Vera Graff answered the phone.

"Thank God," Gina blurted, upon hearing the woman's quick hello. "How are you feeling, Vera?"

"Just fine," she said, brushing off Gina's concern as if it was an unwanted breadcrumb. "How are plans for the store progressing?"

"Moving right along. I hope you can keep the first of June free. That's when we plan to have our opening."

"I'll try." Vera waited, no doubt wondering why the young woman had called.

"I wanted to talk to you about the missing sword," Gina said. "The one you told me about."

"Surely you aren't selling weapons in your vintage clothing store?"

Gina laughed. "No. Not yet, anyway." She cleared her throat. "Vera, I was thinking that you ought to tell the police about the theft, if you haven't already."

"It seems so trivial. Why?"

"Because it may be important. The Russian student — the one who lives in the penthouse — her fiancé was murdered with an antique sword. What if it was yours?"

"What if it is?"

"Don't you see, the murder and the robbery could be related. Perhaps the same person who stole your sword killed Alec Rodin."

"But I hate talking to policemen," Vera scoffed. "I don't like having them snoop around my things . . ."

"They aren't going to snoop. They'll appreciate the lead. And if you don't want them to come to your apartment, I could go with you to the station."

"Absolutely not." Vera sighed. "I suppose I should do my civic duty and call them. Will you come over when they're here? You know the whole thing will terrify poor Yvette. She can't stand anyone in a uniform."

"Yes," said Gina, thinking that it was going to be enjoyable, in a perverse way, to see Yvette's face when law enforcement appeared. She hoped to heck they wore their uniforms, with big, shiny guns strapped to their hips.

"Call me when you hear from them," Gina

said. "I'm at the Coopers' house until noon."

"You're sure about this, Gina?"

"I am. Make a list of anything else that's missing. Let's see if we can help the cops catch this guy."

When ET called and gave Darby the news that Carl and Jill Davenport were suing Pacific Coast Realty over a mold infestation, she surprised herself by feeling philosophical, rather than panicked.

"It's out of my hands," she told her assistant. "I feel I treated them honestly and fairly, and if indeed there is a mold problem in their home, it was not something I knew about, nor could have reasonably known about."

"Very well said," ET murmured. "Attorney Hitchings has voiced the same sentiment to myself and Claudia. We won't discuss it, but you should know that we are both in your court."

"Pun intended?"

ET groaned. "Darby, I never use puns intentionally, you know that."

"Hey, lighten up. If I can make a joke about this, you can, too."

"I suppose." ET gave a little cough. "Are you still coming home on Thursday?"

"Yes. Time to face the music."

"I hope you've enjoyed yourself."

Darby thought about the moments she'd wasted worrying about the lawsuit and shrugged them off. "Yes, Miles has been a wonderful host. We've eaten great meals, seen a show, and toured MOMA. And, I met with Hideki yesterday and put an offer in on a fabulous building in the Flatiron district of the city."

"And how are you managing to sell real estate in New York without a license from that state?" he asked delicately.

"Relax," she laughed. "I'm just getting a referral."

"Good. You're somehow keeping yourself out of trouble?"

"Yes. For all its glitz and glamour, this city isn't all that exciting."

"Meaning no one has asked you to solve any crimes."

Again she laughed. She hadn't told ET about Alec Rodin. "Right."

"Let's hope your uneventful stay continues, and you come home in one piece to California." ET was silent a few moments. He knew all too well his friend's propensity for putting herself in harm's way. "I mean it, Darby. Keep yourself safe."

"No worries," she said blithely. "I laugh in

271

the face of danger."

On the other end of the phone, ET groaned.

"That's just the attitude that worries me."

Fourteen

Vera's call came just as Gina was making her third peanut butter and jelly sandwich. Luckily Alison, one of the afternoon nannies, had just arrived.

"Allie, I need to scoot right out," Gina explained, hugging the boys while simultaneously licking peanut butter from her thumb. "See you in the morning, super-duper-party-poopers."

The giggles over any rhyming words were so satisfying, thought Gina. She grabbed one of the sandwich halves and her satchel and headed out the door. On an impulse, she decided to run down some of the floors to Vera's apartment, taking the stairs two at a time.

She was winded when she arrived, but the sandwich tasted even better.

Vera opened the door with a whoosh and beckoned her inside. "Lunch on the run?" She shook her head as if making a comment on the whole sorry state of the world. "We've already had our midday meal, and Yvette has gone out for a few items at the pharmacy," she explained. "Come in, come in."

Gina entered the apartment, struck, as always, by the Old World elegance of the ornate furnishings. Although located smack in the center of Manhattan, the main salon could be in Vienna, or Paris, Rome, or Budapest.

"I do hope these officers are respectful," Vera fretted, plumping the cushions on a curvy loveseat. "I cannot abide rudeness, you know."

"I'm sure they'll be very courteous," Gina assured her, realizing that she had no idea how the police officers would act. "If they're not, we'll hand them over to Yvette."

Vera gave her a look that was shocked, and then she did an unexpected thing. She blurted out a huge guffaw.

"Oh my word, oh my word," she laughed. "I hope I don't split one of my seams." She wiped her eyes with her fingers, the mirth etched on her wizened face like an engraving. "Gina, you are a funny one."

A knock on the door interrupted their chuckles.

"Go ahead," Vera instructed. "Let them in."

Gina jumped up and pulled open the door, but the figure standing before her was not a police detective.

Miles's voice on the phone was incredulous.

"An apron," he fumed. "A butcher apron, and my wool scarf. They were found this morning in a planter in the lobby of Pulitzer Hall."

"But how . . . ?" Darby struggled to understand the bizarre news Miles was trying to relay. "Your scarf was with an apron?"

"Yes. And it's covered with blood. The apron, I presume, but who knows? Maybe the scarf as well."

"How strange."

"Indeed! I'm headed down to the police station now to talk to them about it."

"Do you think you should call a lawyer?"

"Whatever for? It's the most ludicrous thing I've ever heard of."

"Agreed." Darby knew, though, that evidence, no matter how ridiculous, could cast suspicion on innocent people.

"Can I meet you there, Miles?"

"Oh, I suppose so. Total waste of time, though." He gave her the address and the tone of his voice softened. "Thanks. It will be nice to have your support, no matter how crazy this whole thing is."

She hung up and thought about the odd news. A white butcher apron, stained with blood, and a wool scarf belonging to Miles . . . how had they been linked, and who had put them in the building's lobby?

Darby knew that Miles had nothing to do with placing the items in the planter. So who, then? Someone with an axe to grid against the lanky Brit?

Her thoughts went to Miles's students. He'd called some of their papers "drivel." Did his disdain for their work mean that at least one of them harbored anger? Was it a random prank? Miles said his scarf had been inside his office for days, although he hadn't noticed when it had gone missing. How had it been removed, and when?

Darby pulled on her sneakers and a black lightweight jacket. She ran a brush though her hair, tied it into a ponytail, grabbed a small pocketbook, and headed out the door.

"I'm sorry," said Natalia Kazakova, shaking her head. "I didn't realize you had company, Vera."

"That's all right, dear, come in." From her perch on the couch, Vera waved a graceful arm. "Introduce yourselves — unless you are already acquainted?"

"Not really," Gina said, smiling. "I know your dog, Korbut, but you and I met only briefly several months ago."

"Korbut, my ill-mannered wolfhound," Natalia lamented. "He lunged at someone's sneaker this morning. He is developing a bad reputation, I'm afraid." She looked confused. "You say we've met before?"

"In the locker room of the gym, at Halloween. I was with a friend and we asked you to come out with us for a few drinks. Completely random, now that I think of it."

"But very nice."

"Sit down, Natalia." Vera waved at the satin-covered couch.

"No, I won't disturb you. I came only to see if we could work on our project again?" She asked it delicately, waiting for the older woman to respond.

"Of course." She turned to Gina. "Natalia and I are doing some historical documentation," she explained. Swiveling back to the Russian woman, she sighed and said, "I should think I'll be too tired this afternoon, but we can meet tomorrow." She took a breath. "I might as well tell you, Natalia. Some months ago, an antique sword was taken from this apartment. Gina has convinced me to call the police, mainly because of the death of your fiancé."

The girl's face grew pale. "But that is terrible. Could it be the same sword used to kill Alec?"

"I have no idea. The police are bringing a photograph."

Natalia shuddered. "I do not wish to be here when they come," she said simply, moving toward the exit.

But it was too late. A knock on the door signaled the arrival of someone and this time, Gina knew as she opened the door that the man waiting on the other side was a cop.

He stood in the doorway of Vera Graff's apartment, clutching a manila folder.

"Come in," Gina said. She was about to introduce Vera when the man started.

"Ms. Kazakova," he said, a note of surprise in his voice. "I did not expect to see you."

"And who exactly are you?" Vera Graff had a commanding presence when she wanted, and Gina could see from the way the man hung his head for a split second that he felt chastised.

"Hello, Mrs. Graff. I'm Detective Benedetti, New York Police Department. Thank you for your call."

"Come in, Detective." She moved slowly but deliberately to the couch and eased herself back down. "Natalia was here for a visit and I told her about the sword." She indicated Gina. "This is Ms. Trovata, a friend who works in the building. She is here for moral support." She gave a wry smile and sighed. "My housemaid, Yvette, will be returning from errands very shortly. She's bound to be surprised at your presence. She doesn't take well to strangers in our home."

The detective pursed his lips. "Thank you for the warning."

"Please, sit down."

In contrast to Vera's graceful movements, Detective Benedetti lowered himself like a breaching baby whale. Gina thought she saw a flicker of amusement in the older woman's eyes.

"Let me start off with first things, first, Mrs. Graff. You've called because an antique sword is missing from your apartment."

"Yes, along with a few other things."

"Such as . . . ?"

"A little figurine of a horse, some old coins, and an egg."

He was taking notes. "An egg?"

"That's right." Her blue eyes were sharp. "Encrusted with precious gems. As is the case with the onyx horse, it's rather valuable."

The detective looked up from his jottings. "And this happened . . . ?"

"About a month ago." She paused. "I know your next question, Detective. You're going to ask why I did not report this theft."

He gave her a level gaze. "I was wondering. Especially if the items are valuable. Surely you would want to report them stolen so that your insurance company would cover your losses."

Vera seemed to be choosing her words, but then the door opened and Yvette stood in the threshold. Her face sagged when she saw the assembled guests.

"Madame . . ." she said. Her voice quavered. She swayed on thin legs and Gina feared she would drop the groceries clutched in her arm. Gina sprang up and lent a steadying hand.

"It's okay, Yvette," she whispered. "You don't need to be afraid." She guided the terrified woman to the couch and coaxed her to sit down. She pointed at Benedetti. "This man is from the police department. He's here because of the things that are missing from the apartment."

Yvette jerked her head toward Vera, her eyes wide and questioning.

"*Ça va,*" the older woman said. "*Ne t'inquiete pas.*"

Yvette nodded slowly.

The detective sighed as if he'd had enough of the maid's dramatic entrance. "As I was saying, I'm surprised and disheartened that you did not report this crime. Be that as it may, this is a photograph of the sword we have at headquarters." He took a glossy photo from the file folder and handed it to Vera.

She scrutinized the photo, nodded, and passed it to Yvette, who touched only the edges, as if afraid it would bite her. Gina watched the maid's face carefully but she betrayed nothing.

"Detective, this sword certainly looks like the weapon that was removed from this apartment," she said. She handed him back the photo. "I am saddened to think it may have been involved in a crime."

Benedetti slid the photograph back into the folder, but not before glancing at Natalia. "Where did this sword come from?"

Yvette's eyes darted toward her employer.

"It's an old family piece," Vera said. "I know little more than that."

"I see." The detective consulted his notebook. "On the day that you noticed the sword and the other items were missing, was there anything else strange? Were your doors or locks harmed, for example?"

"Forced entry, is that what you are asking?" Vera Graff shook her head. "No. Nothing like that."

"Who, besides the two of you, has a key to the apartment?"

"No one."

"And you have been here how long?"

"Why — we have been in the building since it opened."

"Did you, or do you, have any suspicions about who may have been involved in this theft?"

Again Vera shook her head. "I'm afraid we were as stymied then as we are now, Detective. No idea." She smoothed the front of her wool slacks with a hand. "If that is all . . ."

The detective took her hint and rose heavily from the couch. "Thank you for your time, Mrs. Graff." He glanced around the room. "Ladies — I would ask that you keep the information about this weapon confidential. We are in the midst of a murder investigation."

Gina stole a glance at Natalia, whose eyes were downcast. Without further word, Detective Benedetti crossed the room and left the apartment.

"Well," Vera said, as the door closed behind him. "I'm sorry you had to hear all that, Natalia. This must be very difficult for you."

Her choppy bangs bobbed as she nodded. "It's not easy, but perhaps with more information the police will solve Alec's murder." She bit her lip and rose to her feet. "The missing egg . . . ?"

Again Yvette's eyes flew to Vera, who answered.

"Yes?"

"Was it . . . is it . . . a creation of Faberge?"

"So you know of the famous jeweled eggs," Vera said softly. She took a breath, looked down at her hands. "It was not genuine, but very beautiful nonetheless. Have you seen these masterpieces before?"

"When I was very young, in a museum in Moscow." She stood and nodded to the women. "I must go. Tomorrow, Vera."

"Goodbye."

"Goodbye, Natalia. I'm glad to see you again." Gina smiled and the young Russian woman smiled as well.

"Perhaps we will meet again," Natalia said.

Sergei Bokeria glanced at his cell phone. Mikhail Kazakova, checking in. He stepped out of the hallway and the cook's inquisitive ears.

"Da," he answered.

"Sergei, I am coming back to New York late tonight." Mikhail's voice sounded weary, as if he were already in the midst of the flight.

"Do you need me to meet you at the airport?"

"No, that will not be necessary. I have arranged a driver. Please let Natalia know I will join her for breakfast."

Bokeria nodded, he would tell the cook as well. "Yes," he said simply. He thought of asking his employer about his deception regarding his whereabouts Thursday night, but decided it was better discussed in person. He waited until Mikhail said good-bye before hanging up.

"Mr. Kazakova wishes breakfast in the morning," he informed the cook in Russian. She scowled, her habitual response.

"And the daughter?"

"Natalia will take breakfast as well." Sergei decided to let Natalia know of her father's plans right away, and continued down the hallway to her room.

American music was playing behind the closed doors. Bokeria could pick out some of the English words, which was strange. Not because Natalia did not favor the pop stars of the United States, but because she usually listened with tiny earphones. He listened more closely and heard the sound of running water. So that was it. Natalia had returned from her outing to the neighboring apartment and decided to take a shower.

He headed back down the hallway to his room. *I will inform Natalia later,* he told himself. He opened his door and closed it, without ever seeing his charge slip from the confines of her room, close the door, and creep silently down the hall.

Miles was waiting outside of the police station when Darby arrived. After a quick peck on the cheek, she took his hand. "Have you heard anything else?"

He shook his head. "No. Let's go get it over with."

They entered the station and Miles indicated a long window with sliding glass doors. A uniformed officer stood and slid open the window. Her face was inquisitive, but serene, despite the piles of papers surrounding her desk and the chaotic jumble of sounds released by the sliding window: ringing phones, the cacophony of male voices, the hum of a computer server.

"Help you, sir?" She waited.

"I'm Miles Porter. Detective Ryan called

and asked for me."

She pointed with an elegantly manicured hand to another door. "His office is right over there," she said. "He will meet you."

They crossed the room. The door opened and Detective Ryan, holding a mug of coffee, nodded.

"Miles Porter." He gave the classic "follow me" gesture and they headed down a busy hallway. He opened the door to a conference room and waved a hand. "Take a seat."

The room had a metal table, six chairs, and glass walls. Detective Ryan closed the door and the three sat down.

"Detective Benedetti isn't in, so you're stuck with me."

Miles shot a look at Darby. Neither one of them liked the sarcastic Ryan, but they had little choice in the situation.

Miles cleared his throat. "Detective Ryan, I have no idea how my scarf came to be . . ."

"Save it, Porter." He brought his hands down on the metal table. Darby flinched.

"Look," he continued. "We've got a piece of your clothing and a blood-spattered apron. These items were found in your building, barely a block from where Alec Rodin was murdered, and only one flight of stairs from your office. You not only saw the victim before his death, but you argued with him, so vehemently that a secretary heard your words. In fact, she heard you say you'd kill him."

"I didn't —"

"Porter, please." Ryan held up his hand like a traffic cop. "You were the last one to see him alive."

"Not quite," Darby said quietly. "The secretary saw him going down the stairs."

"Yes," Ryan said dryly. "She now says she went back into her office and heard another person going down the stairs. You."

"That's ludicrous!" Miles said.

"Really?" Ryan cocked an eyebrow. "She went to the stairs and looked down, and said she saw a male wearing a plaid scarf. Your plaid scarf, Porter."

"Rubbish! She's lying."

"And why would that be?"

"I have absolutely no idea, but I know this: I didn't leave Pulitzer Hall until two hours after Rodin had gone. And I wasn't wearing that scarf."

Darby looked at Ryan. The detective was silent, his hands folded tightly in front of his mouth. Miles expelled a long breath.

"Perhaps I need a lawyer."

"Why?" The question was muffled behind Ryan's hands.

"Because you think I had something to do with this." Miles shook his head.

"No."

"Beg your pardon?" Miles leaned in closer.

"No, you don't need a lawyer, and no, I don't think you had anything to do with the scarf. Nor the apron, which incidentally, is splattered with bovine — that is to say, cow's — blood. It's an honest-to-goodness butcher's apron. Not a trace of human blood on it."

"I don't understand."

"It's simple. Someone's tried to frame you. It's a clumsy attempt to make it look like you killed Alec Rodin."

"But why?"

"Obviously they don't like you, Porter." He narrowed his eyes. "Look, I don't know, but I do know this: you gotta tell me right now why you and Rodin argued." He paused. "The whole story."

Darby shot a glance in Miles's direction.

"All right," Miles said heavily. "I will."

FIFTEEN

Without remembering how she had done it, Rona had boarded a bus to Devin's apartment, gotten off at the nearest stop, and climbed the stairs to the second floor. Now she was standing in front of the door, the key she'd copied from her daughter's ring the year before clutched tightly in her hand.

She had no idea how long she would stand at the doorway. She felt empty, barren, as if all of the fluid had been drained from her body and she was a hollow shell. She remembered the carapace of a beetle that Devin had once found on the sidewalk, how intrigued she had been by the find.

Rona shuddered. Whatever relief she'd felt in finding the insurance policy (and noting the payoff she would receive) had vanished. Devin was dead. The three words repeated like a gong sounding in her skull. She stood motionless, her hands clenched, the key digging into her flesh.

Why am I here? She looked at the door of Devin's apartment, without really seeing it, the scratches and dents on the worn wood registering, and yet not. *I am here . . .* she tried to complete the sentence. And couldn't.

Only a few hours had passed since the fateful phone call with the awful news. Like a sleepwalker, Rona had climbed in a taxi and gone to the hospital. She'd leaned on the arm of a young male nurse who had led her down the hall, and then pulled back a sheet, revealing Devin's peaceful face. Somehow she had nodded when he'd suggested places that could help with funeral arrangements. She remembered his voice had been kind.

A dribble of saliva formed on her lip and dripped down her chin. She shut her mouth, swallowed, tried to recall why coming to Devin's apartment had seemed important. Before her was the scuffed door, in her hand the metal key biting into her flesh.

"Mrs. Finnegan?"

Rona started, dropping the key.

"I'm sorry, I didn't mean to scare you."

It was a young woman in her early twenties, her hair chopped short, her eyes ringed with navy blue eyeliner. She wore jeans and clunky motorcycle boots, a pink tee shirt, and a thick black belt. She picked up the key and held it out to Rona.

"I'm Heather. Heather Cox. I'm — I'm friends with Devin."

"You know." It was more a statement than a question. Rona could tell from the catch in Heather's voice that the girl had heard the news.

"Yes."

"How?"

"The super." She bit her lip. "I used to live in the building. That's how Devin and I became friends."

"I see."

"Mrs. Finnegan —"

"Rona. Call me Rona."

"Rona, I want to tell you how sorry I am. Devin was a great girl, and we'll all miss her."

"Oh?"

She nodded sadly. "I'm on my lunch break, so I can't stay too long, but I'm glad I caught you. I just can't believe it." She wiped her eyes with the back of a hand. "When is the celebration?"

"I don't know what you're talking about."

"The celebration of her life? I could help you plan it. At the very least, I can post it on my page so that everyone knows."

Rona remained standing and the girl gave

her a curious glance — pity, mingled with something like surprise. She wiggled the key. "Let me unlock the door for you." She inserted it and turned the handle. "There."

Heather tossed her chopped hair and crossed into the apartment. As if in a dream, Rona followed.

The apartment was as Rona remembered it — a studio, with high ceilings and a miniscule kitchen — but she saw that Devin had been creative with paints and thrift-store findings, so that the place had a hip, urban feel. Rona's gaze swept the room, settling, without her intending, upon the queen-sized bed.

She moaned.

Heather reached out a hand, steadying her.

"There's no way she did it on purpose," the girl said softly. "If that helps at all. Devin had a good thing going. She was okay."

"It was an accident," Rona said. She gulped and repeated the words. "It was an accident."

"Yeah." The girl steered Rona to a small loveseat. "Want to sit down a minute?"

Rona shook her head, although she was not sure how much longer she could remain standing. "No."

"Do you want me to work on this for

you?" The girl eyed Rona, as if she was afraid the woman would collapse. "I could clean out the kitchen, stuff like that." She paused. "I'd like to help."

Rona nodded numbly. She needed help, she knew it, and perhaps this Heather had been sent to be her angel. The girl's face was open, guileless. She had been Devin's friend.

Rona remembered the two thousand dollars Devin had given her only the day before. What if Heather knew something she didn't? Had Devin stumbled upon some money, and was Heather out to get it?

She'd accept the girl's help, but she'd keep an eye on her as well. No lending her the key so she could copy it, no letting her root through drawers unsupervised.

"I'm not up to much today, Heather," Rona said. "But if you're willing, I'd like to make a small start. Maybe in the kitchen, as you suggested."

The girl nodded. "Shall I go through the fridge? Get rid of the perishables, things like that?"

"Yes," Rona said. "Good idea." She held out her palm. "But first, I'll take the key."

"She has used up the hot water," the cook complained, her Russian low and angry.

"All this time showering, the water constantly running, and now there is nothing but cold."

Bokeria frowned. How long had it been since he'd noticed Natalia's music and the water? A half hour? He put down the bodybuilding magazine he'd been reading and read his watch. *Nearly an hour.*

The bodyguard bounced to his feet and sprinted down the hallway. Out of the corner of his eye he saw the cook hurrying after him.

The pop music still blared inside Natalia's room, something about a party on the beach. He pounded at Natalia's door, yelling her name over the noise. No answer. He rattled the handle of her door. It was locked.

"*Klyuch,*" he barked at the cook. She shrugged, and he thought he detected a gleam of amusement in her cold eyes. He spat out the question. "Where is the key?"

"I do not know." Her voice was a whine that he felt like obliterating with his fists. "Should I call Mikhail?"

Bokeria bashed against the door in response. The cook drew in a quick breath, her mouth a round "o" of disapproval. Again he heaved his considerable weight, and heard the door groan. Once more, and it splintered open.

He rushed in and yanked open the door of the bathroom.

Warm vapor engulfed his face. The place was like a steam room, the walls dripping with moisture, the air heavy with fog. He slid on the slick tile floor, recovered his balance, and pulled open the glass doors of the shower. Empty. He swore and thrust in his arm, turning off the water.

Shaking droplets from his hand, he surveyed the bedroom, stooping to check under the bed and the expansive walk-in closets. When he saw nothing awry, he knew that she was gone. Natalia had left the apartment.

Darby listened as Miles relayed his meeting with Natalia at Pulitzer Hall to an attentive Detective Ryan.

"And this was what time of day?" Ryan asked.

"About ten in the morning," Miles answered.

"Fine. Now tell me about your conversation with Alec Rodin, even if you think you are repeating yourself."

Miles told him as accurately as possible about the conversation, which grew into a heated argument, looking occasionally at Darby to confirm his words.

"Did Rodin ever say that he was in danger?" Ryan asked.

"No. He focused solely on Nat."

The detective raised his eyebrows. "You mean, Natalia?"

"Yes." Miles uncrossed his gangly legs and leaned closer to the detective. "Is she still in danger?"

"I don't know. If Rodin thought her investigation was going to expose some high level officials, perhaps she is."

Darby cocked her head. She was thinking of the threatening note, the one which Natalia had subsequently dismissed.

Miles nodded, as if he could read her thoughts. He described the note and Detective Ryan's face hardened. "Why didn't she tell us about this?"

He made a note on his folder. "One last thing, Porter, and then I'll let you go. Can you think of anyone who would have a reason to embarrass you by planting evidence against you?"

Miles shook his head. "I haven't been here long enough to make enemies," he joked.

The detective frowned. "Apparently you have. The bloody apron alone would have been one thing, but someone stole that scarf and planted it deliberately so that you would be a suspect."

"What kind of a person does that?" Darby mused.

"My guess?" He ticked off items on his finger. "Middle-aged woman, lives alone, not many friends. Some sort of low-level mental illness hovering in the background, probably depression. Ring any bells?"

Miles sighed. " 'If music be the food of love, play on,' " he quoted. " 'Give me excess of it; that surfeiting, the appetite may sicken, and so die.' "

"*Twelfth Night*." The detective said, meeting Miles's eyes.

"Yes," Miles said softly. "I think I've got my enemy."

On the walk back to the apartment, Darby asked Miles to once again recite the Shakespearean quotation. When he finished, she cocked her head to the side, her ponytail swinging.

"Unrequited love," said Darby, dodging a man who had stopped abruptly to pull out a tourist map. "Is that the gist of it?"

"Yes. It's a passage that has always struck me. To love another, without their returning that love, or perhaps even guessing . . ."

"And you suspect that's how someone at Pulitzer Hall feels?"

Miles rolled his eyes, his face russet. "As

embarrassing as it is, I'm afraid so." He exhaled. "The department secretary, Peggy Babson. When I think back on it, I realize she's had a little crush on me. Up until the other day, she was — well, flirty, and I thought it was just her way. I guess it may have been something more."

"Hmm." Darby thought a moment. "What made her change from liking you to wanting to incriminate you in a murder investigation?"

Miles slowed his pace. "I keep asking myself if it was your visit, but I don't think so." He pointed at a food truck selling Latin American fare. "Fancy some lunch?"

Darby nodded. They waited in line to order and Miles continued to think.

"Hang on, I think I've got it — Natalia's visit. Perhaps Peggy thought I was chasing after one of my students." He placed their order and paid.

"Not like it hasn't been done before," Darby said wryly.

"Not by me!" Miles took their tacos, his face abashed. "The whole thing is so bloody stupid, isn't it, and creates a giant distraction from the real question: who killed Alec Rodin?"

"I agree." Darby was nodding, her face pensive. She unwrapped her taco and took a satisfying bite. After she'd chewed for a few minutes, she said, "No matter how disturbed Peggy might be, she isn't the murderer. She didn't even know him, never mind have a motive. Plus, you would have heard her leave Pulitzer Hall, right?"

"Exactly. She's not a killer." He pointed at a small cart selling hot pretzels. "Just twisted, that's all."

They looked at each other and grinned.

"I'll give her one thing," Darby said, squeezing the journalist's hand.

He paused, about to take another bite of his lunch. "And what's that?"

"However twisted she may be, Peggy's got darn good taste."

Sixteen

The girl slung the plastic bag bulging with half-eaten leftovers from Devin's refrigerator over a slender shoulder. "I'll toss this in the dumpster at work," she said, eyeing Rona. "You gonna be okay?"

She shrugged.

"Let me give you my number." Heather put out a hand. "Give me your cell and I'll put it in your contacts folder."

Rona handed her the phone. A moment later it was back in her hand.

"Thanks." Rona wasn't sure what else to say, but Heather was not at a loss for words.

"Devin had a new guy she was seeing, someone with some money," Heather said. "She liked him, said he was nice to her."

"Do you think he gave her the drugs?"

"No way. She didn't do drugs. I mean, she took sleeping stuff once in a while, I know that. And she had an old injury that could be excruciating. She just messed up the dosage, is all."

Rona nodded. She was still numb, and yet Heather's chatter had helped to make her feel less like a zombie.

"Talking about phones, did you find Devin's?" Heather shifted the weight of the garbage bag to her other hip. It was obviously getting heavy. " 'Cause that would be a good way to let people know about her celebration."

Rona shook her head. "Maybe tomorrow." She wasn't sure when — if ever — she would be up to planning this celebration Heather kept mentioning. She did not have the energy to contemplate it, much less explain, so she said nothing. "I will be back in the morning, I think."

"That's good." Heather reached out, awkwardly touched Rona's shoulder. "I'm sorry."

"I know."

"I'll call you."

"That would be good." Rona felt hot tears welling in her eyes, a sensation she rarely experienced. She let them fall down her cheeks as Heather bumped down the stairs with the bulging bag.

"I will call Mikhail?" The cook's voice wheedled again, and Sergei turned on her, his face murderous, his fists ready to silence her jubilation. Hours had passed since they'd discovered Natalia's disappearance, and despite repeated phone calls and texts, Sergei did not know where she was.

Reluctantly he took up his phone, ready to call Mikhail Kazakova, when the sound of the door opening made him pause, and Natalia, humming, strolled in.

Sergei Bokeria got to his feet. He stood, legs akimbo, while Natalia said a calm hello.

In terse words he asked where she had been for five hours.

"I went to see a friend — that's all," she said, hanging a yellow jacket on the coat tree. She turned and seemed to notice the bodyguard's dark expression for the first time. "I didn't mean to make you worry."

His fists hung at his side, clenching and unclenching, as he debated how best to handle her. She was not a girl any more, she was a young woman, and it was natural that she should want more privacy. And yet he had a job to do, a job that involved keeping track of her at all times. It was a task that he took very seriously, as did his employer.

And Sergei did not wish to displease his employer.

He willed himself to calm down. "Was it

an enjoyable outing?" His voice sounded stiff, but she smiled nonetheless.

"Very. We went out to Coney Island, walked around, and had a hot dog. The weather was so nice and there were lots of families — tourists, I suppose — taking rides at the amusement park. We explored a section of the city called 'Little Russia,' and looked at the items for sale. I had a wonderful afternoon."

And who were you with? Bokeria longed to ask, and yet he bit his tongue.

She started toward the other end of the penthouse, then stopped.

"I'm sorry, Sergei, for deceiving you. It was a silly, childish thing to do." She turned to face him, bit her lip. "I am going to speak to my father about my wish for more privacy. I promise you I will no longer play these games."

"Your father arrives late tonight. He would like to breakfast with you in the morning."

"Then I shall speak to him then." Natalia ran a hand through her choppy streaked hair. "Forgive me — and thank you, Sergei."

The bodyguard watched her walk down the hall.

"Our nights together are dwindling down," Miles said, ruffling Darby's glossy hair.

303

"Anything special you'd like to do?"

They were seated in Charles Burrows's living room, a carafe of sparkling water before them, enjoying the late afternoon sun and the bustling city.

"I'd like to solve a mystery," Darby said.

"That beastly Babson woman, you mean? Figure out why she tried to throw me under the bus?"

"Not really, although maybe it's somehow connected. The murder of Alec Rodin. Maybe we can figure something out that the police have missed."

"Hang on — I have just the ticket." Miles stood and jogged to the bedroom, returning with a stack of sticky-backed notes and a marker.

RODIN, he wrote on one square, and stuck it in the middle of the table. NATALIA, MIKHAIL, and SERGEI, soon followed.

"There's Natalia's unnamed source," Darby said, pointing at the pads. "John or Jane Doe."

Miles wrote down a name on another sticky square and stuck it down.

"Vera Graff," Darby read. She thought a moment. "She's the one with the French poodle and maid?"

"I think you mean 'poodle and French

maid,' " Miles corrected, smiling.

"I saw Natalia going in there Saturday night. Did you worm her identity out of Natalia?"

"No," he confessed. "I asked the doorman."

"Ramon?"

"George, the chap who works at night. Ramon is a gossip, but George turns out to be the one who really knows what's going on." He paused. "George told me last night, and I was hoping to get some confirmation before I said anything." He smiled. "That's what we journalists do — we get our facts confirmed."

"Okay. So based on what I saw, and what George has said, we have a hunch that Vera Graff is Natalia's source for the information that rattled Alec Rodin, enough to send him to your office in an attempt to get Natalia's paper."

"Right. Who else?"

"Rona Reichels."

Miles jotted down her name.

"According to Todd Stockton and others, she's still angry over losing a big chunk of commission money when Mikhail bought his penthouse."

"And her anger was focused on one person — Rodin."

"Exactly." Darby reached for her laptop and connected to the Internet. "Do you think there's any chance that Rodin could have been killed randomly?"

"Not with a Russian saber. That seems too coincidental — and too theatrical."

"I agree. It's almost as if the choice of the murder weapon was to make it appear that a Russian killed him." She frowned down at her computer.

"What are you looking for, love?"

"I'm not sure, but if it wasn't a random killing, I'm wondering if we can find any ties to Rodin."

"In general?"

"I guess I'm wondering who in this building, besides Rona and Vera Graff, has connections to the Kazakovas? Or Rodin? It's far-fetched, I know. For all we know, Rodin has enemies crawling out of the woodwork, right? But . . ."

"You have an inkling . . ."

"I wish it was that substantial! It's more like a realization. I'm starting to see that this was a very personal murder. Someone chose to use that sword, right? They followed Rodin, or somehow lured him, to that alley. This feels different from a random killing."

Miles nodded. "Agreed."

She picked up her phone and sent a quick text. "I'm asking Todd Stockton if he can tell me which sales Rona has been involved with in the building," she explained. "We've already got a motive for Rona, but who knows? Maybe it will lead somewhere."

"Good idea. Didn't you tell me you met someone who works for a family in the building? A nanny?"

Darby nodded. "On Friday, when I was in the park." She stood and crossed the room to her purse. "Here's her card. Gina Trovata." She crossed back to the couch. "Should I call her?"

"Why not? Tell you what. You call her and I'll track down the dog walker. Later we can email Charles Burrows, too, and see what he knows."

"Deal."

While Miles went in the bedroom to phone Natalia for the number, Darby dialed Gina. She was not exactly sure what she would say, but excited to be doing a little detective work. *I like this,* she admitted. *I enjoy trying to figure out a puzzle.*

The vintage clothing collector answered the phone with a quizzical hello. Darby quickly identified herself, and then told Gina why she was calling.

"Natalia Kazakova is a student of my

friend Miles," she began. "And we're trying to piece together details about her fiancé's murder. We thought if we could explore some connections within the building . . ."

"You think someone living in the building killed him, huh? Guess it makes sense with the theft of the sword . . ."

Darby's heart pounded. "What sword?"

Gina's voice lowered. "The detective told me not to say anything, but I don't see how it can hurt." She paused. "I'm friends with Mrs. Graff, and she told me that an antique sword was stolen from her apartment a few months ago. This morning she looked at pictures of the weapon that killed Alec Rodin, and she said it's hers."

"What did the detective say?"

"Not much, except that we needed to keep it quiet."

"Who else knows about the sword?"

"Besides Detective Benedetti, Vera, her maid, me, and Natalia."

"Natalia was there?"

"Yes. She and Vera are working on some sort of project."

Darby smiled. This call was more productive than she'd dreamed.

"Thanks so much, Gina. Out of curiosity, who did you say you worked for?"

"The Coopers, in eighteen-twenty-two.

Sherry and Penn. They're both attorneys, with four kids, so they need a few helping hands."

"How are plans for your shop coming?"

"Great, thanks for asking. We've got a location in Brooklyn and are negotiating the lease." She paused. "Did you ask your boyfriend about the sweaters?"

"Not yet. But I promise I will."

Darby said goodbye, and got up to find Miles. He was closing his laptop as she entered the room.

"You'll never guess what Gina told me," Darby began, before seeing the look of anguish on Miles's face.

"What is it?"

His eyes looked up at hers. "Something's happened," he said, his voice shaken.

She waited, went to the bed and sat near him.

"What?"

"I don't think I can talk about it." He looked off to the side. "Not just yet."

"Is it your family? Your friend Jagdish?"

"No, no. It's — something else. Darby, I want to tell you — I will tell you — when the time is right, but not now."

"I see." Darby tried to keep her voice level. "If this is about trust —"

"Trust has nothing to do with it. I trust

you completely."

"What, then?"

"I've just received some very shocking news, and I need a little time to process it. That's all."

"So I'm supposed to wonder what has happened? Wonder if it has to do with your health, or your family, or your profession?"

"I know I'm being unfair, but I need to sort this out." He was contrite even as her temper flared.

"How much time do you need, Miles? Should I just go back to California now?"

"No, God no — I don't want that." He shook his head. "Please, bear with me. I need just a little time to wrap my head around this, and then we'll talk. I promise."

Darby thought back to her own challenges and how Miles had helped her. He'd been patient as she'd confronted her demons on Hurricane Harbor; understanding when she'd balked at commitment. She swallowed and rose to her feet.

"I'm sorry that something has happened to upset you so much." She clasped her hands in front of her torso, surprised to see they were shaking. "I'm going for a walk so that you can have some time alone. I'll be back in an hour or so, and if you want to talk, I'll be here to listen." She kissed the top of his forehead, the scent of him nearly making her swoon.

"Thanks," he said, looking into her eyes.

She turned, grabbed her purse and a jacket, and headed out.

Rona wondered when — if ever — the numbness would wear off.

It was as if she was in a thick layer of fog, so dense and impenetrable that she could feel nothing. She was stretched across her bed, and snatches of her conversation — if you could call it that — with Heather kept ricocheting through her brain, as if her skull was a pinball machine and the thoughts the silver balls. Devin had a new love interest. Devin was making some money. Devin was on the right track . . .

And yet she was dead. Accidentally. How did that happen? How did a beautiful girl like her daughter take a pile of pills and die?

What if it was not an accident, a voice inside her head intoned. What if she did it on purpose?

"No, no," she said aloud. "No, she would not have done that."

Meaning suicide. Every single cell in Rona's body rebelled against the idea. *Is it because you can't admit she was unhappy?*

But she wasn't unhappy! She'd been

confident, upbeat, in control of her destiny. You don't act like that if you're going to take your own life! *No,* Rona thought, *Devin did not kill herself deliberately. She took those pills by accident.*

She gave a heavy sigh. It was tempting to stay in her room, sprawled on the bed, but that was not how she was going to act. Devin, at the very least, deserved a mother who could mourn in style.

She found a black knit dress in her closet and pulled it out. There were calls to make, sympathy to garner, and who knows . . . perhaps business, too.

Miranda Styles listened to her voice mail and frowned. She tried to place the caller, a Miles Porter, and remembered Korbut lunging at his sneaker. *Oh, yeah. The British guy staying in Burrows's apartment.*

His message was puzzling. *I'm trying to gather information about the murder of Alec Rodin.* She rolled her dark eyes. *Oh yeah? Well get in line, buddy.*

Miranda placed a call to one of the building's classically trained chefs who prepared meals for residents lucky enough to afford them, and checked on the dinner she'd ordered that morning. "We'll bring it up at eight, Ms. Styles," he assured her. "And it will be delicious."

"I have no doubt," she said, hanging up. There was plenty of time to take a shower and lay out a negligee, set the intimate table for two, and light the candles. She poured herself a glass of wine and looked out at the park.

The light was just starting to fade, the traffic from rush hour starting to subside. She sipped a crisp Sauvignon Blanc and thought again of the Brit's strange message. Why was he interested in the murder of Alec, she wondered? And what could he possibly know?

A small smile playing about her lips, Miranda crossed the room to her phone, her lean legs moving fast across the plush carpeting. "Mr. Porter?" she asked as the phone was answered. "It's Miranda Styles. I heard your message, and thought I'd call back."

She listened as Miles Porter explained that he was a friend of Natalia's, and he was looking for any information regarding her fiancé's tragedy.

"Aren't the police looking into that?" she asked innocently.

He explained that they were, but that he was trying to lend a hand.

"I see," she said. "I'm afraid I can't think of anything useful, but if I do, I'll be sure to call."

She hung up and took a sip of wine. Odd. Why should Porter be at all interested in Rodin's murder, other than the usual voyeuristic enjoyment everyone got from an act of violence?

She took her tablet from its case and typed in his name. Up came dozens of references, many of them bylines to stories in the *Financial Times.*

He's a reporter, she realized. No wonder he was interested in Alec Rodin's death. And the fact that the murdered man had been on track to be the son-in-law of one of the richest men in the world made it an especially intriguing story.

Miranda put the tablet aside and thought a moment. It was very likely that Rodin had been killed by Mikhail Kazakova, stabbed in broad daylight in an alley four miles from here. The possibility didn't scare her. In fact, she found it a turn-on.

Her reasoning was sound. In the past few months, Mikhail had realized that the arrangement for his only daughter to marry Rodin was a mistake. The Cyrillic writing was on the wall: Natalia's honeymoon would barely be over before she'd be whisked back to Russia, ensconced in a lovely home, and sealed off from the Western world. A marriage to Rodin meant Mikhail might never see his daughter again, much less any grandchildren.

For all Miranda knew, there were other reasons Mikhail had grown to see Rodin as problematic. Reasons that could easily have driven the powerful oligarch to end his future son-in-law's life.

The big question, Miranda thought, as she regarded her stun gun on the kitchen counter, was why he'd chosen such a ridiculous murder weapon. An antique Russian saber! Why such theatrics? Did he picture himself as some sort of avenging Cossack?

She chuckled, picked up a slim remote, and pushed a button, so that strains of light jazz filled the airy space.

Maybe I'll ask him tonight.

SEVENTEEN

Darby walked at a rapid clip through Central Park, trying not to guess the reasons for Miles's strange behavior. *If I keep guessing, I'll drive myself nuts,* she reasoned. *I've got to forget about it — think about something else.*

Like the mold lawsuit? She grimaced. Fortunately her cell phone rang, preventing her from having to dwell on the Davenports and their claims against her.

"Darby, it's Todd Stockton." The real estate agent's voice was brisk.

"Yes, Todd. Have you got that list of sales at Central Park Place for me?"

"I do. I'm going to email it as an attachment, if that's okay."

"So there are that many?"

"Yeah."

"Todd, what's up? You sound strange."

"I'm afraid I have some bad news concerning Rona Reichels."

Darby stopped walking. "Go on."

"Her daughter is dead. We all got the report a little while ago."

"How terrible. I didn't know her — I don't really know Rona, for that matter — but I'm sorry. What happened?"

"Overdose of prescription pills." He sighed heavily. "Apparently it was an accident. There was no note, and no indication that Devin was suicidal."

"How old was she?"

"Mid-twenties, I guess." He paused. "She and Rona were very close."

"I appreciate your call, Todd. Miles may run into her in the building, and it's good to be aware of tragedies like this."

"I suppose. I'm not fond of Rona, but this really stinks." He sighed. "On another note, I'll be sending you some paperwork for Hideki tomorrow. Let me know if you have any questions."

"I will. Thanks." Darby hung up and thought about the compact, no-nonsense woman she'd seen in Natalia Kazakova's apartment. The one who'd baked a cake for the grieving girl. She shoved her phone into her purse. *Poor Rona,* she thought.

Gina Trovata said goodbye to Bethany, turned off her phone, and slid a frozen dinner into the microwave. Plans were going smoothly for the retail space in Brooklyn, and all aspects of the lease had been ironed out. "We can start moving things in next week!" Bethany had squealed. Gina agreed. It was all going well.

Why then, did she feel a nagging sense of something that was keeping her from being really happy? She examined the areas of her life for any snags and found nothing. She was in good communication with her adoptive parents and would see them at a family party in July. Her employer, Sherry Cooper, was happy with the job she was doing as morning nanny for the boys. Vera, her new friend, was not in the best of health, but the woman was in her eighties, after all, and seemed at peace with her condition.

What was it, then? Something that had happened recently, she felt. She poured herself a Diet Dr Pepper and then it hit her: the phone call regarding Alec Rodin's murder.

Darby Farr, the one staying in the professor's apartment, had said she wanted to "explore some connections within the building." Gina had told her about the sword, but now that she thought about it, there was another link, and that was what was bugging her.

The connection was Sherry Cooper. She

wanted the Kazakova penthouse, and it was not just an idle desire: she wanted it the way a dog wants a bone. Hers wasn't a recent obsession, either — it was going on four years ago that she had lost the opportunity to buy it, and had been forced to settle for five thousand square feet instead of six-something.

Why had the Coopers lost out on the penthouse? Gina thought back to the various arguments she'd heard while working for Penn and Sherry. Financing? Could that have been it? The Coopers had needed to finance their purchase of the penthouse, while Mikhail Kazakova had come along and offered cold, hard cash.

Nobody's got eighty billion dollars in cash, Gina said to herself. Or did they? Rumor had it that the Kazakova billions were safely tucked away in Cyprus, the offshore haven of choice for Russians of extreme wealth.

Surely this was the kind of connection Darby Farr was talking about. But did it matter when it came down to Alec Rodin's murder? Would killing Alec help the Coopers scoop up the penthouse? How?

With Alec out of the way, chances were that Natalia was more committed than ever to life in New York. Who wouldn't want to hang out in that luxurious pad at the top of one of the city's best buildings? Did it harbor bad memories? Could Alec and she have spent too much time there for Natalia to feel comfortable after his death?

Gina let her thoughts ramble, knowing that any conclusions she reached were most likely far-fetched.

What if Sherry and Natalia had made a deal? *I'll kill him if you get me the penthouse?* Thursday afternoon, when Alec Rodin had been stabbed, was Sherry's scheduled time off. It was her weekly time to run errands, she claimed. Gina pursed her lips. Was killing Alec Rodin just another pesky task?

She laughed out loud and removed her eggplant parmesan from the microwave. *Gina, you have a devious mind.*

A little voice in her head piped up in protest.

This is Sherry you're talking about! The voice admonished. *Sherry, the mom of four golden-haired little angels.* Gina pulled a fork from the drawer; grabbed a napkin. Quick as a flash, another voice responded: *Sherry, who threatened her hairdresser with a lawsuit the time her highlights came out wrong. Sherry, the one who sabotaged a five-year-old's birthday party because her son hadn't been invited. Sherry, who stole a nanny right out from under one of her best friends, while the friend was having chemo.*

Gina knew that story intimately, because she was the nanny.

She sighed. There was a way to get more information, and that was to hang out with Natalia Kazakova. When she finished her dinner, she'd call Vera for the Russian girl's phone number. Maybe they could meet in the morning, while she took care of the little Coopers. The thought made her smile. She liked Natalia.

As Gina carried her entrée to her small table, she had another thought, and this one, although true, did not make her smile.

Sherry Cooper could not be trusted.

"I'm so glad you're back," Miles said, meeting Darby at the door. "I know I acted very strangely, and I'm sorry. I hope you'll hear me out and forgive me."

Darby shrugged off her jacket and looked into Miles's eyes. There was something there she couldn't quite name. Disbelief? Sorrow?

"Of course I'll hear you out, Miles, and I can't imagine your doing anything that I wouldn't forgive."

"Let's sit down, then, and let me tell you the whole thing."

Darby took a seat on one end of the sofa

and waited. She had no idea what to expect, and told herself that what was required was listening, and then, hopefully, understanding.

"I'm listening."

Miles took a deep breath. "After I graduated from Columbia and worked for the *New York Times,* I got a job in their London office doing investigative reporting. I think I told you about a murder that took place in Piccadilly Square, a cold case involving a very dear friend of mine."

Darby thought back. She recalled one of the first real conversations she'd had with Miles, back in Maine, an intimate dinner at a restaurant in Westerly. "Yes," she said. "A woman named Sarah, who'd been one of your most trusted sources."

"That's right. Her name was Sarah Winterbridge. When she died, I spent nearly two years trying to solve the case, with no real leads. In the course of those two years, I became very close to Sarah's parents and siblings."

"Naturally."

"Sarah came from a very old, respected English family, but her relatives disapproved of her edgy life. She ran with a bad crowd, and was an addict, but she was trying desperately to get clean. The last time we met, she looked healthier than I'd ever seen her. The drugs were behind her. She'd been clean and sober for two weeks, and ready to start a new life."

"But that didn't happen," Darby said gently.

"No." His face registered pain, even after all the years.

"Were you in love with Sarah?"

He shook his head. "No. I cared about her deeply. We were friends, and I admired her spirit. She refused to give up, that girl, and I feel she would have made it, had perhaps already made it . . ."

His mouth was dry, and he licked his lips. Darby handed him a glass of water, and he took it gratefully and drank.

"About a year after her death, I began seeing Sarah's older sister, Violet. I didn't plan for it to happen — it just did. We had a kind of hunger for each other, and it lasted about a year. Never lived together, and never spoke about the future. I think, in hindsight, our relationship was a way for us both to try and make sense of Sarah's death."

He closed his eyes. "Violet broke it off and began dating a Scottish businessman. Shortly after that, I traveled to India to see a cousin. I ended up staying the better part of a year. When I came back to London, I avoided the Winterbridge family. I felt it was for the best."

"But now they have contacted you?"

He looked up quickly. "Yes. Violet tracked me down a month ago. She told me something crazy, something that I did not believe at first, until at last, tonight, she has given me proof."

He paused.

"I have a son back in England. He's called Simon."

Darby exhaled and looked into his eyes. She wanted to keep quiet, wanted to refrain from blurting anything out, but her mind could not keep her mouth shut.

"This changes everything," she said.

Pete pulled on his leash, anxious to sniff the pile of debris Peggy's neighbor had dragged to the street corner.

"Leave it, Pete, leave it," Peggy admonished, not wanting the dog to lift his leg and ruin anything of value. She lifted some flaps of mildewing cardboard, peering into the piles with interest. A child's wooden puzzle, a few detective novels, and a barefoot plastic doll. She picked up a stick and poked the doll. It stared at her with open eyes, its hair splayed out like a fan.

Peggy looked up and down the street, but

no one else was outside. The familiar itchy feeling came over her, the sensation that was only satisfied by collecting. She reached for the doll, grabbing a naked leg. "You can come home with me," she said softly. Although Peggy's one-car garage was stuffed and her former den was nearly full to capacity, there was a guest bedroom that still had floor space. *I'll use only a corner of it,* she vowed, but even as she said it, she knew it was a promise she couldn't keep.

Darby and Miles sat in silence for what seemed like several minutes.

"I realize everything is different now," Miles finally said. "And I completely understand if you want to end our relationship. I have no clue as to how this will play out. I don't know whether I want to meet him, or if he wants to meet me."

"How old is Simon?" Darby's tongue felt very thick.

"Twelve."

She nodded. *A good age, better than thirteen . . .*

The memory of her parents' death, occurring the summer she became a teen, came back in a rush. Darby watched it unfold before her as if it were a movie projected onto her brain. There was her father, John

Farr, tanned and handsome, climbing into the dinghy, her mother, Jada, wearing white shorts and a red-checked blouse. She saw her mother wave a jaunty goodbye. She saw herself climbing on to her bicycle, one knee skinned from where she had scraped it at the little beach. *I pedaled off to find my friend Lucy, never dreaming it would be the last time I'd see them.*

She willed the movie to stop.

Why am I thinking of this now? Is it the shock of the news? It's the same kind of shock this poor kid will get when he learns that Miles Porter is his father. Out of the blue, out of nowhere, his whole life will change . . .

She blinked. Was it the same? She was informed at age thirteen that her parents were gone, lost at sea, while Simon would be told of a new adult in his life, a man who had never known about him, but who was now anxious to meet him.

She looked up. That man was sitting next to her.

A kind and generous man. A smart, brave, and strong man.

Darby swallowed. It was not at all the same.

"Simon will be surprised, to say the least," she said. "It'll be a bit of a shock at first. But I know he'll want to meet you, and I bet it won't take him long to realize he's won the British Lottery." She smiled. "That is, if they have that sort of thing over there."

Miles looked away, clearly moved. He cleared his throat. "Will you come with me?" His voice was thick. "Will you come with me and meet him?"

Darby wiped her eyes, thinking back to that thirteen-year-old girl who had managed to survive, somehow, despite it all, survive and open her heart again.

"I'll be there," she said.

EIGHTEEN

The sound of the front door's bolts unlocking woke Sergei Bokeria. He glanced at his watch. *Four a.m.*

He opened the door of his bedroom and stepped into the hall. In the dim light he could see his employer fastening the apartment door's locks.

"Mikhail." He said his name to keep from frightening the man, but still Mikhail Kazakova whirled around, a look of surprise on his wide face.

"Sergei. It is late."

"Da." The bodyguard stood still while Kazakova picked up his overnight bag and began heading toward him.

"I must speak with you."

"Now? It is the middle of the night. We can talk in the morning, after breakfast. I hope you told Natalia to join me?"

The big man nodded. He moved slowly to the side of the hall, blocking Mikhail's path, and saw the man look up, astonished.

His surprise turned to anger. "What is this, Sergei? I am very tired."

"As am I," Bokeria said. "Tired of your lies."

"Whatever do you mean? You are talking nonsense."

"You arrived in New York last Wednesday, and yet you let Natalia believe you were still in Russia on Thursday."

"What? How do you know this?"

"I have made inquiries." Sergei shifted his massive weight from one foot to another. "Natalia believes you arrived in the city on Friday morning. Where were you the day before? Wiping the blood of Alec Rodin from a sword?"

Kazakova's face turned crimson and he shook a fist at Bokeria. "Sergei, our friendship is not so strong that this kind of foolish talk will not break it."

"And what of your bond with Natalia? Can that be severed if she knows of your deception?"

Kazakova's glower seemed to soften. "Come, come, into the study. We will not talk like peasants in the hallway."

Sergei followed Mikhail into his den, a room that Americans called a "man cave." The scent of rich leather and fine cigars pervaded the space, which was furnished in dark hunter green with mahogany accents.

"Vodka?"

Bokeria shook his head. "No."

Mikhail fixed a drink for himself and strolled over to Sergei. "Please, sit," he said. "I would offer you a cigar, but I know that Sergei Bokeria does not smoke."

The big man said nothing.

"So, you have realized that I am not always where my daughter Natalia thinks I am." He lowered himself onto a leather armchair and took a gulp of his drink. "The answer is simple, and one anyone would expect from a man in my position: I have a female friend, with whom I enjoy spending evenings, and I am often in her company." He placed the tumbler of vodka down on a polished table.

"And for this you lie to Natalia?" He did not add, although he wanted to, "and me?"

"I did not wish to complicate my situation with Natalia by telling her of this special friend." He reached for the drink and knocked it back. "I think it would be difficult for her to hear, especially because of her unsatisfactory relationship with Alec Rodin." He looked thoughtful. "Although now it may be of little consequence."

"Yes. Conveniently for you, the man is dead."

Kazakova laughed out loud. "Such dramatics, Sergei! Are you imagining yourself in the starring role of an opera?" His laughter turned menacing and his jaw clenched. "How dare you talk like this to me!" The words were like little daggers. "Have you forgotten your role in this household? You are my daughter's bodyguard. Your job is to keep her safe, not to comment on current events." He reached for his glass, slamming it down when he remembered it was empty. He stood. "I'm going to bed."

"I don't think so. Not so quickly." Bokeria reached into his pocket and pulled out a gun. "Sit down."

Mikhail Kazakova chuckled, but it was a mean, low, sound. "You will regret this, Bokeria. I promise you, you will live to regret these actions."

"Shut up and listen." The bodyguard kept the gun trained on his employer. "While you are out sleeping with lady friends and I am here protecting your daughter, her fiancé finds himself stabbed in an alley and she receives a death threat."

Kazakova's face went white. "I was not told!"

"Of course you were not told. You were

not here. You were too busy putting your private parts into your lover." He narrowed his eyes, a difficult feat considering the lumps of flesh on his enormous face. "Before Alec was murdered, Natalia had made a friend, a boy named Jeremy, who works on Wall Street as a securities broker. He appears to live beyond his means and has many loans to his university. I am sure Natalia's fortune must be appealing." He shifted his bulk in the leather armchair. Across from him, Kazakova's face was intent. *At last I have his interest,* Sergei thought.

"So far they have gone on a few innocent outings, nothing serious. He is a likeable boy and he makes Natalia happy." He paused. "But I think back about this note, the one she received shortly after Rodin's death, and I ask myself who would send such a thing."

"Yes?"

"And I believe it was you."

Bokeria waited for the outburst, the outraged denial that he was sure would accost his ears, but to his surprise, there was nothing.

"How did you know?" Mikhail pursed his lips, waiting.

Sergei ignored the question, because the

truth was, he hadn't known, only guessed. "If I am to keep your daughter safe, Mikhail, I must know if you are Rodin's killer."

"A difficult question."

Bokeria waited. At last Kazakova expelled a long breath of air.

"I did not kill Alec, although I cannot say I did not consider it."

"Because of Natalia."

"He was going to take her back to Russia. After all of her years in America, she would not survive."

"Yes." Bokeria knew he meant that not only would Natalia dislike it, but that she would be in actual physical danger.

"I offered him — incentives — but he would not agree. The house in Palm Beach, a share of the casino in Monaco, but he laughed, said he was a wealthy man in his own right."

"The power he had in Moscow — it changed him."

Kazakova looked up, surprised. "Yes, that's right."

"But Natalia is not the only reason to have Rodin killed."

"I am amazed, Bokeria."

"Because you expect me to be ignorant of what is going on? I know more than you realize."

"I see that. And yet you have never tried to extort anything from me."

"I care only for Natalia's welfare. She is my job."

"But it is more than that —"

"Never mind." He waved the gun. "We are not discussing Sergei Bokeria. Tell me the whole story. Start at the beginning so that I know it all."

Mikhail Kazakova nodded heavily. "First I will get us both a drink."

NINETEEN

Sherry and Penn Cooper were fighting again. After working for them for more than a year, Gina Trovata could see the signs, as clear as a billboard on the New Jersey Turnpike.

On this Tuesday morning, Penn wore his customary "I'm super pissed-off" pout. He poured his coffee and stirred his steel-cut oats while wearing it, managed to gulp them down while pouting, and relented only when kissing the boys goodbye. To his wife he gave a curt nod, much like one would give a leper.

Sherry was not so subtle. She slammed every single thing she came in contact with, including Honey's water dish, which caused a pool of water to spread like a small farm pond across the kitchen floor. "Jesus @$%*&# Christ," she screamed, in all her profane glory, and then a chorus of Cooper boys (three of them anyway, because the littlest could not yet speak) repeated her handiwork.

Gina had to pinch her thigh — very hard — to keep from laughing.

When the so-called adults had finally left, and the Designated Car Pool Mom had come to pick up the older ones, Gina looked at Sam and Trevor and clapped her hands. "Let's do something fun, okay, boys?"

She'd already called Natalia, and invited her on a quick outing which dovetailed nicely with Natalia's last investigative journalism class. "We're going to go through Central Park," Gina confided, "and look for everything we can find that digs."

"Digs?" Natalia had been confused.

Gina laughed. "These are little boys, Natalia. They are all about trucks, destruction, flying dirt — you name it. The baby can't even talk and he practically poops himself when he sees an excavator. It's in their DNA."

Natalia had sounded dubious, but she agreed.

"Where should we meet?" Natalia asked.

Without even trying she sounds like a KGB spy, thought Gina.

"Come to our residence," Gina suggested. "Eighteen — twenty-two. See how the other half lives for a change."

"The other half?"

"Oh, never mind. Just get on over here at nine o'clock. That way we'll have some time together before your class starts at eleven."

Natalia came and the little Coopers took curious peeks from their stroller. Gina steered everyone down to the lobby, past Ramon, and out to the park. "Truck," Trevor was saying, his blonde head ready to find the first front-loader or dump truck that came his way. Gina smiled.

"So," she began, looking at Natalia. "How are you doing, you know, since your fiancé was killed?"

The Russian girl shrugged. "Okay, I guess. I am sad that Alec is gone, but I cannot deny that the marriage was not something I wanted."

"Then why were you in it?"

Again the shrug. "It was arranged for me, many years ago."

Gina stopped pushing the stroller and looked into Natalia's eyes. "Okay, so this is what I don't get. You're a smart girl, taking advanced journalism classes at Columbia, right? You let yourself get stuck in some archaic arranged marriage, and the only way you escaped was because the guy conveniently got stabbed?"

Natalia's brown eyes flashed. "I do not

need interrogations, thank you. I will head home."

"No." Gina reached out a hand. "I'm sorry. I'm like that — too outspoken. I shouldn't comment on things I know nothing about."

Natalia watched her awhile, and then jerked her head, indicating that they should resume walking. "I am really not so — how do you say — thin-skinned, but . . ."

"It's okay. I was out of line."

The women walked in silence for several minutes, the only noises coming from Trevor, as he attempted to identify nearly everything they passed.

"Have you ever been overweight," Natalia asked, "but it has been long enough that you have clothes that fit you, and people who expect you to look a certain way. You don't feel particularly bad, you just don't feel totally like yourself."

Gina nodded.

"Then one day you look at yourself in the mirror, and you say, 'This just isn't me.' " She turned to Gina. "That was how it was with my engagement to Alec Rodin. One day I looked at my situation and I said, 'This is not Natalia Kazakova.' I do not want to be this man's wife, I do not want to be the mother of his children, and I do not want to be his property."

"And what did you do?"

She smiled. "At first? Absolutely nothing. What could I do? My father had arranged the marriage. I'd known Alec for years and years. He was like a big brother to me, giving me advice, always watching out. I was just a pawn in their chess game." She grinned. "But luckily, I was a pawn with brains."

"Go on . . ."

"I realized that I was doing very well in my English classes, and that I loved to write. And so I begged the School of Journalism to let me take an advanced course." She rolled her eyes. "It doesn't hurt when I ask for things that my father is a billionaire, and sometimes I use this to my advantage." A quick shrug. "In any case, I was enrolled in the school, and I began my course of studies. The work, the research, it made me feel . . ." she paused, grew quiet, sought Gina's eyes. "I felt completely happy, as never before."

"You found your passion," said Gina.

"Yes, I believe that is right. I am meant to be a journalist. I am meant to uncover the story, the truth."

Gina nodded. "I understand. I really do." She thought of the day she found her first vintage suit and realized that she was not the only one who saw the value in the design and fine workmanship. It was validation for her longings, her inklings — the first assurance that what she imagined could be her life's work.

"And then what happened?"

Natalia tilted her head. "Instead of feeling happy for me, Alec was dismissive. He insisted that I wrap up 'my little classes' and help plan the wedding. He told me that I would be coming back to Russia, and that my American schoolwork would be unnecessary."

Gina's dark eyes smoldered. If this kind of thing could happen to the daughter of a billionaire, no wonder the women of the world were so challenged. She took a breath. "What did you do next?"

"Next?" Natalia shrugged. "I made a plan. An idea of how to be rid of him." She put up a finger. "No, wait a minute — first I met someone with an interesting story."

"Vera Graff?"

"I see I am not the only one with a good working brain." She grinned. "Vera gave me the idea for my final Investigative Journalism paper. Her story had everything — greed, revenge, honor, and patriotism. I knew instantly that this was an account only

I could tell."

"Yes?"

"And Alec put his foot down, saying I was way out of line with such irresponsible reporting, and that I would get many innocent people in trouble, including himself and me. He explained the power of a new organization in Russia, the FSB, and warned me that their reach was long and wide. He knew better than to forbid me to publish the story, but he told me that if I did it, I would be ruined, and possibly killed." Her voice grew softer. "I knew I had found my way out. I would pursue my research."

"What is this all about, anyway?"

"Real estate that was stolen after the Russian Revolution."

"Isn't that ancient history?"

She shook her head. "In Russia, the past is always with us."

"Yes, but what makes it important today?"

"Those buildings that were stolen from so many are being resold for millions of dollars, and the families of exiles are finally speaking out."

"And Vera belongs to one of those families?"

"Apparently so."

Gina bit her lip. "Did you hire someone to kill your fiancé?" she asked.

Natalia paused. "No. I thought about it, when I was angry, and I may have spoken to someone close to me, but it wasn't a serious conversation. I could not kill Alec because I know that he did care for me." Her lips curled upward. "However, it is true that someone killed Alec Rodin."

"How do you know you're not responsible?"

"The person I spoke to would never have used a saber." She looked across the path, a short distance from where they were walking, and Gina followed her gaze. The hulking form of Sergei Bokeria loomed over the other walkers.

"I see," Gina said.

"Believe me," Natalia said, nodding toward her bodyguard. "He would have used his bare hands."

Beside them, in the stroller, Trevor let out an excited squeal. Two men with shovels were digging an enormous hole, probably to replace a tree that had perished during the winter. To Gina it looked as if it could easily hold a body.

"Dig! Dig! Dig!" Trevor yelled.

Gina took a deep breath. Things were getting surreal.

On the other side of the path, Sergei Bokeria kept watch over Natalia, the nanny, and the enormous stroller. He thought of the story Mikhail had told him in the early hours of the morning, a story that reminded Bokeria of a deadly game of roulette.

Mikhail admitted that he had decided the impending marriage between his daughter and Alec Rodin was a huge mistake. After Natalia's four years in America, attending an American university, Mikhail had come to the conclusion that she would never again fit in Russian society. "She is too liberal," he said, "too outspoken." And so he had tried to convince Rodin to live in the States, offering his many real estate holdings as enticement. But Rodin had not taken the bait.

"I decided that if Alec would not come willingly, perhaps he needed to be forced out of Russia," Mikhail admitted. As part of this plan, Mikhail started a covert campaign with Russian authorities to cast Rodin in an unflattering light. "I thought that if they began asking him questions about his real estate dealings, his investments, he might decide it was no longer wise to stay in Moscow." Although he hadn't known about it until after Rodin's death, he realized that Natalia's research paper had played perfectly into this scheme. "I know she thinks that I have been against her career, but I have kept up this pretense so that Rodin would not suspect."

And yet, Mikhail had admitted to Sergei, his machinations against Rodin did not seem to be working. "He was more determined than ever to return to Russia, with Natalia as his bride."

Mikhail said that the night before Rodin was killed, he'd decided that the only way to keep from losing his daughter forever was to tell Rodin the truth. "I thought of Irina, and knew that I must do whatever was necessary."

"Including murder?" Sergei had asked.

Mikhail's eyes were more hooded than usual. He downed the last of his third vodka and faced the bodyguard. "Yes, including murder. But I tell you, I did not do it. I had not yet spoken to Alec. I had been prepared to offer him my fortune if need be."

Sergei could not envision Mikhail giving up his fortune for Natalia, but stranger things had happened. The men had stood, embraced in a bear hug, and gone to bed.

Now Sergei regarded the young women across the stone path, glad that — at least for the moment — her world was safe.

Rona let herself in to Devin's apartment,

feeling the hush of the space settle on her shoulders like a lacy shawl. The morning sun was coming through the windows and the noises from the street below were muffled. *It really is a peaceful place to have lived,* she thought.

She moved through the few rooms slowly, lifting objects that caught her attention, holding them, and putting them back in their places. She wasn't sure why she was doing it, but it felt right, and so she continued.

Here, on the window shelf in the bedroom, was Devin's small stuffed alligator, her go-to cuddle toy since age three. Rona remembered buying it in a tourist trap in Fort Lauderdale. They had gone to Florida for the funeral of Rona's aunt Sylvia, and Devin had squealed when she saw the green gator. Rona picked it up, held it for a few moments, noticing how the tail looked as if it had been chewed.

Devin's watch, which the girl had hardly ever worn, was on the dresser, along with her collection of earrings, and a lipstick, *Crazy for Cappuccino.* Rona smiled, looked at the color. She pulled open the top drawer. Birth control, a passport, and a small ring of keys, along with a few pair of underwear. Rona picked up the keys and noticed they were labeled. Under them was a business-sized envelope, puffed up as if it contained something. She peered inside. A neat stack of hundred dollar bills — at least twenty of them — were tucked inside.

Rona took the envelope and the keys and shoved them in her pocket. Where had her daughter been getting this cash? Selling drugs? Her friend Heather had mentioned something about a new man in her life — was he the one showering her with money?

Distracted, she let her eyes sweep over the rest of the room. Devin's phone was on the nightstand, atop a thick textbook, and Rona put the phone in her pocket with the other items. Her hand brushed a few knickknacks but she was no longer interested. Suddenly the apartment's walls were too close, and she felt as if she could not breathe. She stumbled to the door and locked it behind her, hoping to escape before she ran into Heather or anyone else.

Miles and Darby were washing the dishes from a late morning breakfast when Miles's phone rang. Earlier that morning, he'd told Darby what he knew of Violet and Simon. Apparently Violet had never intended to tell the boy of his true father, but circumstances — and Miles wasn't sure what they were —

346

had intervened. "I don't know whether he'll even want to meet me," Miles had said. "It's a lot to absorb, just the same."

Miles picked up the ringing cell phone and glanced at his display. "It's Jagdish, about Russia," he said. "Finally."

Darby rinsed the pan they had used to make scrambled eggs, dried it, and went to sip another cup of coffee on the couch, next to Miles. She heard him asking about Mikhail Kazakova and the FSB, watched him taking notes, nodding, and furrowing his brow. When the call was over, he turned to her with a look of amazement.

"Kazakova has not set foot in Russia for at least three years," Miles said. "Jagdish says that all of his money is held in off-shore accounts in Cyprus or has been put in foreign real estate. He's not even considered a resident of Russia."

"You're kidding! Then where is he flying off to when he's not in New York?"

"His other properties?"

Darby thought a moment. "I wonder how he liked the idea of Natalia marrying a Russian businessman?"

"Jagdish says the scuttlebutt in Moscow is that Mikhail owed Alec Rodin some kind of favor — something having to do with his fertilizer companies in the Ural Mountains.

He says there's no real evidence, but it's widely believed Rodin greased some wheels for Kazakova — something that helped him achieve his vast wealth."

"Or maybe he hushed something up?"

"Perhaps. Jagdish did mention an environmental scandal at a factory. He didn't have much information on that, but what he did talk about was Rodin and the FSB."

Darby leaned forward. "And . . . ?"

"He said Rodin made a big show about being a real estate developer in Moscow, and other Russian cities, but that it's long been rumored that his real work is with the new and improved KGB."

"The FSB."

"Exactly. They have their fingers in so many bowls of borscht it isn't funny. Selling the old palaces of the exiled nobility is just a sideline, Jagdish said."

"Hmm. Correct me if I'm wrong, but didn't Natalia's story focus on the real estate?"

"Yes."

"Then why do you think Alec got so upset when he read the story? Doesn't it seem as if he overreacted?"

"Maybe his actions had nothing to do with Vera's allegations after all."

"That's what I'm starting to think. Alec

didn't care that she was talking about the palaces or exiled royals. He didn't want her talking about the FSB."

Miles nodded. "We may be on to something." He glanced at his watch. "I've got to go, love, but I'll be back shortly after lunch. Meet me here?"

"Sounds good." They kissed, tenderly, as if nothing could come between them.

As Gina and Natalia made their way back to Central Park Place, Gina posed the question she'd been wondering for a while. "Natalia, what happened to your mother?"

The girl stopped and stared.

"I'm sorry," Gina blurted. "I didn't mean to upset you."

Natalia began to smile. "I am not upset, only stunned. You don't know how often I long to talk about her, and yet no one ever breathes a word." She sighed. "It is as if she never existed."

Gina thought of her own experience as an orphan. Her adoptive parents had gone out of their way to honor the birth parents that Gina would never even know.

Natalia took a deep breath. "Are you sure you want to listen? Once I begin, I may find it hard to end."

"Please. I'd like to know about her."

"Okay." Another breath. "First: her name. It was Irina. She was smart — a good student, and not afraid to work. She met my father when they were in college."

"What was she studying?"

"Medicine. She became an obstetrician. A good one."

Gina smiled.

"My father," Natalia continued, "was studying business, and they fell in love and got married. I was not born until my mother finished her schooling. My father does not talk about it, but my grandmother told me that they were quite happy." She paused. "We were quite happy."

"How did she die?"

"A car accident, when I was nearly four. She was driving home after delivering a baby. Perhaps she was tired, or found a patch of ice on the road. It was nearly spring but the pavement was still slippery, especially late at night."

"A truck driver found her car, smashed against a guardrail. She died instantly, they said."

"How awful for you, and your father."

"Especially my father. After all, I was very small. It was then that he became very fearful for me, for my safety. I think he felt that he had not protected my mother, and so he was going to make sure I was constantly guarded." Her eyes drifted to Sergei, standing nearby. "If anything, his obsession with me has gotten worse."

"I suppose it's understandable, although I don't agree with it," said Gina.

Natalia sighed. "My father is not a bad man. Here in America I think people assume that because we are Russian and wealthy that Papa made his money by stealing from poor Russians. It's true that many of the billions made during the 1990s were created in just such a way. But my father did not do that. He built his company from the bottom up during this century, and he gave jobs to a great many people. When he sold it, his only crime — if indeed it is a crime — was in taking his money out of Russia."

"I see. Was that because he didn't feel it was safe?"

Natalia nodded. She glanced quickly at her cell phone. "Gina, I did not notice the time. I'd better get going to my class. Thank you — for the conversation, and the friendship."

They were now in front of the building, and both little boys were asleep.

"My pleasure. We'll have to do it again." Gina watched as Natalia headed toward

Sergei, who hailed them a cab. She waved as they got into the car and sped off.

A voice by her elbow made her jump. "Are you the Gina who wants my jumpers?"

She turned and saw the rugged face of Miles Porter.

"Yes! I'm glad your girlfriend told you."

"She did. Darby also mentioned that you two have been putting your heads together regarding Alec Rodin's death. She's in the apartment now if you want to chat."

Gina nodded. "I'll bring my little men home and head over. Which one are you in?"

"Nine-thirty. I'll text her and tell her you'll be coming by."

He headed for a cab and Gina pushed the stroller toward the building.

Gina made the boys some lunch and tidied up before the afternoon nanny, Allie, arrived. By the coffee machine she spotted a cell phone, the red indicator light blinking to show messages. She picked it up. It was Penn's phone, and he was probably irate over leaving it home.

That's what happens when you start the day angry, Gina thought, feeling as if it were something the nuns at the orphanage might have said. Out of curiosity, she touched Penn's screen and it sprang to life.

That's odd, Gina thought. You would think that with all of his sensitive info he'd have his phone password protected. It had opened right up to text messages, and without really intending to, Gina could read many of the headings. She shrugged, went to put the phone down, when one of the headings caught her eye.

DODGED A BULLET.

What a strange heading. Gina listened to hear if Allie was coming, but heard nothing. She touched the screen and saw a long conversation between Penn and an associate at his firm named Jack. She was about to close the screen when a name jumped out at her.

RODIN.

Gina gasped. This was too strange. Knowing that Allie could arrive at any moment, she tried to speed read the line of texts.

WAS GOING TO BE MESSY.

IMPLICATED THE FIRM.

And then, at the end: SO LUCKY HE'S GONE.

"What are you doing?"

Gina dropped the phone and it clattered onto the counter. She whirled around, her heart beating fast.

"Jeez, Allie, you scared me!" The noon nanny was five minutes early. "Penn forgot

353

his phone and I just found it. I was checking to see if I could find his work number to let him know."

"They're on the bulletin board, Gina." She said it with an air of superiority, as if she knew everything and lowly Gina was a complete dolt. Gina smiled sweetly. She happened to know she made more money than Allie, and she loved the fact that Miss High and Mighty didn't have a clue.

"Gosh, you're right. Thanks loads." Gina called Penn's office and left a message with his secretary, alerting her that the phone was at home, in case he was concerned.

She gathered up her backpack, hoping Allie could not see the odd mixture of emotions flitting over her face, and hugged the boys goodbye. "Thanks again for your help, Allie."

"Yeah, whatever," she replied, collapsing on the couch and opening a magazine.

Gina slipped out the door before Trevor could start calling her name.

TWENTY

On Tuesday morning, Peggy Babson called Columbia University and said she was sick.

She wasn't really sure why she'd done it. She wasn't sick at all — she felt fine, but the idea of getting to the train and slogging through a full day of work, only to take the train home again did not have any appeal.

She supposed that the reason she did not feel like going to work could have something to do with the bloody butcher apron. She had a sneaking suspicion that her plan had failed, that the detectives had ignored the evidence linking Miles to the murder of the Russian man. She wasn't positively sure why law enforcement was choosing to look the other way, but she had an inkling that it had to do with secret trade agreements with the Queen.

Peggy decided to make herself a cup of tea, but it was getting more and more difficult to find a clean mug. It didn't occur to her to wash one of the dozen mugs that were crowding her counter. Instead, she took a small bowl down from the cupboard.

Yes, she thought. *This will do nicely.*

When the water had boiled, she pushed aside piles to find the familiar plaid box, pulled out a bag, and placed it in the bowl. She poured in some water and waited for it to steep. Poor Pete was following her around, looking for his morning meal, but so far she'd been unable to locate his dog food. "We'll get you something in a bit, Sport," she said.

Sport. That was something that her Dad would have said. She smiled, thinking of him and her mother. This had been their house, up until their death, and since moving in Peggy had tried her darnedest to keep it just as nice and tidy as they had done.

But the compulsion to collect was getting stronger. Even as she removed the tea bag from her bowl and prepared to throw it away, she felt the urge to save it instead. "Why?" she asked aloud. Almost immediately she heard the answer. *You never know what will happen . . .*

It was true! You never did know what would happen. One day you lived in beautiful Rockaway with your neighbors, and the next a terrible storm had blown in and destroyed the place forever. Oh sure, individual houses survived, some of them anyway, but the spirit of the town was broken. A tiredness settled on the people like a fine sprinkling of dust.

Peggy put the damp tea bag on top of a stack of boxes. She'd try to remember it was there, in case she needed it.

Gina walked into Charles Burrows's apartment and immediately saw the sticky notes that were still on the coffee table. She read the names aloud: "Rodin, Natalia, Mikhail, Sergei, Vera Graff, Rona Reichels."

"Crap, you guys are serious about this!" She took off her back pack. "Good. Give me that marker, I've got two more names."

Darby watched as she wrote down "Sherry Cooper."

"Your boss?"

Gina nodded, still scribbling. "And her husband, Penn." Triumphantly she handed Darby the two notes. "Sherry has wanted to live in the Kazakovas' penthouse for four years. The first thing she said when we heard Rodin was dead was that she was calling Rona Reichels to see if it was free."

"Interesting," Darby said. "Go on."

"She has Thursday afternoons off and is used to getting what she wants."

"And Penn?"

"His firm was in some sort of litigation with Alec Rodin. I don't know much about it, but they were relieved when he died. One of them said they'd 'dodged a bullet.' "

Gina wasn't about to tell Darby how she'd obtained this information, and the real estate agent didn't ask.

"Excellent. We'll need to dig deeper on that, see if we can find out what that litigation was about." If Darby was thinking about her own pending lawsuit, she didn't show it.

Gina lifted two of the squares and waggled them in front of Darby.

"I don't think Natalia killed him, nor do I think it was Sergei." She told Darby about her conversation with Natalia, especially the remark that Sergei would have used his bare hands if he'd been the one to kill Alec. "I suppose we need to keep them on the list, but I don't think either one of them did it."

"What about this new friend of Natalia's? Jeremy?"

"She didn't even mention him when we talked today. I don't think they are very serious, but perhaps we should put him down. I'll ask her about him next time we talk."

Gina took the marker and a square and wrote down Jeremy's name.

Darby remembered what Todd Stockton had told her earlier. "Did you hear about Rona's daughter? She died on Sunday night of an accidental overdose."

"You're kidding." Gina couldn't recall ever meeting Devin Finnegan, but she knew the Coopers would take the news hard. "That stinks, but I still see Rona as the number-one suspect. She's the only one we know who had a real reason to hate Rodin."

"Besides Natalia?" Darby teased.

"Good point."

"What about Mikhail? We heard that he owed Rodin something, some kind of payback to do with his fertilizer factories in Russia. Did Natalia say anything about that?"

"Only that her father is a good guy, and that he's a self-made man who did not pillage the country to amass his fortune." Gina's phone buzzed and she picked it up. "How sweet. Sherry Cooper is my new friend on Facebook." She clicked on something, scanned it, and then sat bolt upright. "Sweet Lord! You are not going to believe this!"

Darby felt her scalp tingling. "What is it?"

Gina's eyes were wide. "Guess who was a champion collegiate fencer?"

■ ■ ■ ■

Rona emptied her pockets back in her apartment. Devin's cell phone, her set of keys, and the money all went on the table. Rona sat down heavily and looked at the items.

Cash was cash, Rona figured, and Lord, did she need some. Where it came from was of little consequence. She needed money, and she'd look at this windfall as another little gift from Devin.

The keys. Rona picked them up, noticing the little tags affixed to each one. 677. 834. 515. 930. 1822 . . .

Why in the world had her daughter possessed so many keys?

She froze. The numbers . . . they were familiar.

She looked at the sequence again. And then it hit her.

The numbers were units she had sold in the building.

This building. *Her* building.

Rona felt her blood run cold. If anyone knew these keys existed, her real estate license could be in jeopardy. How had they found their way into Devin's apartment?

She stood up, tried to clear her head.

Somehow Devin had gotten her hands on keys from her old listings. The Graff apartment, Charlie Burrows's, the Coopers . . . but how?

She looked down at the keys. And then she knew the answer.

Devin had made copies.

It would not have been that difficult. Rona had always kept the keys to her properties together, on a sterling silver key ring, neatly labeled so that she could get into a listing at a moment's notice. Devin could have taken a key, had it copied, and then returned it to the ring.

But why?

Rona racked her brain. She could almost hear Devin, a senior in high school, asking innocently, "What properties have you sold?" Had the girl copied the keys because she was thinking ahead?

Of course, some buyers changed the locks the minute the ink on their deed was dry. She thought of the Coopers. Surely these keys would no longer work in apartment 1822. Others, Rona knew, never changed their locks, putting their faith in doormen and God knew what else.

Like Vera Graff.

The phone on the coffee table vibrated, making Rona jump. Someone was trying to reach Devin. Someone who did not know she was dead.

Perhaps her mysterious new friend?

Rona looked at the phone, wondered if there was any way in the world she could answer it. The vibrating continued, insistent. She shook her head. *No . . .*

It vibrated again.

Rona reached down and picked up the phone.

"We need to tell Detectives Benedetti and Ryan what we know," Darby said, letting the implications of Gina's words sink in. *Sherry was an expert fencer. Sherry knew how to handle a sword . . .*

She looked over at Gina, who was hugging her knees to her chest, as if she were trying to make herself very small. "You okay?"

"Yeah, yeah." Gina nodded her head, and yet she still retained the fetal position.

"I'm calling the detectives." Darby punched in the numbers she'd added to her phone earlier, when she and Miles had gone to the station. She waited while the phone rang.

At last the voice of Detective Benedetti answered. Darby explained the new evidence and asked if the detectives would come by.

"Love to, but we're no longer on the case," he said.

"Why?"

"Whole thing's been reassigned."

"To another detective?" Darby was puzzled.

"To a whole new division," Benedetti said. "FBI."

"Why?"

"I'm afraid I can't say, Ms. Farr."

"Let me make sure I understand. The FBI is now handling the murder of Alec Rodin?"

"Put it this way, things are a little deeper than they seem."

"Was Rodin an agent?"

A pause. "I don't know. I really don't know. But there's something going on."

"Did you learn anything about the perpetrator? Anything you can share?"

"The only thing we can say with real certainty is that Rodin was killed by a woman. A woman, or a very slight, short guy."

"Explain."

"His wounds were consistent with the thrust of a person between five-foot four and five-foot eight inches tall. Someone with quickness, rather than strength."

"What about suspects? Can you tell me

anything?"

"What's your interest in this, Ms. Farr? I mean, apart from the loony tune who tried to frame Professor Porter?"

"We've discovered some links within the building, connections that seem worthwhile for follow-up."

"Humph. Interesting. Police work involves tracking down every single lead, many of them useless, but I tell you — if the Feds have been brought in, and I assure you they have, there's something else going on. We're not talking a little spat over parking at Central Park Place."

"I understand. One more thing — can you tell me the name of the lead FBI investigator?"

"Yeah, he's a guy out of D.C. Cardazzo."

Darby's stomach clenched. She'd wanted Benedetti to say that the agent working the case was Ed Landis, but that would have been impossible. Landis, a Special Agent with whom she'd worked several times, had been killed in a freak helicopter accident two months ago.

Darby thought back. She'd met Agent Cardazzo the summer before, when a buyer for a waterfront estate turned out to have connections with organized crime. "Detective, may I have his number?"

"Sure." He rattled it off and wished her good luck. "My personal guess is that this is a hit by the Russian mob," he confided. "They're an equal-opportunity racket, so why not get a woman to snuff Rodin out?" He sighed. "I gotta go work some other cases. You and your friends over on Central Park West stay safe."

Darby hung up and noticed Gina peering at her notes. "Sherry got me to measure a pair of pants she needed hemmed," she said. "Without her power heels, she's five-foot-five."

"Everything fits except her motive. How does killing Rodin ensure she'll get the apartment?"

"I'll have to think about it. Who are you calling now?"

"This guy Cardazzo. Just so happens I met him in Maine."

"What's he like?"

"On the brusque side." She waited to see if he would answer, got a recording, and left a message. There was the sound of the door being unlocked. "Great — Miles is back."

He entered with a cheery hello and stopped short when he saw Gina. "Darby, don't tell me you've given away all my clothes," he joked.

"Yes, everything down to your last sock.

Sit down, we've got lots to tell you."

She and Gina brought him up to date on what they'd learned and he gave a low whistle

"The FBI, eh? There's more to this case than we think." He perused the square sticky-backed notes on the table, stopping to point at the one labeled "Jeremy."

"He picked Natalia up from class for a late lunch," Miles noted.

"Today?"

"That's right. I asked him where he worked, and he gave me the name of the firm. On the way home I called, pretending to be looking for a reference. I got a very chatty fellow who told me Jeremy is one of the best traders on the floor, putting in crazy hours and the like."

"Not if he's taking late lunches with Natalia," Darby said dryly.

"True, but I think it's because he's smitten with her." Miles gave a little smile. "Happens, you know."

"What else did the chatty co-worker say?" Gina asked.

"He said that Jeremy isn't afraid to take a chance, even if it doesn't always pan out, and that his attitude is exactly what one needs in the cutthroat world of trading." He thought a moment. "I nearly forgot the most important thing. Jeremy was in the office, on the floor trading, all afternoon on Thursday. This guy was completely positive."

"Okay, so he is one of the few with an alibi." Darby consulted her notepad. "Seems like we have a few things to check up on. Hopefully Agent Cardazzo will call me back, number one. Then there is the litigation with Penn's firm and Rodin. Who wants to look into it? I'm curious about Mikhail's fertilizer companies, especially this little environmental problem he had with the locals, so I'm going to see what I can find on that."

"But Mikhail sold his companies, didn't he?" Gina was rooting in her backpack for a granola bar. It was hours since she'd munched on animal crackers with the boys and she was starved.

"True, but if Rodin bailed him out of something, maybe it had to do with his businesses."

Miles cocked his head. "Should I look into the litigation, Gina? I've got some time."

"Great." She unwrapped a snack bar and took a bite. "Penn's firm is Corcoran, Corcoran, and Sterling." She looked at her watch, took another bite. "I've got to go and meet Bethany to sign our leases for the store."

"How about those jumpers? Do you want them now?" Miles stood and queried Gina, his hands on his hips.

"I thought you'd never ask."

"You know that when he says 'jumpers' he means 'sweaters'?" Darby couldn't help but tease.

"Jolly right," Gina said. "Let's go get them."

Time for lunch, thought Peggy Babson, following the narrow path that led through the living room piles to the stove. She opened the refrigerator and then shut it, quickly, as the stench of something rotten assailed her nostrils. *Well, I'm not eating anything from there!* She recoiled from the fridge and opened a cupboard. Perhaps a nice bowl of soup?

There was a whole stack of cans in the cupboard, and at least a few of them were condensed soup. She nodded with satisfaction. The only issue now would be a clean pot.

She rummaged in a lower cabinet until she found a pot that looked reasonably clean. She moved stacks of newspapers and boxes around on her range until she had cleared a small radius around one burner, and then she turned on the gas.

The blue flames shot up hungrily while Peggy picked her soup. The cans were all appealing, but in the end she decided on cream of mushroom. Naturally, it was the can near the bottom of the stack, but she was confident she could dislodge it without too much trouble.

Somewhere in the house she heard the cries of Pete and remembered that she owed him some food. He could have a bowl of cream of mushroom soup, too, she decided. He'd enjoy a change from plain old dog food.

She put her hands on the can of soup and yanked it quickly from the stack. For a minute she thought her rapid tug had worked, that the mound of cans would not topple. She thought of magicians who performed similar tricks and decided it was not very difficult. Just then, the entire stack of metal cans came down, straight at her head.

Diced tomatoes in their own juices and tender niblets of corn tumbled from the shelf, but it was a five-pound can of baked beans that did the damage. It struck her just above the right eye, knocking her to the floor, where her head whammed into a foot-high stone bunny. The statue was a relatively new acquisition, and missing one ear, but

Peggy had spotted it on a neighbor's front porch and felt the familiar itch that meant she had to have it.

Later, those same neighbors would find Pete outside their door, looking as if he needed a good meal but otherwise fine. The house down the street had not fared as well. The fire department described the structure and its contents as a total loss. As for Peggy Babson, she was found to have perished in the blaze.

TWENTY-ONE

A deep, resonant male voice on the other end of the phone said Devin's name.

Rona held her breath, her mind racing. The voice said the name again, this time in a questioning tone.

"Hey," she said, in that breathless way her daughter said it.

"Well hey to you, too." The man sounded older — as in Rona's age — but she couldn't be sure. "I was hoping you could come and keep me company later on. Say, dessert and drinks? I can't wait to spoil my little angel."

"Yeah." She tried to sound eager, hoping he'd say more.

"Come to the townhouse, okay?"

"Hmmm . . ." She hoped that she sounded indecisive.

"Ah, come on baby, I know you prefer the Upper East Side, but Midtown isn't that bad." He gave the address, which Rona scribbled down.

"See you at eight, sugar," the voice said.

Rona hung up, her head pounding. Was this the source of Devin's pocket change? Had he supplied her with drugs, too?

Rona licked her lips. This mystery man was in for the shock of his life.

Miranda pushed the buzzer of the penthouse. Beside her, panting on his leash, was Korbut. He whined.

"I know, I know, you need a drink," she said to the wolfhound, stroking the top of his head. She'd already dropped off Mimi and Honey, after putting all three dogs through a brisk two-mile walk. At Vera Graff's she'd asked Yvette if the rumor about an antique sword having been stolen from their apartment was true.

The maid, her whole body quaking, had said yes, and that it was the weapon used to kill the Russian man.

"Was anything else taken?"

A jittery Gallic shrug and then Yvette had surprised her by answering, "Some coins, a little horse, a crystal paperweight, and a small jeweled egg."

Miranda had thanked her, given her Mimi, and climbed the elevator to the penthouse. She once more pushed the buzzer.

"Okay, Korbut, I guess I get to root

around again for the key." She found it, inserted into the door, and she and Korbut entered.

The apartment was not entirely quiet. Down the hallway, Miranda could hear music from behind a closed door. She reached over and unclasped Korbut's leash.

The dog went bounding down the hallway, nudging open a doorway and bursting in. Instantly the music was louder. Miranda was wondering if that was where his water bowl was kept when Natalia appeared in the room's door frame.

Naked.

She didn't look down the hallway, didn't see Miranda, but instead tugged the door closed, this time more securely. Miranda heard the click of the latch, said a quiet "huh," and clutching the leash, left the apartment, re-locking the door behind her.

As Rona approached the door of Devin's apartment, she heard the chirpy voice of Heather Cox saying hello.

"Are you — I mean, I know you're really upset — but is it, like, any easier today?"

Rona met her wide eyes with an unsmiling face. "No."

"Oh. I get it." She stood behind Rona as she unlocked the door. "Well, I'm glad I'm here to help."

Rona was about to say she didn't need or want any help when she stopped herself. Maybe she could use Heather's help after all.

"Yes, I'm glad, too."

The smile on the girl's face was pathetic.

Rona pushed open the door and the two went in. "I wonder if you can look through the kitchen drawers and cabinets, Heather, for anything that looks valuable. The insurance company has asked me to make a list of items, and they need it right away."

"What about valuable kitchen stuff? Like good knives? Or a Panini maker?"

"That might be good. Tell you what: look for some paper and keep track of those kinds of things, okay?"

The girl nodded and got right to work. Rona sighed and headed into the bedroom. Heather would be out of her hair for a while at least.

She started first with the nightstands, opening the little drawers and poking around on the shelves. She found a heavy crystal paper weight, decided it could be valuable, wrapped it in one of Devin's old tee shirts and slipped it into her bag.

On the dresser, she opened a brightly colored cigar box and found some jewelry.

Nothing caught her eye until she picked up a familiar-looking watch. She flipped it over. "To CB from RR."

The watch brought back a series of memories. She remembered finding it downtown and having it engraved with the inscription. Giving it to Charles after he bought the apartment — actually, the day he moved in — right after his wife had skedaddled. She and Charles had been close for a while there. Maybe they would be again.

How had Devin come to own this watch?

Rona let out a long hiss of air. There was only one explanation. Her daughter had been a thief.

She tossed the watch in her bag and continued looking. She'd forgotten all about Heather, hard at work in the kitchen, and was nearly finished with the dresser, when she came upon a shoebox wedged into the bottom drawer.

She sat on her haunches and opened the box. Inside was a heavy horse figurine, its body smooth and black, with eyes some kind of glittering jewels. Beside it was a small pile of coins, and something wrapped in purple velvet.

Rona unwrapped the object, which was heavy and about the size of her palm. It was an egg — but not just any egg. It was a jeweled Easter egg, light pink in color, encrusted with diamonds and pearls. She held her breath and looked at it. It was truly gorgeous.

"Cool." The voice of Heather from the doorway interrupted her reverie.

Rona shoved the egg in her bag, but then thought better of it. "I'm sorry," she said to Heather. She pulled out the egg and held it out. "You'd probably like to see this. I gave it to Devin a few years ago at Easter. None of these little gems are real, but it's pretty, isn't it?"

Heather knelt down. "They look real, that's for sure." She held out a hand and Rona was forced to hand her the egg. The girl fingered the different enamel panels and Rona was about to tell her to stop when a part of the egg sprung open, revealing a heart-shaped frame and three tiny portraits.

"Wow! This is really amazing!"

"Yes!" Rona backpedaled, amazed at what the girl had discovered. "I forgot about that!"

"Who are these people?"

"Old family members," Rona answered. She stuck out her hand. "Better get back to work," she said, taking back the egg and wrapping it in the velvet.

Heather handed her a steno-sized notebook. "Here's what I found. Nothing too valuable." She stood. "I've got to go. Have you figured out what to do about the apartment?"

"No — I'll just break the lease, I guess."

"I'd be interested in renting it, if you want someone to see Devin's lease through." She smiled. "I wrote my number down on the list. And I wouldn't be creeped out that Devin died here, because she was my friend."

"Uh-huh." Rona supposed this was a compliment. "Thanks. And thanks a lot for your help."

"No problem."

Rona went back into Devin's bedroom. She put the shoebox back into the drawer and continued looking through the closets, the glittering pink egg impossible to forget.

Corcoran, Corcoran, and Sterling proved an easy place to obtain information, at least for Miles Porter. Darby marveled at the way he chatted up a paralegal, telling her that he was a new guy, helping out with the discovery. "I'm making sure the case is well and truly dropped," he explained. "I'm supposed to take my little sister out for dinner for her sweet sixteenth, and I was afraid I'd have to cancel given this whole thing." She heard him say that yes, they'd been lucky that Rodin was now out of the picture, and yes, it had been a frivolous claim to begin with, but what could you do. A minute later, he hung up.

"Penn Cooper's firm gave Alec Rodin bad advice on an investment," he said, "and Rodin was ready to sue."

"What kind of investment?"

"Condos in Miami. There were several investors — including Mikhail Kazakova."

"No way! So Mikhail was probably annoyed about these condos, too, right?"

"I imagine so. I wonder whether his beef would have been with Alec, the one who got him into it?"

"Interesting. Was Penn Cooper directly on the line?"

"Doesn't appear so, but who knows. What are you finding out?"

"I'm reading about Mikhail's fertilizer company in the Chelyabinsk region of the Ural Mountains. The local residents claimed that toxic substances were leaching into their water supply from the disposal of chemicals used at the factory. There were lots of protests, but it doesn't look like it really went anywhere."

"Any familiar names?"

"Mikhail is mentioned quite a bit as the

then president of the company, but nothing else." She looked a moment more and then said, "Hang on. One of the leaders of the opposition against the factory — her name is Elena Bokeria."

"Bokeria? Isn't that Sergei's family name?"

"Exactly. Perhaps it's common in the Urals."

"We need to find out if there is any connection. Certainly would give Sergei a reason to dislike Mikhail."

Darby nodded. "Not sure how it helps us with Alec Rodin's murder, though." She rubbed her temples and scrunched up her nose. "I need some fresh air. What about you?"

"Capital idea. Let's go for a stroll, maybe find some of those warm chestnuts." He held Darby's jacket for her and then shrugged on his own as well. "I'm going to need to take you for a good dinner tonight, too."

"You've got it." She turned and faced him. "Maybe we'll talk more about Simon tonight?"

Miles shrugged. "There's not much to talk about until we see what happens, love. If he doesn't want to see me, that's pretty much the end of it."

"He'll want to see you."

"Then we'll figure out the timing and make a plan."

"Okay." She reached up on her tiptoes and kissed him. "Off we go to find chestnuts."

"I saw the strangest thing today." Mikhail Kazakova was standing before the window in Miranda Style's apartment, gazing out at the view.

She appeared with a drink and handed it to him. "What's that?"

He took the glass and reached a hand around her waist. "Thank you, my dear." He took a sip. "It's quite terrible, really. I was standing on the street corner, near Wall Street, waiting with a horde of people to cross, and suddenly there was a kind of a scream, and this man next to me flew into the line of traffic."

Miranda put her drink down. She looked at his profile, until he turned to her and laughed.

"It's okay, I wasn't hurt at all," he said.

"What about the other guy?"

"He didn't fare so well, I'm afraid. Some sort of delivery truck was coming through and he landed right in front of it."

"He was pushed."

"Apparently so."

Miranda took a sip of her drink. "Do you think that shove was meant for you?"

"Me? No, I do not." He took a long gulp of the drink. "Why do you say that?"

She sighed and sat down gracefully on a white leather couch, her long brown legs folded elegantly in front of her. "Alec was murdered five days ago in broad daylight. You're describing an accident today in the closest proximity possible, also in the middle of the day. Yes, I think there's a possibility that you're a target."

He turned from the window. "I don't see why."

"It could be any number of reasons, couldn't it, Mikhail?"

"I don't know." He made an exasperated sound. "I suppose. What do you think I should do?"

"Have Sergei guard you."

"Absolutely not. He's Natalia's bodyguard. She's the one in danger."

"From whom?"

Mikhail shrugged. "The world is a treacherous place. I will not remove her protection."

"Then arrange for your own. Immediately."

"You really think I should?"

"Yes."

"I'll make a call tomorrow."

"Did you see anything or anyone when this man was pushed?"

He shook his head. "It happened so fast. I heard the noise of his yell, felt him brush by me, and then the screech of brakes . . . A very brutal way to die."

"And virtually impossible to solve, unless there were witnesses or a security or traffic camera."

"Yes. But let's leave all that and talk of other things. You are busy? Our Korbut is keeping you in fine shape, I see."

"Korbut, and my other clients."

"And your other business?"

Mikhail knew that Miranda had another life, but he did not pry. She had made it clear to him that those were the ground rules, and other than some innocent questions, he did not press the issue.

"Yes," she said, smiling. "My little business on the side is going fine."

He finished his drink. "I think we should dine out tonight. Somewhere opulent. In fact, I want to surprise you."

"Sounds exciting. I'll get dressed while you make the arrangements." As Miranda chose a pale ivory dress from her closet and proceeded to put it on, she remembered seeing Natalia naked, obviously in the middle of some afternoon delight.

She decided she would not tell Mikhail, at least not now. He had enough to worry about.

Special Agent David Cardazzo called just as Miles and Darby had finished their walk. They had stopped to admire the outside of Central Park Place, and were seated on a bench directly in front of the building.

"Can you talk?" The agent asked, his voice gruff.

"Yes."

"I imagine you're calling about the murder of Alec Rodin, am I correct?"

"Yes." Darby could not keep the surprise out of her voice. "I'm amazed that you know."

"Detective Benedetti provided us with a list of anyone he'd spoken with. When I saw your name, I put two and two together." He paused. "Not difficult."

"I see." She frowned at Miles. So far this wasn't going very well.

"I certainly appreciate your taking the time, Agent Cardazzo. I don't remember if you recall our meeting in Maine —"

"Of course I do. Listen: here's the deal. We've taken over this case, so any information you discover should come directly to me."

"I see." Quickly Darby ran through the discoveries she, Gina, and Miles had made over the course of the last few days. Were any of them really facts, or were they just conjecture, or even worse, interesting tidbits? It was a fact that Penn Cooper's firm had been engaged in a lawsuit with Alec Rodin, but was that FBI worthy information? Sherry Cooper had been a standout fencer in college. Did that mean she'd murdered someone?

"You know about the sword coming from Vera Graff's apartment," she said lamely.

"Yes." His tone was impatient. "It was what killed Rodin."

Her heart fluttered a little. Had they possessed real confirmation of this fact before?

"Alec Rodin was in a lawsuit over some investment advice," she offered.

"Yes, Corcoran, Corcoran, and Sterling. They've been forthcoming."

"Penn Cooper lives in the building where the Kazakovas live."

"Huh." He sounded unimpressed. "Listen, Darby, I recall that you seemed to enjoy playing detective back on Hurricane Harbor. Ed Landis humored you, I know. But this isn't Maine. This is New York. You're way out of your league here, and things aren't what they seem. I suggest you enjoy the rest of your visit with Mr. Porter, and then head on back to California." He paused. "Call me if you have some real information. Goodbye."

The line went dead. Darby turned to Miles, her mouth agape.

"Now that was a brush-off," she said, her voice becoming angry. "I remember that guy was annoying, but . . . ugh!"

Miles gave a small smile. "As frustrating as that was, Cardazzo's call gave us yet another piece of the puzzle."

"Not really. All he did was confirm that the sword was the murder weapon. I guess that's something, sure —"

"No, I mean that because of the timing of his call, we were still sitting here on this bench, and I happened to see Kazakova's driver leave the building from the private exit. Do you know who was seated behind the driver?"

"Mikhail? Natalia?"

"The dog walker."

"No! Miranda Styles?"

"I'm pretty positive."

"How could you tell?"

"She leaned forward, and I saw her arm

and part of her face. I'm sure it was Miranda."

"Maybe they're taking Korbut to the vet." Darby started giggling, and Miles joined in.

"Or off to buy him some dog treats." He grinned. "If anyone will know what's going on, it's Ramon. Let's go pick his brain."

They practically ran across Central Park West until they met up with the doorman. As usual, he ribbed Miles and flattered Darby.

"Still here with this broken-down Brit, eh? Well sometimes I think the redcoats won after all. Women hear an English accent and they go all gooey. Isn't that right, Mr. Bean?"

"True, my friend. I'm tempted to give you some lessons so that you, too, can charm the — uh — knickers off the ladies in your life."

"Deal." He gave a broad smile and then narrowed his eyes. "Okay, watcha looking for?"

"Miranda Styles and Mikhail Kazakova. We just saw them leaving together."

Ramon shifted uncomfortably and let out a sigh. "That's a toughie." His dark eyes darted around the opulent lobby. "I could get in big trouble for saying something."

"Let me ask the questions, then, and you

won't say anything." It was a technique Miles taught his students in the beginning investigative journalism class. He found that once a source gave a few nods, they were more likely to start talking without any prompts.

"Are Mikhail and Miranda romantically involved?"

A quick nod from Ramon.

"Has this been going on for some time, say a year?"

Another nod. "At least." Ramon chewed the inside of his lip. "They are super discreet, but still . . ." he paused, looked around again. "I know Kazakova's driver."

"I see." Miles thought a moment. "Miranda walks his dog, too, along with several others."

More nods. "She does something else, too, but I don't know what it is. In between walking dogs she has another life."

Another life. Darby thought about that as she and Miles rode in silence up to the ninth floor. What was Miranda Styles doing with her time, when she wasn't with Mikhail or her canine charges?

"Personal trainer," Miles said aloud as the elevator doors opened. "She's extremely fit."

"That's as good a guess as any." Darby yawned.

"Nap before dinner? I've got my sights set on a little Indian place tonight."

"You're on. I feel like my brain needs a rest."

"Good idea. Let the brain rest and the body work." He waggled his eyebrows and opened the door.

Rona Reichels found the Midtown address without any trouble. She paused before a nondescript door, her heart pounding. It was eight o'clock and she could not believe she was going to confront the man who'd been Devin's lover.

She gave a discreet knock and the door opened. A balding, middle-aged man in red boxers and a tee shirt stood before her, his face changing from delight to dismay.

"You're not my baby angel," he faltered.

Rona pushed her way in. "No, I'm not. Your baby angel is dead, and I'm her mother."

He deflated like a balloon. "Devin . . . dead?"

"Yes." She looked around the apartment with her appraising real estate eye and thought *Expensive.* Whatever his outward appearance, this guy had money. "We need to talk."

"Let me put on some clothes." He hurried from the room.

Rona thought briefly of her safety and decided she did not really care. *Bring it on,* she thought grimly. *Gun, knife, whatever.* She was ready.

He returned wearing a pair of dark pants and a button-down shirt. "I didn't get your name," he said.

"Rona." She exhaled. "I'm trying to figure out a few things. Were you and Devin a couple?"

He gave a kind of chuckle and sigh at the same time. "I wish. A knockout like Devin . . . and a guy like me." His grin was sappy-sad. "No. We connected through a website service that matches young women with older men."

"A dating site?"

"No, more like . . . companionship."

"And sex?" Rona stared him down. "Is that part of the bargain?"

He looked away. "It can be."

"Ugh."

"Hey, I'm not ashamed. Devin signed up to be an angel of her own free will. We connected, and I showered her with gifts. She seemed to enjoy being with me."

"Money? Did you give her money?"

"Sure. She was struggling to pay back loans, and it was tough. Her mother was always on her back . . ."

He stopped.

Rona shook her head, moved to the door, pulled it open.

"I'm sorry," the man said. "Really, I am. I liked her. She was very sweet."

Rona bit her lip and walked away.

TWENTY-TWO

"Okay, let's get back to basics," said Darby to Miles. They were at a bustling Indian restaurant not far from Central Park Place, enjoying curry and an intriguing Indian beer.

"What do you mean by 'basics'? You mean, who had a motive?"

"Yes, but I was thinking of starting with the murder weapon itself. It's the only piece of evidence we have — the antique sword."

"Saber, really . . ." Miles broke off a piece of a papadum and dabbed it into a green curry.

"Okay, saber. Who could have stolen it? Remember Vera said there was no evidence of a break-in, so either they left their apartment unlocked, or someone used a key."

"Or it was one of them. After all, Detective Benedetti said it was a woman."

"True, but even if those two weren't ensconced in their apartment all afternoon,

I doubt they'd have the physical strength to kill Rodin. That's got to be a pretty forceful thrust to penetrate the chest cavity, puncture the lungs, right?"

Miles looked down at his dinner.

"Sorry if I'm ruining your appetite! Think about it though — who could have gotten into that apartment easily and with a key?"

"The superintendent."

"Yes. And he could have sold the sword to an antique shop."

"I wonder if Benedetti checked any shops nearby? He wouldn't be very good at his job if he hadn't."

"Who else had easy access?"

"Well, Natalia was in there a fair amount, but I doubt she's got a key. Cleaning lady?"

"That's Yvette, remember?"

"Who else gets keys to properties?"

Just then Darby flashed on her lawsuit with the Davenports, how a key she'd had to the house didn't work, because the entire door unit had been changed. A nagging voice said: why had it been changed? She tabled that question for now and turned to Miles.

"Real estate agents have keys, and I bet you that Rona was the listing broker for this apartment when Vera bought it." She grabbed her smartphone and checked the list Todd Stockton had sent her. "Yes!"

"So Rona keeps the keys from when she lists the property, then sneaks in and steals the saber, uses it to kill Alec Rodin because, four years later, she's still angry over losing all that money. The fact that it's an antique weapon makes it look like it's some sort of Russian crime of passion."

"What should we do? Should we try to talk to Rona?"

"Why not?" Miles glanced at his watch. "It's only nine-thirty, early by New York standards. Let's settle up here and go see what she says."

Gina phoned while Darby and Miles were making their way back to Central Park Place.

"Anything new? Seems like ages since we talked."

Darby brought her up to date on the conversation with Agent Cardazzo as well as Miles's spotting of Miranda and Mikhail.

"So they are an item," Gina mused. "Wonder if Natalia knows?" She was silent for a moment. "Something I just remembered about Miranda . . . something I thought was strange at the time. She wears a gun. I saw it when Vera collapsed and she was helping me."

Darby told Miles who frowned. "Perhaps she's worried about being attacked by dogs?"

"I heard that," Gina said. "Pepper spray I can see, but what dog walker wears a gun?" She sighed. "Where are you guys headed now?"

Darby described their hunch that Rona could still possess keys to Vera Graff's apartment.

"Are you going to point blank ask her?" Gina wondered. "Isn't she going to just deny it?" She thought of her ruse with the dog collar. "What if you pound on Rona's door and ask if there is any chance she has a key to Vera's, because you're worried about her and you can't reach the super. Say that you hear weird noises or something, and nobody answers when you knock."

"Great idea, Gina, and it might actually work."

Darby and Miles climbed the stairs to three-twelve. Both were panting slightly from the exertion of climbing, which they thought would add to their performance. "Ready?" Miles whispered.

"Ready."

He pounded on the door.

Almost instantly, Rona opened it. She was

wearing a satin robe over pajamas, and her face was bereft of any makeup. Darby remembered Devin's recent death and her heart clenched for the woman.

"We're checking to see if anyone can help us. The old lady in five-fifteen is making strange noises and we can't get the super. Nobody answers when we knock and we're worried that something is going on."

"Five-fifteen . . . that's Vera Graff. Have you called the police?"

"Not yet," Miles lied. "We were trying to get in there first. We don't want to embarrass the old lady if it's nothing, but all the same, every second counts." He wrung his hands. "Somebody mentioned that you are a real estate agent and that you might have a key."

Rona started, glanced into her apartment and back. "I don't think so."

Inwardly, Darby groaned. It was not going to work.

"I know Mrs. Graff will be thankful if we don't have to call the authorities, make a big fuss . . ."

Rona must have seen dollar signs because she put up a finger. "Let me just check. Sometimes I do have old keys rattling around."

She returned minutes later, handing him

a key with a flourish. "Didn't even know I had it. Bring it back as soon as you can and let me know how she is."

Miles muttered a thank you and grabbed the key. He and Darby ran to the elevator. When the doors were safely closed they looked at each other with amazement.

"What now?" Miles asked.

"Fifth floor. We need to see if it works."

At first, no one answered the buzzer at Vera's, but then a frightened voice asked what they wanted. Darby explained and the woman told them to go away. A moment later, another voice, more commanding than the first, requested their names.

A moment later the door opened and Vera Graff stood scowling into the hallway.

"What is this all about?"

Miles brandished the key. "We are trying to figure out who stole your saber," he said.

"That rusty old thing?" She frowned. "I hardly think it is worth waking my housemaid and I up in the middle of the night . . ."

"That sword was used to kill a man," Darby said quietly. "And this key may help us find the killer. May we see if it works?"

"Now? Be my guest," Vera said, shaking her head as if the whole thing was ridiculous.

Miles inserted the key and turned the lock. "I'd say it works perfectly."

Yvette murmured something in French and put a trembling hand to her lips.

"Why don't you go and sit down, Yvette," Vera suggested. "I'll handle this."

The woman scurried away. As soon as she was out of earshot, Vera gave them a fierce look. "Just what kind of game are you playing, coming here like this and terrorizing my maid?" Her voice was a raspy hiss. "Where did you get that key?"

"Rona Reichels."

"The real estate woman? What is she doing with a key to our apartment?"

"We think she's had it since she listed the property," Darby explained. "The point is, someone could have used it to come in and take the sword."

The old woman's scowl faded.

Darby and Miles exchanged glances.

"We've become friends with Gina Trovata, and I know you and she have spent time together," Darby said. "We're trying to get to the bottom of this, with Gina's help."

Vera Graff nodded. "Gina knows about other things that went missing as well. You can ask her." She seemed to sway on her feet slightly. "I'm too tired to talk about this now. I'm heading back to bed, but I'd ask that you keep us posted on what you find out. In the morning, that is." She held out her hand. "We'll change our locks as soon as possible, but in the meantime, I'll have that key."

The door closed and Miles gave a low whistle. "Back to Rona's for the confrontation?"

Darby nodded. "Let's go."

Across town, in one of the city's most expensive restaurants, Mikhail Kazakova took a bite of his quail. "Are you enjoying yourself, my dear?" He offered his companion a taste. "This is absolutely marvelous. Try a bite."

"No, thank you," Miranda said. She looked around the quiet dining room, searching for anything or anyone out of the ordinary. She'd felt unsettled ever since Mikhail's admission of the violent push he'd witnessed, a push she was sure had been meant for him.

A man across the room caught her eye. He was thin, and short, with a neatly trimmed goatee and glasses. Several times she'd seen him glance in their direction. Now he was rising to his feet, crossing the room . . . and stopping at a table in the center of the room. He spoke to the diners who rose and hugged him, obviously friends.

She turned her attention back to Mikhail.

"My red snapper is exquisite," she said, smiling at him. "I'm just a little jumpy, that's all."

"You're not still concerned about that incident I told you about, are you?"

"Actually, I am." Miranda gave him a level look. "I think your life is in danger."

"Miranda, really —"

"Hear me out. Someone killed Alec, and since I know it wasn't you, I have to surmise that you are now the one whose life is on the line."

He gave a mischievous grin. "You are sure I did not slip into that alley and kill Rodin? God knows there were times I thought about it."

"Yes, I'm sure."

"I will play what you call the devil's advocate and ask how you know I am not the killer."

Her face was deadly serious. "I know you didn't do it because I've been tailing you."

"Me? You've had me under surveillance? Whatever for?"

"I was hired to investigate you." She picked up her wine glass. "I'm a private investigator."

"Aha!" He said, bringing his hand down

on the table. "I knew you were in some sort of covert work." His eyes twinkled. "Dog walking! What a red herring." He chuckled, shaking his head. "Only one question remains: who are you working for?"

Miranda reached out and traced the shape of a letter on his powerful hand. "Someone who cared about you very much, it turns out." She paused. "Alec Rodin."

"I don't understand."

"Alec hired me to find out whether you were planting misinformation about him with the Russian authorities. When I gave him proof that you were discrediting him with the FSB, he understood it was to protect Natalia and prevent her from going back to Russia."

"Then why did he insist on going through with the marriage? Why not break it off?"

"He struggled with the decision, I know, but he needed Natalia for his cover."

"Cover? I do not understand."

"Alec was an informant for the FBI," she said. "He uncovered evidence of massive fraud in several Russian cities, but he knew that to go to the authorities would be futile. As you know, several have tried to work within the Russian legal system, and have been tortured and killed for their honesty. Alec thought he could go through different channels, but I'm convinced that's why he was killed, and why your life is now expendable."

Mikhail's face was pale. "This has the ring of truth to it. I always trusted and admired Rodin. This is why I wanted Natalia to be his wife in the first place." He put his head in his hands. "Poor Alec. Can we find his killer?"

"I don't know," Miranda said, "but I'm trying."

"There is one more thing I need to know. Is our relationship part of *your* cover?"

"No," she smiled. "I'm off the job. For good." She touched his hand again. "Now I'm involved because I care."

The Russian oligarch grinned. "Then I am one very lucky man."

"I've had those keys tucked in a drawer," Rona said to Darby and Miles. "I only just found them the other day. If someone got into Vera's apartment and took things, they didn't do it with my key." She rubbed her eyes. "I can't believe this. I ought to call the police. My daughter died two days ago and you're pulling this crap on me? You ought to be ashamed."

The door slammed.

"Well," said Miles. "That didn't go very well."

"No." Darby grimaced. "I do feel badly. She did just lose her daughter."

"Yes, but she's lying, Darby. Did you see the way her eyes were darting back and forth? Plus she said 'keys.' Plural. Trust me, they did not just turn up in her drawer. She copied and kept them for a reason."

"You're right. There's more behind it." She stifled a yawn. "Come on, Sherlock. Let's call it a day."

Twenty-Three

"I've always felt it was a random crime," Detective Benedetti said. It was early Wednesday morning, and Miles and Darby had decided they needed to see him as soon as the station opened.

Miles shifted in his seat. "Why is that?"

"The murder weapon may have belonged to the old lady, but whoever stole it could have turned around and sold it to any number of retail establishments. There are hundreds of shops selling antique swords in the city, not to mention the hundreds available on-line. That's how the murderer got the weapon."

"And now?" Darby leaned forward in the hard metal chair. "Do you still feel it was a random act of violence?"

"I do. I think someone with a sick mind thought it would be fun to stab someone."

"No copycats," Miles said. "No other crimes like this one have occurred."

"Exactly. A random crime, committed by a woman or a small man. That's what I told the private eye, too."

"What private eye?" Darby asked.

"A woman — tall, athletic build." He fished in his desk. "Eagle Eye Investigations."

"Interesting. Can you tell us her name?"

"Sure." He squinted at the card. "Miranda Styles."

"Okay, I'm confused," Miles said. "Miranda the dog walker is a private investigator?"

"Apparently so," Darby said. "I'll admit it — I never saw that coming, although Gina did tell us she saw Miranda wearing a gun."

"That's right. Speaking of Gina, shall we fill her in?"

"Definitely. Let me give her a call." She pulled out her phone, dialed, and left a message. Gina called back almost instantly.

"I'm at the Coopers'," she said, "What's up?"

"Miranda is not only Mikhail's snuggle buddy, but she's a PI, too," Darby said.

"No way." Gina was silent a moment. "Actually, when I think about it, that makes a lot of sense. There's no way you could afford to live at Central Park Place on a dog walker's salary, right?" She sighed. "What now? She hasn't come for Honey yet, so I guess she's running behind. Do we try to pool our information?"

"Yes. When Miranda comes, see if you can stall her. We'll join you to speak with her."

"Great. By the way, I called Natalia this morning. She's been hanging out with her new boyfriend and is meeting Vera today. Hasn't seen much of her father, but says that's par for the course when he's in New York. He's very busy with business."

"Business of a romantic nature," Darby said dryly. "See you soon."

Gina hung up and continued connecting the wooden train track for Trevor. Beside them, Sam clapped his hands in his little jump-seat, while Honey lay sprawled on the floor at the baby's feet. Gina frowned. Miranda was much later than usual. She hoped nothing was wrong.

Her phone buzzed and Gina saw that Sherry Cooper had sent a text. Something was on Facebook about Devin Finnegan, and Sherry had forwarded Gina the link. Idly she clicked on it and took a look.

The Facebook page was a memorial site for Devin Finnegan, with photos of the young woman and her favorite quote: *"All I ask is the chance to prove that money can't make me happy."* An event was posted: a gathering that would take place at a bar Friday night to celebrate the young woman's life. The person posting the information was named Heather Cox, and Gina promptly requested to be her friend.

Heather had tagged a list of people so that they, too, would get the event announcement, and Gina read through them, her mind wondering about Miranda. It was strange she hadn't called . . .

"Come on boys," she said to Trevor and Sam. "Let's go for a ride in the elevator."

They clapped their hands, ready for anything that sounded like adventure. Gina strapped them both in the stroller and gave Sam a bottle. Honey stood up and stretched, wagging her tail hopefully. "You'd better stay, girl, just in case Miranda and I miss each other." She had a sinking feeling that wouldn't happen.

It was only two floors up to Miranda's apartment, but the boys loved going in the elevator, no matter how long the trip. Gina pushed them down the hallway a few doors and paused before 2005.

She rang the buzzer.

There was no answer, and Gina leaned in closer to the door and rang it again. A horrible smell accosted her nostrils. Sulfur? She recoiled, wondering why there was such a stench . . .

And then she knew. She grabbed the front of the stroller and raced down the hall, pushing the boys as if she were in a race. She hit the button to call for an elevator, and waited. Usually one was right there! Why was it taking so long?

It seemed as if the odor of sulfur had followed her down the hall. She put a hand in front of her mouth and realized her fingers were shaking. *Where was the elevator?* She did something she hadn't done in a long time: she prayed, a litany of pleas from her heart to God, Mary, Jesus, and whomever else might be listening. And finally, the elevator was there.

Gina rushed in and closed the doors.

And waited.

"Oh, my God," she wailed, realizing she'd forgotten to indicate a floor. She punched L for lobby and felt the reassuring descent.

"Down," Trevor said, pounding on the frame of the stroller. "Go down."

"That's right, sweetie," Gina panted. She could hardly speak. Her heart was racing and her mouth very dry. She felt a buzzing feeling and realized it was her phone, vibrating against her thigh.

She yanked it out. Heather Cox had accepted her friend request. Big deal! Gina was about to shove the phone back in her pocket when she had another thought. As the elevator continued its descent downward, she called 911.

The elevator stopped at the seventh floor and an elderly couple came on, using canes and moving slowly. Gina bit her lip, trying to keep from screaming. They looked up and nodded and she managed a tight smile. A very tight smile.

Finally the doors opened on the opulent lobby and the elderly couple began shuffling out. Gina dug her fingernails into her palm to keep from pushing them. Instead, she waited until there was enough room to brush by them. She glanced around for Ramon and saw him at the door, greeting Miles and Darby.

"Call the building superintendent," she cried, breathing hard.

"Gina, what is it?" Darby put a steadying hand on her shoulder.

"I went up to Miranda's apartment and there's a terrible smell of sulfur . . . I've called 911 . . ." She gulped for air. "I'm pretty sure it's a gas leak."

The evacuation of Central Park Place stopped traffic on the street and brought throngs of paparazzi, hoping to see some of the building's more famous occupants. Darby and Miles stood with Gina and the boys, hoping the news from Miranda's apartment would be good.

"I feel terrible for Honey, too," Gina said. "If something happens . . ."

"The gas has been turned off, Gina," Miles said. "Thanks to your quick thinking the rest of the building will be fine."

No one said anything. They knew the danger lurked in Miranda's unit on the twentieth floor.

"I wonder why we haven't seen Natalia?" Gina asked. "Or Sergei?"

"You've called, right?" Darby asked.

"Yes. No answer." Gina looked down at her charges, who sat in the stroller, fascinated by the ambulance and fire trucks. A moment later there was a strangled sob and a blur of blonde hair.

"Damn, I'm glad to see you!" Sherry Cooper hugged Gina before swooping down to kiss her sons. "I came as soon as I could. I've been so worried! Does it look like everyone inside is okay?"

"We don't know about Miranda yet," Gina said. "We're waiting."

"Oh my God," she seemed to notice Darby and Miles and introduced herself. "I hope she's okay. Carbon monoxide poisoning . . ."

She swallowed, left it hanging.

A cheer went up as a stretcher, flanked by medical personnel, emerged from the building.

"Looks like they are working on her," Sherry said hopefully. "That's a good sign."

And then another stretcher, also surrounded by emergency medical technicians, was rolled out the entrance. Darby and Miles exchanged a glance. *Mikhail.*

"I thought Miranda lived alone," Sherry said, craning her neck. "Whoever that is seems to be in worse shape, judging by the number of EMTs."

Gina looked at Miles and Darby. Her very countenance seemed to ask, *Freak accident? Or had Alec Rodin's killer struck again?*

Once the building had been declared safe to re-enter, Sherry and the boys headed inside, while Darby, Miles and Gina walked to a little café around the corner. All three were quiet, each trying to make sense of what had just happened at Central Park Place.

The authorities confirmed what Gina had surmised: gas had been seeping into Miranda's apartment for most of the night, and foul play was almost certainly to blame. It was known that the two victims were alive, one of them, just barely. Natalia and Sergei had been located, and were now at the hospital. Miles requested and received an update on Mikhail's and Miranda's conditions: Miranda was recovering rapidly, while Mikhail was in the intensive care unit.

"Is Sergei at the hospital?" Darby asked.

"Yes, he and Natalia. Her friend Jeremy left his office as soon as he heard, and, according to Sergei, he's the one keeping Natalia from hysterics."

"That's good at least," Gina huffed. She stirred her coffee. "I just can't figure out how someone could get into Miranda's apartment, number one, and then sabotage the gas, number two?"

"I know," Darby said. She sighed. "We need some sort of insight . . . something to help us see the way."

"Not sure if this helps, but it looks like Miranda's getting discharged," Miles said, looking at his phone.

"Already?" Darby and Gina exchanged glances.

He nodded. "Natalia's sent me a text. Miranda insists that she's fine, and I suppose they think she's well enough to leave."

"Guess a private investigator doesn't stay

down for too long," Gina quipped. "Maybe we should have some sort of welcome home thing for her." She frowned. "Speaking of parties, I hate to be morbid but there's a gathering for Devin Finnegan on Friday night."

"That doesn't sound like an event Rona would organize," said Darby.

"No — it's a friend of Devin's named Heather Cox. She's got a list of people she's invited, but Rona doesn't seem to be on it." Idly she pulled out her phone and clicked on the memorial site. "No one I know, but that's to be expected."

Suddenly she sat bolt upright. "Wait a minute . . ." she handed Darby the phone. "Take a look at that name."

Darby glanced down, read the list of invitees. "How odd." Her eyes flew up to meet Gina's. "Oh, my goodness — I've been blind. All this time . . ." She grabbed her phone. "We've got to speak with Cardazzo right away. If what I'm thinking is right — we may already be too late."

Special Agent Cardazzo met them at the entrance to the hospital. "This better be good," he muttered.

"It is," Darby said. She turned to Gina. "Head on upstairs and make sure nobody leaves. We'll be up as soon as we've briefed Detective Cardazzo."

His eyes were quizzical. "What are you planning here? Some sort of bust?"

"Yes, actually," she said. "In a few minutes, you'll have the person who masterminded Alec Rodin's death, as well as the nearly fatal poisoning of Mikhail Kazakova and Miranda Styles."

"I hope 'nearly fatal' is still accurate," Miles said quietly. He put down his phone and sighed. "Natalia just texted. Mikhail Kazakova's dying."

TWENTY-FOUR

Ramon could not understand why one of the private chef uniforms was missing. He knew that he'd spoken to the laundry service and that they were all in Monday's delivery. Where had the misplaced one disappeared?

Of course, dealing with linen was not a duty of a doorman, but at Central Park Place, the staff members pitched in, no matter what the situation. The head housekeeper wanted Ramon's assistance in tracking down the uniform, and he was happy to lend a hand. They were a team, and, if anything, the disaster with the gas leak had brought them closer.

He once again checked the closet where the uniforms were kept. One was definitely absent. He stroked his chin and headed back upstairs to his post. Yes, it was perplexing.

The private waiting room was quiet, except for the soft sobs of Natalia Kazakova. She was flanked by Sergei Bokeria, whose enormous bulk could barely be contained in his chair, and Jeremy Hale, who was holding her hand and murmuring in a soft voice. Across the room stood Miranda, her eyes rimmed with red, although Darby didn't know if it was from sorrow or from her exposure to the fumes of gas.

Gina sat by the door, waiting. She said nothing when Darby and Miles entered, but her eyes reflected gratitude that they'd arrived. A moment later the door to the waiting room opened, and all eyes turned to see Rona Reichels.

"I was told to come —" she looked around the room. "What's this about?"

"Have a seat, Rona," Miles said. "We'll explain in a moment."

Again the door opened and Sherry and Penn Cooper stood on the threshold. "Gina, what's up?" Penn asked.

"Come in," she said. "Have a seat."

"What's going on?"

"You'll find out in a minute."

"I don't have 'a minute,'" Penn said, "I'm

in the middle of a merger . . ."

"Oh, Penn," Sherry said, "Just sit down."

The last person to arrive was Todd Stockton. He nodded, slipped in, and took a seat without speaking.

Darby cleared her throat. "I want to tell you all some good news. Mikhail is on life support, but it looks as if he may pull through."

"Papa?" Natalia cried out. "I must go to him." She rose to her feet, along with Jeremy.

"I know, Natalia, but please, wait a few minutes. It's very important — for his and your safety."

Beside her, Sergei Bokeria frowned. "Safety?"

"Yes." Darby looked around the room. "The gas leak in Miranda's apartment that nearly killed her and Mikhail was no accident. Someone gained access to the unit and destroyed a valve, letting gas flow freely into the apartment."

"The doctor said one of the things that saved us was an open window, right by the bed," Miranda said softly. She gave a tired smile. "Mikhail insists on opening the window, no matter what the season, regardless of the temperature. He has to have fresh air." She looked at Gina. "The other thing that saved us was Gina Trovata's quick actions."

There was a murmur of approval from the assembled group.

"Who was the target?" asked Jeremy. "Miranda?"

"No," Darby said. "Despite the fact that this happened in Miranda's apartment, the person who turned on that gas was trying to kill Mikhail."

"It wasn't the first time, either," said Miranda. "Earlier in the day a man was pushed into traffic and killed. Mikhail had the distinct impression it was supposed to have been him."

"Where?" Sherry Cooper cried. "At Central Park Place?"

"Downtown."

"This is interesting as hell, but I have to get back to my office," Penn Cooper said, standing up. "If you'd excuse me."

"Can we first talk about the lawsuit Alec Rodin brought against you?" Darby asked.

"Not me, my company," Penn huffed.

Darby's look was somewhat sympathetic — after all, she knew how he felt. "Your name was on the suit. Something about bad investment advice?"

"Yes, but — that's been dismissed."

"Only because Rodin is dead."

There was an uncomfortable silence. Rona Reichels pulled out her phone.

"Are we boring you, Rona?" Miles asked.

"I don't even know you," she glared. "Are you the guy staying in Charles Burrows's apartment?"

"That's right. Charles is the one whose marriage you broke up when you sold him the condo, isn't that right?"

Her eyes smoldered. "I don't have to sit here and listen to this," she said, rising to her feet. She shoved her phone in a voluminous pocketbook.

"Oh, but you do," Miles said. "Because you've broken just about every real estate rule in the book. Maybe sleeping with your clients doesn't violate any laws, but keeping keys to their apartments certainly does." He waved in Todd Stockton's direction. "I think you know Todd? He's on the board of the New York Real Estate Commission."

"I never even used those keys!"

"You may not have," Miles said. "But someone else did. Someone used those keys to break into Vera Graff's apartment and steal an antique saber, along with several other items worth thousands of dollars."

She started. "I don't know what you're talking about."

"Really? Then you won't mind if the

authorities search your apartment when we're through."

Darby, ignoring Rona's protests, glanced around the room. "Solving the murder of Alec Rodin involves answering one big question: who could have gotten those keys from Rona and stolen that sword? This was a question I pondered for a long time. Finally I realized there was only one answer, because there was only one person who could have known those keys existed: Devin, Rona's daughter."

"But Yvette and Vera hardly ever leave their apartment," Gina said. "Did Devin go in at night, while they were sleeping?"

"I doubt it. That would have been extremely risky, since both women are elderly and light sleepers. Chances are she watched and waited until she saw them leave Central Park Place together. Devin had been in the apartment before, years earlier, when she fed their cat for a few days. She might have remembered that they had an antique sword — a saber — along with some other antiques. Or maybe she happened across the valuables by accident. In any case, Devin unlocked the door, went in, and stole the weapon. There was no sign of forced entry, nothing to indicate any theft, because she'd used a key."

Natalia rose, visibly upset. "I must see my father."

"In a minute, Nat," Miles said. "Please — it's important."

She sunk back into her chair.

"So Devin possessed the murder weapon," Darby said. "Was she Alec Rodin's killer? What possible motive would she have had?" Darby thought a moment. "We know that Detective Benedetti believes the murderer was a woman, right? He looked at the thrusts of the sword and did calculations to determine the height of the attacker. Devin fits that profile perfectly."

"Devin could have killed Rodin to avenge her mother," Gina said.

"It's true that Rona was cheated out of a large commission when Mikhail bought the penthouse," Darby said. "How much was it, Rona? A million dollars? After all, it was Rodin who counseled Mikhail not to use Rona as a broker. Rodin was the deal killer. Revenge could have been Devin's motive."

"But the more I thought about it," Darby continued, "the more I realized that helping out her mom didn't seem like the kind of thing Devin would do. This was a woman who, by all accounts, did not have a close relationship with her mother, who could be, well — rather selfish."

Rona swallowed.

"It certainly appeared that Devin killed Alec. She had the weapon, she fit the size of the killer, and she did not have an alibi. But why? What would have been her motive?"

"Before we could answer any of these questions, Devin died of an accidental drug overdose. That would seem to be the sad end of it, right? But then, immediately following her death, two attempts were made on Mikhail Kazakova's life. That started me thinking: What if Devin's death was not an accident?"

Rona shook her head at Darby. "What are you saying?"

"Devin Finnegan had an accomplice — more than that, really — a mastermind. This person planned the murder of Alec Rodin with her, giving her encouragement and helping her practice the swordplay itself."

Rona remembered the textbook in Devin's apartment. She closed her eyes. It had been anatomy and physiology . . .

"Once Devin successfully killed Rodin, this person decided she was expendable. Maybe Devin had gotten cocky, or regretful — or maybe it was always what the mastermind had planned all along. And so, she was drugged and killed."

Rona put her face in her hands.

"The mastermind now had one more person to kill: Mikhail Kazakova. Again, we ask ourselves, why?"

The room was absolutely silent, as if no one dared to breathe.

Darby continued. "Was Mikhail hated by someone whose family member had suffered health affects due to an environmental accident at a fertilizer company in the Ural Mountains?" Darby looked pointedly at Sergei, and then shifted her gaze to Sherry Cooper. "Or was murdering him a temptation because the lure of owning the penthouse was just so strong?"

Sherry Cooper shifted uncomfortably in her seat. "You can't suspect me of any of this."

"Really?" Miles asked. "But aren't you a champion fencer?"

She glowered. "Sure, back in college. But I had no reason to kill either one of them. May I go back to work now?"

"Yes," Jeremy Hale said, standing, "some of us have jobs to do . . ."

"And what's yours, Jeremy?" Miles said.

"I'm a trader on Wall Street." He looked around the room. "Really, this is ludicrous . . ."

He bolted for the door of the waiting room and yanked it open. Natalia screamed and Miles sprang across the room. There was a scuffle, and several seconds later Special Agent Cardazzo pulled Jeremy Hale to his feet.

Darby Farr strode across the room. "Here's how you saw your job, Jeremy. Eliminating Mikhail Kazakova so that you could marry his daughter."

Natalia gasped, shook her head. "No," she moaned.

"Yes," said Darby gently. "And the reason you were told earlier that your father was so close to death was because we were worried for his safety. It would have been so easy for Jeremy to finalize his plan."

Natalia put her head against Sergei's bicep, as if the massive bodyguard was her only form of support.

Agent Cardazzo tightened his hold on Jeremy Hale.

"Before I cart him away, I have to ask: How did you make the connection?"

"It was something you said, actually," Darby admitted. "*Things aren't what they seem.* I was trying to find links between Devin and an accomplice, and then Gina found proof that Devin and Jeremy knew each other. I realized things weren't what they seemed. Not only did these two know each other, but they were partners in crime."

"It won't stand up in court," Jeremy Hale boasted. "You'll see. I'll be a free man."

"Shut up!" Cardazzo ordered.

"Did you love her?" Rona demanded, easing slowly from her seat. Tears were rolling down her face. "Did you love my baby?"

Jeremy's lips curled in scorn. "Devin? Sure. After all, she'd do anything for money. What wasn't to love?"

It was all Darby could do to keep from punching his smug face.

After Jeremy Hale had been handcuffed, read his rights, and dragged from the hospital, the rest of the room exhaled, practically in unison. Rona wobbled unsteadily out of the room. The Coopers and Gina followed.

"I can't believe it," Miranda said. "He hatched this whole thing?"

Darby nodded, her heart clenching for Rona.

"I feel like an idiot," said Natalia. "A total idiot."

Beside her, Sergei frowned.

"You shouldn't," Darby said. "Jeremy Hale exhibits all the qualities of a psychopath. He's charming and manipulative, plus a pathological liar. Clearly he has no remorse for his actions." She looked into Natalia's eyes. "People are taken in by psychopaths all the time. You're certainly not the first. Luckily he didn't get the chance to succeed with his plan."

"After my father, I might have been next," she said grimly, then shuddered. "I must go see Papa now, but I don't know how I can thank you."

"Thank Miles and Gina," Darby said. "It was a team effort."

Natalia stood and bowed her head slightly, as if words weren't enough. Beside her, Sergei Bokeria shifted his massive weight.

"You did not get everything quite right, Darby Farr," he said gruffly. "The relative you found in the Ural Mountains? She is a distant cousin, from a branch of the family the rest of us do not like." His face contorted in what Darby imagined was a smile.

"And Sergei would never do anything to harm my father, because he knows it would hurt me," Natalia said. "Come on, let's go see him." She took his elbow and steered the big man out the door.

Miranda watched them walk down the hallway to Mikhail's room. "Good work, Darby. Very impressive. I started thinking along these same lines after a little episode that happened yesterday. I'd stopped at the penthouse to get Korbut and saw Natalia — well, let's just say I came to the conclusion that her relationship with Jeremy had really heated up. And that got me wondering whether it had developed as innocently as it seemed."

Darby nodded. "I hope Natalia doesn't blame herself too much for falling for him. We checked with several associates at Jeremy's office. He's known as an impulsive risk taker."

"The ideal characteristics of a successful trader, right?" Miranda grimaced. "I'll make sure Natalia gets some support with this whole situation, starting with some face time with her father." She gave a little wave, her long legs striding down the hallway.

Todd Stockton came up beside Darby and Miles. "I'm heading out too. Other than a slap on the wrist, I'm not going to go too hard on Rona. I think she's learned her lesson. I will make sure she returns those valuables, though. What did you say they were?"

"Not to worry," Darby said. "I believe she'll find Detective Benedetti waiting for her at Central Park Place."

"Will he arrest her?" Miles asked.

"No. She found the antiques in Devin's apartment. But Gina will be on hand to help Vera identify them and get them back."

"Whew," Todd Stockton said. "This is

crazy. I've had more than my share of excitement for a while. If I don't see you before you head back to California, have a safe trip, Darby, and I'll be in touch with details on Hideki's purchase."

"Great."

At last Darby and Miles were alone.

"Well done, love," Miles said.

"Well done, love, to you," she said.

"Your last day in New York," he said. "Any requests?"

"Tiffany's. I feel like ogling expensive jewelry and channeling Audrey Hepburn."

Miles grinned. "Let's go."

Gina helped Vera carry the stolen objects back into her apartment, under the watchful eyes of Yvette. She looked on as Vera placed the items carefully on a shelf, saving for last something wrapped in purple velvet.

It was a light pink enameled egg, encrusted with diamonds and pearls. Lovingly Vera fingered the egg, touching one of the panels, so that it sprang open. Gina peered at the jeweled egg, amazed. Inside was a heart-shaped frame and three tiny portraits.

"Beautiful," Gina breathed. She glanced toward Yvette who was smiling — a sight the younger woman had never seen.

"I heard Natalia ask you if this was an egg

created by the famous Russian artist," Gina said softly.

"Faberge," said Vera. She glanced at Yvette, said something in rapid French. Yvette scowled but then nodded.

"The truth is," Vera continued, "we don't know, and we don't care, do we?"

Gina gave a small smile. "Your own little mystery."

"Yes," Vera said, glancing first at Yvette and then back to Gina. "Sometimes a mystery is good." She said something again to Yvette and the maid scurried out. "I've sent her for tea," she said, her voice conspiratorial. "It's the only way she'll leave me alone." She sighed. "Oh, I'm tired, Gina, and I'm sorry to hear that Natalia has undergone such troubles. Please tell her that if my health allows, I wish to continue our interview sessions. Will you do that?"

"Yes, but . . . you're fine, aren't you Vera?"

"You remember what I told you, Gina. If anything happens to me, I want you to have all of my clothing, handbags, shoes — the works. Just come in here right away and take it. I've told Yvette those are my wishes."

"I understand. But hopefully that day is a long way off."

"Hopefully." She brightened. "I would like

to be able to come to your new store's opening."

"That would be fabulous!" Gina clapped her hands as Yvette entered with the tea. "I would love it if you came." She looked up at the French woman. "And you, too, Yvette. I hope you'll attend the party when my store opens."

Yvette looked as if she would drop the tray of teacups. With considerable effort, she lowered it down and scooted from the room, her pale eyes full of tears.

"Spring in Manhattan," Miles said, wrapping an arm around Darby and bringing her close. "I think it's the nicest night so far. I can't decide if it's because I'm with a top-notch sleuth who just solved two murders, or if the temperature is really warmer."

She laughed. "We did it, Miles, didn't we? Thanks to Gina and her discoveries, plus the fact that she found Mikhail and Miranda before it was too late . . ."

Miles clenched his teeth. "I hope that Hale gets exactly what he deserves, like life in prison. How do you think he gained access to Miranda's apartment?"

"I'm afraid it was rather easy for a con man like Jeremy. Somehow he knew of their penchant for ordering from Central Park

Place's private chefs, so he stole a uniform, and delivered their dessert. I suspect he added something — probably the same chemical he used to drug Devin — so that they'd get groggy fast." Darby passed a bag to Miles. "Popcorn?"

"Sure." He grabbed a handful from the gourmet bag they'd purchased and they munched in silence. "And then he turned on the gas."

She nodded. "Luckily he didn't expect someone in a climate-controlled building would have a window open."

"On a cheerier subject . . . I can't believe you're coming back in June," Miles said. "Even better, you're coming with me to merry old England."

"I can't wait." She grinned. "It's going to be fun."

"What about Maine?"

"I'll get there, too. I miss Tina and Donny, and I want to see how Bitsy Carmichael is doing, too." *And,* she thought, *I miss my cove.*

"Let's head back to the Burrows pad," Miles suggested, grabbing another handful of popcorn. "Unless you want to hit another ritzy store?"

"No," she laughed. "I've had enough excitement for one day."

Twenty-Five

Gina got the call from Sherry Cooper as she was about to meet Bethany for an early dinner.

"I hate to be the bearer of bad news, but something's up on the fifth floor," she said.

"What do you mean?" Gina's heart started to race. *Vera,* she thought. *Vera lives on the fifth floor . . .*

"I was just heading out to meet Penn for drinks and there's an ambulance out front. Ramon said it's an emergency with someone on the fifth floor."

"Did he say who?"

"No."

Gina called Darby.

"We're on our way," Darby said. "I'll let you know what I find out as soon as we get back to the building."

"Okay," said Gina, but even as she hung up she knew she was headed back to Central Park Place. She had to see for herself if Vera

431

was okay.

She called Bethany and cancelled their plans, then grabbed a taxi.

The ambulance was pulling away as Gina's taxi approached the building. She craned her neck for a clue that would tell her who was inside, but saw nothing.

Outside Central Park Place, Ramon was wringing his hands. "Such a sweet lady," he said, as Gina approached. "To have to go through this . . ."

"Vera Graff?" Gina asked, not wanting to know the answer.

Ramon nodded, and Gina felt the pit of her stomach drop.

"Is — she — dead?"

Again the sad nod from the doorman. Gina put her hands to her face. "Why did Vera have to die?" she said softly, shaking her head.

"Wait a minute," Ramon said. "She didn't die."

"What do you mean?"

"I mean, Vera didn't die. Her maid did. Poor Vera's got to find new live-in help, and you know that ain't going to be easy. Especially not at her age."

Gina's mouth was open. "Let me get this straight: Yvette was the one in the ambulance? Vera Graff is okay?"

"Well, as okay as you can be when . . ."

You have to find a new maid. Gina couldn't believe what she was hearing.

Before she lost it entirely, she headed for the elevators and the fifth floor.

TWENTY-SIX

Natalia Kazakova was already at apartment five-fifteen, sitting on the stiff couch talking with Vera. Both women gave sad smiles as Gina knocked and entered.

"You heard about Yvette?" Vera asked, her voice breaking.

"I did." Gina went to her and gave her a hug. "What happened?"

"Heart attack," she said, her lips trembling. She looked around the room as if reconstructing the scene. "I was taking a bath, and I came out . . ." she wiped her eyes. "She was lying there . . ."

"At least she did not suffer," Natalia said. She patted Vera's arm. "You would not have wanted her to be in pain."

"No." Vera sniffled. She cleared her throat. "You know, I'm upset, but I'm also so *surprised*. I always assumed I would die first. I never dreamed something would happen to Yvette!"

Tears rolled down her face. "We've been friends for so long. Through so many tough times. All the moves, all over the place, for my husband's posts. His death." She sniffled again. "My miscarriages. Yvette was always there for me, holding my hand. Wiping the tears, telling me not to give up."

"Just as you were there for her," Gina said.

"I suppose so," Vera agreed. She looked at the two women and took a deep breath. "You know, Yvette asked me to keep a promise, and I did it, for sixty years. I never told a soul, not even my husband."

On the other side of Vera, Natalia raised her eyebrows.

"I suppose it will all come out, now," Vera said, quietly.

A quizzical glance passed between the young women.

"What are you talking about, Vera?" asked Gina.

"Who I am," she said, with a rueful smile.

Natalia gave a knowing nod. "Perhaps you want to tell Gina first, before it becomes public knowledge."

"What, exactly?" asked Gina.

Natalia looked at Vera expectantly. When the older woman kept silent, Natalia sighed. Finally she said, her voice low, "Vera is the source of my story about stolen royal palaces in Russia."

"I see," said Gina, who had already sur-mised as much.

Natalia paused. "Vera is of 34th genera-tion Russian nobility. She is the Princess Anastasia Bolensky . . ."

Beside her, Vera shook her head. "No, dear. I'm afraid you're mistaken."

"Vera, you said yourself it was all going to come out."

"It's just that I'm not Princess Bolensky."

"I don't have the name wrong, do I?" Natalia sounded like a true journalist, want-ing to be sure of her facts.

"It isn't me," Vera persisted.

"Really, Vera," Natalia chided. "You have given me all of the information on your story!"

"Yes, I provided you with the information, and I believe it is accurate," the old woman said. "But I am not the princess." She moistened her lips. "That was my dear friend, Yvette."

"Some secrets are so well hidden it's impos-sible to know them," Darby said, when Gina told her the story an hour later. "Yvette — or Princess Bolensky — was in hiding her whole life."

"Yes," Gina said. "After the 1917 Revolution, Yvette's family estates were seized by the authorities and their owners arrested. The ones who weren't killed or captured fled Russia disguised as peasants. They settled in Paris, where Yvette was born and raised. Only after the fall of Communism did some of her family go back to live in St. Petersburg."

"But Yvette . . ."

"Yvette couldn't do it. She was terrified that what had befallen her family might happen again."

"Did her relatives recover their property?"

"Some assets were obtained, and shared with the rest of the surviving family members. You would not have guessed it, but Yvette was not a poor woman. She not only owned most of the furniture and antiques — including the saber — but the apartment itself!"

"Unbelievable." Miles shook his head in disbelief. "What happens to Vera?"

"She's all set. Yvette left everything to her in her will."

"You're saying that Yvette remained incognito, working as Vera's maid, virtually her whole life?" Darby asked.

"She chose security over freedom," Miles said.

"In a sense that's true," agreed Gina, "but

remember, Yvette and Vera were very close friends. I suspect that behind closed doors the roles of housekeeper and employer were ignored. It was only when there were people watching that they put on a charade."

"Did you ever have a clue that this was happening?" Darby asked.

"Not really. Once I heard Vera call Yvette a nickname that I did not recognize. Turns out it was *Nastasia* — a nickname for Anastasia, which, by the way, means 'resurrection.' "

"How apropos." Darby turned to Miles. "Where does this leave Natalia and her story?"

"Vera would still be a source — although not a primary one. It weakens the whole thing somewhat, but Natalia has a good angle, if she chooses to pursue it."

"Oh, she will," Gina said. "Her experience with Jeremy has made her more determined than ever to become an investigative journalist. She's going to be on a quest to make sure the truth gets out."

"I'm glad somebody is," said Miles. He lifted his eyebrows. "Speaking of truth, mine is that I'm famished. Join us for dinner, Gina?"

"No, thanks," she said, looking at her watch. "I'm off to Brooklyn to meet Bethany and make some plans for the store." She reached out and gave Darby a hug. "If you're in the city for High Voltage Vintage's opening, I hope you'll come." She hugged Miles as well. "You're invited, no matter what."

"Brilliant," he said, hugging Gina back. "I can't wait to see my jumpers on display."

"Talk about resurrection," Darby said, rolling her eyes. "I can't believe anyone will actually hand over money for those ratty old sweaters!"

"Not just buy them — wear them!" Gina laughed.

Darby and Miles joined in. It felt good to laugh, and wonderful to look to the future with hope. Rough times were ahead, times that would test them, but today the sun's warmth promised spring, a time of renewal for all.

ABOUT THE AUTHOR

Top-producing Realtor **Vicki Doudera** uses a world she knows well as the setting for her series starring crime-solving, deal-making real estate agent Darby Farr. A broker with a busy coastal firm since 2003 and 2009 Realtor of the Year, Vicki is also the author of several nonfiction guides to her home state of Maine.

When she's not writing or selling houses, Vicki enjoys cycling, hiking, and sailing, as well as volunteering for her favorite charitable cause, Habitat for Humanity. She has pounded nails from Maine to Florida, helping to build simple, affordable Habitat homes, and is currently president of her local affiliate.

Vicki belongs to Mystery Writers of America, Sisters in Crime, and the National Association of Realtors. Sign up for her newsletter, find signing events, book club questions, Darby Farr recipes, and much

more at www.vickidoudera.com, or drop her
a line at vicki@vickidoudera.com.

The employees of Thorndike Press hope you have enjoyed this Large Print book. All our Thorndike, Wheeler, and Kennebec Large Print titles are designed for easy reading, and all our books are made to last. Other Thorndike Press Large Print books are available at your library, through selected bookstores, or directly from us.

For information about titles, please call:
(800) 223-1244

or visit our Web site at:
http://gale.cengage.com/thorndike

To share your comments, please write:
Publisher
Thorndike Press
10 Water St., Suite 310
Waterville, ME 04901

CPSIA information can be obtained
w.ICGtesting.com
d in the USA
05n0552030714

9 781410 470232